WINTER QUEEN

Fairy Queens 1

Also by Amber Argyle

Witch Song Trilogy
Witch Song
Witch Born
Witch Fall

Fairy Queens Trilogy
Winter Queen
Summer Queen
Daughter of Winter

WINTER QUEEN

Fairy Queens 1

AMBER ARGYLE

Starling Publishing

Editing by Linda Prince
Text design by Kathy Beutler
Author photo by Emily Weston
Cover art by Laura Sava
Map by Robert Defendi

Summary: "Becoming a winter queen will make Ilyenna as cold and cruel and deadly as winter itself, but it might be the only way to save her people from a war they have no hope of winning."

ISBN-13: 978-0-9857394-2-3
ISBN-10: 0985739428

Also available as eBook:
eBook ISBN-10: 0985739436
eBook ISBN-13: 978-0-9857394-3-0

Library of Congress Control Number: 2013934665
Printed in the United States of America
10 9 8 7 6 5 4 3 2 1

Visit Amber Argyle at her author Web site: http://www.amberargyle.com

DEDICATION

For Gordon and Gayle Stuart and
George Wesley and Theda Weston

For coming before and showing us the way.

Strong as stone, supple as a sapling.
* —Shyle adage*

1. Clan Mistress

Ilyenna's horse danced nervously beneath her, the animal's hooves clicking against the snow-covered stones that coated the land like dragon eggs. Reaching down, she patted her mare's golden neck. "Easy, Myst. What's the matter, girl?"

"There." Her father pointed at the base of a forested hillock not fifty paces beyond the road. Ilyenna saw the shadowed form of a large animal.

Bratton soundlessly pulled an arrow from his quiver and nocked it. "Bear?" He directed the question at their father.

The word stirred currents of tension in Ilyenna's body. The cold stung her cheeks and formed a vapor no matter how shallowly she breathed. As she glanced up and down the road, her hand gripped the knife belted around her bulky wool coat.

"I think it's a horse," Bratton finally said.

Ilyenna eased her mare forward for a better look. It was a horse—a bay. "Then where is his rider—" The words died in her throat when she spotted a motionless gray lump at the horse's feet. Without thought, she rammed her heels into her mare's ribs.

"Stop!" her father cried at the same time Bratton called, "Ilyenna!"

But the healer in her couldn't be denied. In three of the horse's strides, she was in the forest. She pressed herself flush against Myst's muscular neck. Still, larch trees managed to slap her, leaving the sharp scent of their needles in her hair and clothes. Clumps of snow shook loose from their sagging boughs, falling across her horse's mane and into her face. Yet Ilyenna barely registered the icy shock.

The other horse shied away. Myst tossed her head and balked, but Ilyenna didn't have time to hesitate. She jumped from the saddle, and her heavy boots sank into drifts up to her thighs. Grateful for her riding leggings, she struggled toward the man, whose face was blue with cold.

Her heavy riding skirt spread around her as she knelt beside him. Strangely, even in this frigid weather, he wore no coat. Beneath him, the white snow was stained crimson. An arrow shaft stuck out of his left side, and his mouth was coated with bloody foam.

A quick assessment revealed the arrow head had passed completely through his chest, but the shaft was still lodged inside him. Ilyenna couldn't imagine riding in that kind of pain. Each of the horse's strides would've reopened the wound and spilled more blood.

Fear rose in Ilyenna's gut, and she wondered what had driven this man to ride himself so close to death. The lump rose higher when she recognized the knots in the stranger's clan belt. "An Argon," she announced as her brother and her father reined in behind her. Instantly, her mind went to the Argon clan, and her brother's best friend, Rone.

At the mere thought of the boy from her childhood, a hundred memories came unbidden. Memories she wished to banish forever. But over the last six years, that had proven impossible. She bit the inside of her cheek, forcing herself to concentrate as she pulled her sheepskin-lined mittens from her hands and probed the man for additional wounds.

"You can't just run off," her brother growled as he dropped beside her. "What if his attacker was still here?"

Ilyenna kept her expression neutral. Even though she was seventeen, her brother would never see her as anything but a child—one incapable of caring for herself, let alone their clan. Thankfully, the calm sureness that always accompanied her healing steeled her voice. "He's not breathing well. Get him on your knees."

"Ilyenna, I don't understand," he finally said. "You told me the clans are like a family, each clan brother to the next. Why would one clan attack another?"

How could she explain war to one so young? She shot a pleading look at Enrid. But months ago, her great-aunt had claimed she was too old for clan-mistress duties. She simply nodded toward the boy with her customary "You're the clan mistress now—you handle it" glance.

Holding back a sigh, Ilyenna heaved some rolled blankets onto the back of a saddle and used the straps to tie them on. "Otrok, sometimes people do bad things."

His brow furrowed. He was no more than ten, but his soul often seemed much older. "But why would the Tyrans attack their brothers?"

This time, Ilyenna let her sigh escape. She bent next to Otrok and put her hands on his shoulders. "You remember what we talked about . . . with your father." Otrok's expression turned wary. She continued carefully, "Sometimes people hurt each other—even people who should be family—and there's never a good reason for it."

Otrok pursed his lips and nodded. He would understand that all too well. It had taken Ilyenna weeks to nurse him back to health after the last beating his father had given him.

She looked up to see Otrok's older brother run toward her through snow dusted with hearth-fire ash. He wasn't old enough to trim a beard—not yet old enough to fight, and yet too young to leave behind.

She looked past him, searching for the boys' father. As usual, Dobber was drunk. She'd had him at the beating pole not two weeks past for altering some sheep's earmarks to look like they were his. Perhaps he'd manage to kill her horse, giving her an excuse to take his other son as her tiam as well.

Without a word, she handed Otrok's older brother the horses' lead ropes. "Be careful."

He grinned in response and led the horses to a group of boys clustered beside the packhorses. She bit the inside of her cheek.

The men might use the boys in the fight, but only if no other choice remained. Ilyenna hoped it never came to that.

She felt a strong hand on her shoulder. "Remember, Ilyenna, the Shyle are strong as stone—"

"And supple as a sapling," she finished for her father. Had it really only been a few hours since they'd left the dead Argon? Ilyenna hated the tears that threatened to reveal just how frightened she was. Clan mistresses weren't supposed to be frightened. "Let me go with you. You'll need a healer."

He withdrew his hand. "You're our clan mistress, as was your mother once. Your place is here." He stepped closer and whispered, "And clan mistresses don't ask for things they shouldn't."

It was a soft rebuke, but one that stung anyway. Glad she could blame her reddened face on the cold, she tried to memorize his features, the smell of him—pipe smoke, horses, and leather—and the rough texture of his hands.

He mounted Konj. "Send any straggling warriors that come from the outlying homes after us."

Most of the Shyle moved into town for the winter. Only the poor risked the isolation of a harsh winter alone.

His eyes searching, Bratton absently nodded his goodbye and took off. Ilyenna could only guess he was going to say goodbye to Lanna. If their budding romance continued, Ilyenna suspected they'd be married by summer.

Her father sent the scouts out and motioned for the bulk of the men to follow him. The boys brought up the rear, bringing the packhorses and acting as errand boys and healers.

Nearly four hundred of them and not one looked back.

In utter silence, Ilyenna and the women watched the Balance leave the village with the men. Men and women were on opposing sides of the Balance. When they came together, they connected both ends of the Balance in a perfect circle. The Link. Now, every male out of boyhood and beneath old age had left.

The Balance would be off. Bad things happened when the Balance was off.

Ilyenna shook her head. She needed to keep the clan busy, keep their fears buried under a heavy load of work and exhaustion. "You've poultices to make, food to prepare, carding and spinning to do." None of the women seemed to hear her as they stared after their men. "Move to it!" she shouted.

That brought a satisfying round of jumps and purposeful strides. As Otrok passed her, Ilyenna caught his arm. "Round up two other boys. Use some of the horses we have left. Take turns watching the road at the mouth of the canyon. If you even think you see a Tyran, ride here and don't stop for anything."

She hated to ask sentinel duty of one so young that even the men had left him behind. But Otrok's small size would give him many advantages. If he had to run for it, his horse wouldn't tire so quickly, and even the clumsiest Shyle boy was quieter than a deer and left fewer tracks. Besides, he was the closest thing to a warrior she had left.

Otrok's big eyes opened wider. He wet his lips with the tip of his tongue and squeaked, "Yes, Clan Mistress."

It was a risk she had to take, for until the men returned, the safety of the Shyle rested in her hands.

2. The Balance

Wearing only her full-length linen underdress, Ilyenna broke the thin layer of ice in her washbasin and used a cloth to bathe her face and body before taking the salt to her teeth. She shivered violently and cursed the bitter cold. Winter had strayed far too long into the warming months. The summer fairies were losing the battle to regain their footholds in the clan lands—another indication the Balance was off.

Ilyenna quickly pulled on her felt overdress—a long garment that resembled a blanket with an opening for her head. She buckled her clan belt over the dress to keep it in place. As she pulled on her socks and heavy felt and leather boots, she was careful not to look at her feet. They were long and thin. Pretty, really, except the tips of some of her toes—two on each foot. There, only stumps remained. They ached terribly sometimes, a constant reminder of what she'd done.

When she finished dressing, Ilyenna braided her thick hair and tied it off with a leather cord. It had been three days since the men left. Three days without a word. Already knowing what she'd see—tired brown eyes and fair skin even paler than normal—she avoided looking in the mirror altogether.

Moving down the hall, she passed numerous doors. Most led to unoccupied rooms. Once, they'd been filled to the brim with the clan chief's family. But that was before Ilyenna's time. Before the war that killed her grandfather and all his brothers, leaving their valley vulnerable to the raiders who had killed or enslaved a third of the women and children—including her grandmother and three of her aunts—leaving only her father and great-aunt Enrid behind.

Hearing of the attack, the clans had responded with hundreds of men who eventually managed to fight off the invaders. In their rush to leave, the Raiders had left something—or rather someone— behind. Ilyenna's mother.

Now the attic rooms only held Otrok, Bratton, Enrid, Ilyenna's father, and Ilyenna. If what the dying man said was true, she suspected they'd soon be overflowing with Argon refugees. She descended the ladder into the great hall. After crossing the cavernous space, she pushed open the kitchen door on the other side.

The scent of bitter herbs hit her in a hot, steamy wave. Qatcha— garlic, oregano, onions, and salt simmered with chicken organs. It was her mother's recipe for staving off fevers. "The ranker the smell, the better the cure," she'd always said whenever Ilyenna and Bratton complained about the stench. But in the end, even the qatcha hadn't been enough to save Ilyenna's mother.

Great-aunt Enrid glanced up from the hearth, still stirring the qatcha. "Bad night?"

Ilyenna rubbed her eyes. "I'll sleep better when the men return."

Enrid grunted and handed Ilyenna the silver spoon, which was only used for making qatcha. "Have I got enough garlic?"

Ilyenna licked the spoon and made a face. "A little more."

"Much more and the men won't drink it even if they're holding death's hand," Enrid grumbled.

Enrid was one of the few women Ilyenna didn't have to be the clan mistress around. "We'll hold out on the whiskey until they finish their dose," Ilyenna said. "That ought to bring them around to drinking as much as we want."

She pulled her coat from its peg by the door, swung it on, and stuck her knife in the coat's sheath. The women of her clan never went anywhere without the knives they used for cooking, eating, and if needed, defense. She couldn't help but glance down the road leading to the canyon. She didn't see the men returning, but what she did see made her groan.

"What is it?" Enrid asked.

"Trouble," was all Ilyenna had time to mutter before Larina Bend marched into the kitchen.

"Ah, Ilyenna, good. I need to speak with you."

Ilyenna bit the inside of her cheek to keep from snapping at Larina. "Oh?"

"Yes. The other women keep insisting my family take in one of the—" she waved toward the canyon that separated the Shyle from the Argons "—families when they arrive. But as I'm sure you understand, we simply do not have the room or the food."

Ilyenna bit down harder on the inside of her cheek until she tasted blood. "Larina, you've the biggest house in the village, next to the clan house. If you want more room, go to your empty summer home and have all you want. If not, accept a family with all the grace your mother is so renowned for."

Enrid snorted, but covered it well with a cough.

Larina shot a suspicious glance at Enrid. "Of course we are generous, but my poor mother—"

Ilyenna planted both hands on Larina's back and guided her toward the door. "Your poor mother is too kind. Tell her to send you to me the moment she thinks she can fit another family. Now if you don't mind, I've animals to feed."

Larina opened her mouth, but before she could speak, Ilyenna caught sight of three horses galloping through the village toward the clan house. She pushed past Larina and hurried out the door. When she recognized Otrok as one of the riders, she broke into a run.

His face was drawn, his cheeks chapped with cold, but thankfully he didn't appear injured. The moment he saw Ilyenna, he shouted, "Big group of people coming."

"Who are they?" she asked as he and the other two boys reined in beside her. Their horses were blowing hard and shaking with fatigue. Even in the freezing weather, the animals were coated with sweat.

"Clanmen . . . bunch of Argons, most . . . women and kids." Otrok spoke so fast his words blurred together.

Ilyenna felt some of the tension ease from her chest. At least they weren't about to be attacked. "Father and Bratton?" she interrupted. "Are they all right?"

"Dunno, mistress. Didn't see them," one of the other boys responded.

Then, as if ashamed he couldn't tell her more, Otrok stared at his horse's mane. "You said to come back as soon as we saw them. I didn't take time to ask questions."

"Did you see Rone, Clan Chief Seneth, or Clan Mistress Narium?" Ilyenna held her breath.

The boys exchanged glances before finally shaking their heads. Ilyenna's hopes crashed to her feet.

Otrok's eyes welled with tears. "I'm sorry, mistress, I—"

She placed her hand on his leg and gave it a reassuring squeeze. "You did well, Otrok. All of you did well. You and the other boys cool down these horses before they freeze and then get yourselves warmed up and fed." She started toward the bell.

The other two boys moved away, but Otrok dropped from his horse to follow Ilyenna, still talking so fast she only caught snatches of what he said. Something about sending horses and food. But she already knew all that.

"Otrok, what kind of shape are the Argons in?"

He sighed. "Some seemed pretty bad. Others looked a'right."

At least he knew that much. Ilyenna caught Yessa Tuck by the arm as the girl darted past. "I've nine horses left in the barn. Find some girls to help you hitch them to any sleighs you can find. If there are any spare horses left in town, tie them to the sleigh bed."

The girl took off at a run.

Ilyenna gave the bell rope one good tug. It clanged three times before swaying silently. Within seconds, women were pouring from their homes. "The clanmen are coming with injured Argons," she announced. "Load up the sleighs with food, blankets, and medicine for double our number of men. Anyone willing to drive a sleigh or heal the injured, dress warm and wait for me at the bell. The rest of you make a hearty stew and be ready to help in any way you can."

Lifting up her skirt, Ilyenna hurried to the clan house. Great-aunt Enrid met her at the door, disapproval on her stout face.

"Let the others go," the elderly woman said. "A clan mistress mustn't put herself at unnecessary risk."

Ilyenna wanted to remind Enrid just who the clan mistress was, but she'd be better served to ask the burrs not to grow on her mother's grave. Practicality was the way with Enrid, not arguments or whining. "They may need me. And Otrok didn't say anything about Tyrans." She pulled on her fur-lined gloves and tugged a knitted cap over her braid.

Enrid pressed her lips together and stood with her fists on her hips. Gnarled and bent over as she was, she possessed a stubbornness that made her a formidable woman. "I heard him. Didn't sound like he saw much of anything, really. And your father wouldn't approve."

"No," Ilyenna admitted. "He wouldn't. But Father's not here. He left me in charge, and I've made my decision." She held her breath. Enrid no longer held the authority to stop her, but she looked determined to try. "Enrid," she said more softly, "what if Bratton or Father's injured? You know I'm the best healer."

Sagging in defeat, Enrid seemed to age twenty years before Ilyenna's eyes. "If you must."

Ilyenna snatched her medicine satchel and hurried out before Enrid could change her mind. Eighteen grim-faced women in nine sleighs greeted her. The rest of the village's horses were tied to the backs of the sleighs. The women's hands gripped the reins, and each wore a knife strapped over her coat. Most of these women had helped Ilyenna with the healing during times of sickness.

She nodded to gray-haired Sharina as she slid in beside her. The woman had finished Ilyenna's education in birthing after her mother's death. Sharina snapped the reins and the horse took off, the runners slicing smoothly through the snow.

By midday, Ilyenna caught sight of the first dark figures struggling up the curving road. The Argons were easy to recognize. If their clan belts hadn't given them away, their appearance would have. Even from a distance she could see most were disheveled;

some had their feet wrapped in cloth instead of shoes. The worst hunched painfully over a horse's withers or were carried between stretchers.

Ilyenna's father had left with just under four hundred men. Ilyenna could only guess there were at least double that in Argons—mostly women and children. The occasional man she did see wasn't in good shape. Usually, he rode a Shyle horse. Sometimes only the hands of the men and women surrounding him kept him in the saddle.

The village would double in size in one day. In the throes of winter. How could Ilyenna possibly provide healing for so many? Feed so many?

As the two groups drew closer, she stood in the sleigh, searching for her father and brother in the mass of people, but they were as thick as winter wool. Her stomach twisted into knots. Father and Bratton should've been here to greet the sleighs. Then she caught sight of Konj, her father's enormous horse. But it wasn't her father who rode it. Instead, a pale Argon clutched his ribs and winced with every step the horse took.

As the other women fanned out to help load the most severely wounded, Ilyenna launched herself over the side of the sleigh and rushed to the man riding her father's horse. "Where's Clan Chief Otec?" she asked breathlessly.

Straining through the pain, the man tried to turn in the saddle, but then shuddered and simply tipped his head. "When he fell off his horse, they put him in a stretcher."

The words knocked the breath from Ilyenna's lungs. "Fell off his . . ." She whirled in place, her eyes frantically scanning the nearby stretchers. A hand fell on her shoulder. A heavy hand, just like her father's. Her heart aching with hope, she turned.

But it wasn't her father. It was Bratton. Bloody bandages wrapped various parts of his body, and one side of his face was swollen and bruised.

With a small cry, she reached for him, but he held her back. "He needs you, Ilyenna."

With a quick nod, she followed him as he limped through the crowd. Two of her clanmen, bloody and battered themselves, carried a heavy stretcher between them. She fell in beside them, hardly believing the man inside was her father. His skin was ashy and sagging, as if he hadn't moved in hours. "What happened?"

Bratton winced with pain as he struggled to keep up with them. "Took a war hammer to the side of his head."

Ilyenna stepped into the sleigh ahead of the men and helped them load her father. Usually, Ilyenna was the calm one, the one who took charge while other people panicked. But seeing her father being jostled into the sleigh and not so much as stirring . . . She took a deep, biting breath of winter air and forced her mind to still.

She unwrapped his bandages, revealing a wicked knot that began just below his bald spot. The skin had split, and blood crusted the wound. "Father! Father, can you hear me!" He didn't respond. Prying apart his eyelids, she checked his pupils. One was wide, the other narrow.

His brain was swelling.

"Not good," she muttered. Desperate to try anything, she slapped his cheeks. Nothing. Knowing it needed cleaning anyway, she poured some whiskey on his wound. He moaned and shifted a little. She nearly cried out in relief. She barely noticed when the sleigh moved forward. Instead, she gave him five spoonfuls of dandelion tincture to reduce his swelling from the inside. Then she bandaged his head with a compress of mountain daisies, packing it on the outside with snow to help reduce the swelling.

After checking her father for more injuries, she realized there wasn't much else she could do. She tried to rub some warmth into his cold hands, silently hoping death would stay away.

"Ilyenna," Sharina said gently. "There's a little one what needs your help."

Forcing herself to turn away from her father, Ilyenna saw a girl of about seven who cradled her arm as tenderly as if she held a newborn. Her face was gray, her breathing quick and shallow. Reluctantly leaving her father, Ilyenna crawled over to where the girl sat. "What's your name?"

"Dekle," the girl answered weakly.

Ilyenna gently reached for her arm. "Can I see?" Reluctantly, Dekle held it out. It was a mass of swollen, black tissue. A hard knot revealed where the jagged edges of the bone pressed against the swelling muscle. "What happened?"

With a shudder, the girl looked away. "When I wouldn't come out of the wood pile, a Tyran hit me with the butt end of his axe."

Rage flashed hot in Ilyenna's breast.

Balance, she tried to remind herself. For every innocent, there is also evil.

But the adage did nothing to dissuade her anger. She gave the girl a strong dose of dandelion tincture, but she didn't dare wait for the alcohol to take full effect. The girl's eyes were starting to droop—a dangerous sign. "I'm going to have to set it." If I don't, you're going to die, she thought.

Dekle winced. "You're going to hurt me?"

Ilyenna hesitated before discreetly motioning for Sharina to come help. "Sometimes a healer has to hurt in order to heal."

Dekle violently shook her head and shrank into the sleigh bed.

Ilyenna was sorry, but she didn't have time for this. "You may as well be brave, Dekle. We'll do it either way."

Wide-eyed, the girl looked between both healers. She must have believed they meant it, for she finally bit down on the blanket and lay back in Sharina's arms.

Ilyenna nodded to Sharina. "Hold her." To the girl, she said, "It's going to hurt, Dekle, but I need you to hold as still as you can." Dekle nodded. Pushing down on the break while pulling on the girl's hand, Ilyenna felt the bone snap back into place. She fought the nausea that rose within her as the girl arched her back and screamed.

With those screams ringing in her ears, Ilyenna probed the break to see if it had lined up.

Dekle jerked away, clutching her arm and sobbing.

"Dekle," Ilyenna said softly, "I need to make sure it's lined up. I know it hurts, but after I'm done you can rest."

But Dekle was done cooperating. Sharina had to lay herself across the girl so Ilyenna could finish inspecting the break. Satisfied, she allowed the girl to cradle the arm against her stomach. Sharina helped Ilyenna apply a compress of mountain daisy, wrap it with heavy strips of canvas, splint it, and use hemp as a sling. Then they gave Dekle another dose of dandelion tincture. After Dekle, there were more breaks to set and wrap, ointments to rub into wounds, dressings to change, and tinctures to hand out.

Ilyenna regularly checked on her father. She gave him another dose of dandelion tincture and stuffed more snow in his wound. But aside from the occasional moan, there was no change in his condition. Blowing on her numb hands, Ilyenna realized they were crossing into Shyleholm. She'd been so busy she hadn't realized how far they'd come. She jumped down from the sleigh. All these people would have to sleep somewhere, and she was going to displace her clan to do it. With a suppressed sigh, she jogged on ahead.

Women ran out to meet her. Worry and fear added a sharp edge to their normally soft features. When they realized Ilyenna had nothing to tell them, they spread out, searching for their loved ones. She couldn't bring herself to ask for their help with the injured Argons. Not yet. Some of them had lost husbands, sons, fathers. Others would have their own wounded to tend to.

"Bring the most severely injured to the clan house," she called to the sleigh drivers. "The clan will have to take in everyone else for now."

She draped a man's arm over her shoulder and helped him hobble inside. Enrid held the door for her. Inside, broths were already simmering in pots. Ilyenna laid the man next to the warm fire and went back for another. Those in the most distress, she laid before the hearths in the kitchen and hall. Others filled her family's rooms and the rest of the hall. In addition to the overflowing injured, clusters of people hunched over loved ones.

Ilyenna quickly saw how crowded the clan house was becoming and set the hale people to work passing out broths or blankets, gathering more firewood, or washing dirty bandages or clothing. Anything to keep people moving and useful. Even though the great hall was large enough to accommodate a clan feast, there wasn't room to take a single step without stepping over or shuffling around someone. In passing, Ilyenna's brother told her there were over five hundred Argons. She didn't stop to count, but several hundred of those had to be injured.

So the scrubbing, stitching, and amputating began. Her ears rang from their screams. Some were simply beyond her skill to heal, like a man whose foot was nearly cut in half. He adamantly refused amputation. It was hard to tell with all the bleeding, but she tried to align it as best she could before she stitched it closed, added a few leeches to increase the blood flow, wrapped it, and ordered the man to stay off his foot for the better part of a year. She knew from the look in his eyes that he understood. If they did manage to save his foot, he'd never run again. He'd be lucky to hobble, if he lived at all.

After the most dire cases were finally under control, Bratton finally came to her. Without waiting for her to ask, he prostrated himself on the table. "I've a few cuts that won't stop bleeding."

Ilyenna eyed him as she washed the blood from her hands. "You should take some whiskey. Give it time to work before we start."

He shook his head. "Can't be drunk. At least not until Father wakes up and can take over again."

She opened her mouth to say even a little would take off the bite, but Bratton seemed to know what she was thinking. He gave her the look that meant "Leave it alone." Pursing her lips, she nodded. Then she ordered one of the Argon women to get him a cup of tea made from willow bark and other healing herbs. While he drank it, Ilyenna pulled away the bandage from his thigh. She hissed at what she saw—a gouge that cut clean through the muscle. She lined up her bone needle and threaded a strip of sheep intestine through the eye. Then she gave her brother a chunk of leather to bite down on. "You need someone to hold you?"

In answer, he lay back on the table. She poured whiskey on the wound and scrubbed it clean. Bratton arched his back, his whole body straining. His face turned red and the veins stood out on his face. Starting deep, she worked her stitches toward the surface. He cursed her through the leather. Eventually, he started screaming.

When he tried to squirm away from her, Ilyenna nodded for some nearby men to hold him down.

He shoved one. "No!"

"Bratton!" she warned him.

The two gripped his arms and held him while she finished. When it was over, he buried the heels of his hands into his eyes to hide his tears. Ilyenna quietly set a mug of whiskey at his side. Without a word, he drained it.

Lifting a shaking arm to her forehead, she wiped the sweat from her brow. Great-aunt Enrid came over from the hearth and set a plate in front of her and a bowl of qatcha in front of Bratton. Ilyenna wasn't really hungry, but she knew she needed to eat. She washed Bratton's blood from her hands and sat down on a chair. Her legs, feet, and lower back ached from hunching over so many people.

With a crust of bread, she poked at a boiled potato topped with melting sheep cheese. Taking a bite, she suddenly realized she was famished. But one glance at the tight lines around Enrid's face told Ilyenna they had another worry. It wasn't hard to guess what. "How's the food holding out?" she asked softly.

Enrid glanced around before edging closer. "Doubling our clan's numbers in the dead of winter . . . I'm watering down the stew. If we're careful, no one will starve."

Ilyenna pushed the plate away. "Let one of the others have it."

Enrid planted both fists on her hips. "You need your strength as much as anybody."

Ilyenna rubbed her forehead, trying to work out the knot inside her skull as she would a cramped muscle. It didn't help, but she was so weary that closing her eyes for a moment brought some relief.

"You're tired. You and Bratton get some rest," Enrid said.

Ilyenna shook her head. "I'll sleep tonight. The fevers are starting. We're running out of leeches and garlic. I've bandages to change, and I need to make new ointments."

Enrid gestured to the window. "It is night, Ilyenna. If you don't go to bed, you're going to do something foolish."

To placate her, Ilyenna grabbed the plate and began to eat. Enrid threw up her hands in defeat and went back to the hearth.

Bratton's breathing had slowed. "We haven't enough men to guard the canyon," he said. "But we need to send up some sentinels."

Ilyenna nodded. "I'll have Otrok and his friends go up."

"Tell them to light a signal fire if they see any danger and then make a run for it."

"I'll send him now and see that someone in the village takes shifts watching for it."

Tension drained from Bratton's face. The whiskey was working. If he was drunk, she might get some answers. "I've heard bits and pieces of what happened."

The muscles in Bratton's jaw bulged. "We came across them just before Argonholm. Their men were fighting off Tyrans, trying to give the women and children a chance to escape. We drove them off. Would've moved on to the village, but it was already overrun—Tyrans picking off Argons one at a time. All we could do was gather those we could and run."

Ilyenna stared at her hands, still imagining them stained with Bratton's blood. She'd treated the injuries, but imagining how they'd been inflicted made it so much worse. "Why did the Tyrans attack?"

"No one knows." Bratton scrubbed his face with his hands. When he spoke again, his voice sounded raw. "Some of the clanwomen escaped without coats on their backs or shoes on their feet, but not a one left without a weapon. Even the younger children had knives. Without their help, I don't think we'd have made it."

Ilyenna tried to imagine the women and children fighting for their lives. How many had died? Had Rone and his family been among them? She looked away from Bratton and cleared her throat, but her question seemed to lodge there.

Bratton seemed to know what she couldn't ask. "I didn't see Rone or any of his. They were attacked before dawn. Fell just after nightfall."

Trying to hide the color rushing to her cheeks, she nodded

quickly. "Our clanmen?" She scraped the last bite of her dinner off the wooden plate.

Bratton rubbed his eyes. "Thirty-eight dead or unaccounted for. Sixty-seven seriously injured. Not one came away without some kind of wound."

Ilyenna swallowed several times. "Their names?"

Bratton shook his head as if to drive away an unwanted image. "Let the dead care for the dead, Ilyenna," he said coldly. "For now, you need to concentrate on the living."

3. Blood and Ashes

B lood seemed to follow Ilyenna everywhere. When she fell into dreams, she drowned in a river of it. Whenever she blinked, crimson light leaked through her closed eyelids. Even now, the predawn sky was stained the color of bloody water. No matter how many times she scrubbed her hands, she couldn't rinse the hurt from her soul.

With tears stinging her eyes, she lay slumped against the window, blankets wrapped around her. She relished the cold against her aching head as she watched tiny frost flakes fall from the sky. For a moment, she thought they were really winter fairies dancing and spinning on the breeze—fairies who should have long ago given up winter and returned to their homes in the far north.

But that was ridiculous. Even if they were fairies, mere mortals could never see through their glamour. She sniffed and wiped her eyes. The Balance was seriously off when the seasons failed to shift and one clan turned on another. It had been two days since the Argons had arrived. She'd been unable to sleep that night. Sometime in the darkest hours, an idea had formed in her mind. A dangerous one. But after two days of people dying . . .

Bratton moaned and shifted in his bed. After extracting herself from her blankets, Ilyenna went to check on him. He still burned with fever. She leaned over the other bed. Her father was so unnaturally still, no matter how hard she had struggled to wake him, no matter how many medicines and treatments she had tried.

He was worse than ever. They both were. Ilyenna had been healing since she was old enough to thread a needle. She knew how close she was to losing both of them. In the end, that made the choice for her. Before she could change her mind, she tiptoed through the clan house so as not to wake the Argons scattered everywhere.

When she reached the hall where the most severely wounded were kept, she nearly gagged. The air was rank with garlic, whiskey, and a myriad of body odors. Hiking up her skirt, she stepped over a slumbering woman, her arms clutching her child— even in sleep, she was afraid to let go.

Just before Ilyenna reached the door, she caught sight of the old man with the amputated foot. He was dead. All she could feel was relief that there was one less mouth to feed. She covered his face so as not to frighten the children. "So passes a warrior," she whispered. "So passes an Argon."

Brushing the death from her hands, she stood. She'd have to remember to call one of the men to haul him out.

She entered the kitchen and fed the fire. Having the refugees in her home left her feeling like she slept under too many blankets. And the dying hadn't slowed. If anything, it had increased. Already a line of shrouded, frozen bodies waited for the ground to thaw so they could be buried behind the clan house. But Bratton was right. Ilyenna couldn't worry about burying the dead until the living had the time and strength to dig the graves.

Without waiting for the fire to take off, she wrapped her coat over her dress, braced herself against the cold, and stepped outside. The cold immediately took her breath away.

When Ilyenna was a child, Great-aunt Enrid had told her stories of the constant battle between the queens of winter and summer— two women on opposite sides of the Balance. In winter, the summer queen was always forced to retreat to her personal domain far to the south. A place where summer never faded, where no one ever died of cold and where food was always fresh.

Ilyenna thought if she ever came to such a place, she'd never return to her home in the mountains. She hated winter, hated the sickness, hunger, and death it brought. It had tried to break her once. She'd vowed it would never come so close again.

She trudged through the snow to the slight rise behind the clan house. There, snow-covered mounds dotted the hillside far back into the trees. A graveyard was a link between the living and the dead, and she had to speak with her mother. Twilight or morning was best. The dead were tied to night's side of the Balance, as the living were tied to the day's. She stopped at her mother's grave.

"Mother . . ." She hesitated. It was dangerous to seek the dead's attention. Dangerous because they might just decide Ilyenna should join them. "I need you to let Father and Bratton stay with me. I know you miss them. I know you long for them. But I–I'm not strong enough to lead the clan by myself. Please. If you hold any sway with death, let it pass them over."

Wondering if she'd been heard, Ilyenna waited. Nothing happened. It was said that the dead no longer understood the living's fondness for life. Ilyenna's mother had died trying to save her. Perhaps it was selfish to ask for more. Perhaps Matka wouldn't understand why Ilyenna wished her father and brother to remain in a world of cold and cruelty.

But she had watched so many die. She couldn't bear to see her father and brother join them. As she turned to go, a small shadow fell across her. But that was impossible; the sun had yet to rise. She glanced at the sky. Frost was still falling, but one of the flakes was acting strangely, almost as if it was moving of its own will.

Ilyenna stared as it zipped and twisted, moving horizontally instead of downward as falling frost was meant to. But it moved so fast and erratically, Ilyenna kept losing sight of it. She started when she felt a strange pressure at her feet.

In the hollows of the snow, shadows boiled like cauldrons of vapors. Ilyenna's breath caught in her throat. The shadows surged and spilled over her feet like smoke, then stretched up, reaching for her. She cried out as they crawled up her body, covering her like a second skin.

Ilyenna scrubbed at her arms, trying to remove the shadows, but they clung to her. Her heart thudded painfully in her chest as she stumbled and fell back into the snow. Suddenly the shadows returned to the ground. She pulled her sleeves up, revealing her pale skin, no shadows in sight.

She scrambled to her feet and ran from the graveyard. At the clan house, she hurried past Enrid and went straight upstairs to her father. She knelt beside him, pressing her fingers to his face. He shifted away from her cold touch.

Moving to the other bed, she touched her brother. His fever had broken and his color was better. Relief warred with horror inside Ilyenna. She pressed her hands into her stomach and doubled over. It was never a good idea to attract the attention of the dead. But if she was careful, perhaps they would forget about her. Besides, she'd had no choice.

After feeding the qatcha to her father and brother, Ilyenna stumbled back to the kitchen and collapsed in a chair. The first thing she noticed was that someone had already removed the dead man.

Enrid glanced up. "You're up early," she whispered so as not to wake those lying on the floor. As cold as it was outside, heat shimmered from the huge fireplace. Enrid ran a knife through a nutty brown loaf of bread and slapped some lard on a slice; the butter had run out a few days ago. She held the bread out to Ilyenna.

Ilyenna shook her head. "I'm all right." The burden of caring for so many was crashing down on her. She braced herself against the table as panic swelled in her chest.

"Winter's almost up," Enrid said.

Ilyenna grunted. "Just in time to start digging for roots and shriveled berries."

They'd already started killing barren ewes. The dogs would be next. She wondered how they'd survive next year if they were forced to decimate their herds.

Glancing around, she couldn't help but once again notice the Argon's clothes. Most of the people had been forced to flee their homes with what little clothing they'd had on. Ilyenna was still treating their frostbite.

It was cold still, cold enough they'd need warm clothes and coats. At least Ilyenna wouldn't have to worry about finding enough wool. The Shyle's poor, rocky soil didn't offer up much in the way of fields or even gardens. But the steep slopes and harsh winters were perfect for raising sheep and goats, and the Shyle had wool by the bagful. The clan women carded and spun that wool into the finest yarn and cloth in all the clan lands.

Ilyenna stood abruptly, took the bread, and put her hand on the door latch. She had to get away from here—from the dead, the injured, and the emptying foodstores.

"Ilyenna, what's wrong?" Enrid asked.

She paused. She almost considered telling Enrid what she'd done. But it would only anger and frighten the old woman. "I'm going to buy every skein of yarn or bolt of felt Volna Plesti will give me." The woman and her family operated the enormous dye vats far downwind of the village, near the mouth of the canyon.

Enrid smiled and nodded. Just yesterday she'd said Ilyenna needed to get out of the clan house. "Make sure you bring all the knitting needles she has as well."

Ilyenna hesitated. "You're certain you can handle things?"

Enrid cast Ilyenna a look of exasperation. "I was the clan mistress not long ago, remember?"

Ilyenna shouldered open the door and hurried away. The sun had turned the west mountain faces pink, but had yet to touch the valley. A cold wind snaked through the tightly woven fabric of her coat. She hugged it tighter, wishing Otrok hadn't taken Myst with him to guard the entrance to the Shyle.

Already, many figures were about—boys gathering and chopping wood, girls feeding chickens, goats, and sheep. Ilyenna barely noticed them, all her concentration was on getting away from the graveyard. What if she'd brought the attention of the dead on her whole village?

She jumped when someone called out to her. Lanna, a steaming pail of goat's milk in her hand, trotted toward her. This was the beautiful clan woman Ilyenna's brother had taken a fancy to a few months back. But long before her brother had come along and the clan-mistress duties had taken all her free time, Lanna had been Ilyenna's best friend. With pale features, a curvy build, and blond hair as thick as an arm, she fit in everywhere Ilyenna stood out.

Lanna visibly braced herself. "How's Bratton?"

Trying to banish the image of the shadows crawling up her arms, Ilyenna took a deep breath. "He's much better. His fever is broken."

Lanna smiled, revealing slightly crooked teeth. "I'm so glad." Her face fell when she glanced back at her house. "Where are you off to?"

"Volna Plesti's to buy some wool," Ilyenna answered.

"Mind if I come? I'm not sure I can bear going back. We've four sick Argon babies. All they do is cry."

Ilyenna tried to swallow the lump in her throat. She'd visited those babies yesterday. They'd been exposed to too much cold. Two were very young and very ill, and they refused to eat. She doubted either of them would live. If a Tyran had been present at the moment, she'd have gladly taken her knife to his tender parts.

Instead, she forced a smile. "I could use the help."

She waited as Lanna hurried to find another sack for the wool and they set off. As they walked, the sun crept down the mountain slopes into the valley. It wasn't long before the snow softened enough to soak Ilyenna's shoes. She took her coat off, wondering if the winter fairies had finally decided to withdraw. With the warm sun on her face, she could almost forget the Argon refugees crowding Shyleholm and emptying their foodstores, almost forget her worry over Father, Bratton, and the shadows in the graveyard. Almost.

They reached Volna's by midmorning. She opened the door and nodded when she saw them. The old woman's face was as wrinkled as a winter apple. "You'll be looking for my wool skeins," she said.

Ilyenna and Lanna shared a surprised look.

Volna shrugged. "Why else would our clan mistress walk all the way to the mouth of the canyon?" She moved aside and they stepped into the room. Volna tipped her head toward a woman and three small children braiding rags into rugs at the table. "This is Hinley and hers."

They nodded to the Argon woman, who nodded back. Then Ilyenna and Lanna followed Volna into her storerooms. From floor to ceiling, the shelves spilled with colors, everything from skeins of yarn to felt and raw wool. Volna nodded toward their sacks. "I suppose you'll want to fill them."

With a nod, Ilyenna held out a small bag of silver.

The old woman held up her hand. "Old women like to feel wanted. You can pay me after you're sure you can afford to feed all the Argons."

Ilyenna hesitated, the bag dangling between them. "But how will you buy dyes at the spring feast?"

Volna smiled. "Wool's just as warm in cream as it is indigo. We'll make do."

A weight lifted from Ilyenna's shoulders. "Thank you, Volna."

"Take some of the brighter colors, Lanna, " the old woman said. "The Argons could use some cheering up."

With that, she left Lanna and Ilyenna to make their selections. Once their bags were stuffed to overflowing, they said goodbye and started down the road. They chatted softly at first, but a sense of alertness soon grew inside Ilyenna. Even the birds had gone silent. She found herself watching the woods and feeling like they watched back.

Finally, she stopped. "Something's wrong."

Lanna pressed her lips together, a worry line between her eyebrows. "I feel it too."

That's when Ilyenna noticed a soft rumble echoing off the mountain slopes. "Do you hear that?"

They stood in the road and listened.

Lanna shook her head. "It's just the river."

"No, it's growing louder. Besides, the river is frozen over."

Suddenly, Ilyenna recognized the pounding of hooves. She turned to look down the road just in time to see a rider round the corner at full speed. It was Otrok. He'd gone to act as sentinel again. But where were the other two boys she'd sent with him?

He waved his hands frantically. "Hide! Quick, hide!"

Ilyenna sprinted for the trees, the sacks of wool bouncing awkwardly on her back. She whirled at a sharp cry from Lanna. She'd slipped on the ice and fallen, landing on her backside.

Brightly colored skeins spilled across the road. Ilyenna ran back to her and began frantically shoving the skeins inside the sack.

Drawing up his horse, Otrok gaped at Ilyenna. There was dried blood on his face.

"Mistress? What're you doing here?" He held out his hand. "Get on!"

Ilyenna glanced down the road. The echoing distorted the sound, but they couldn't be far. With two riders, the horse would fall behind and the village would have little or no warning. She met Lanna's fearful gaze.

"Go with him." Lanna said.

"No! Tell the men to defend the village," Ilyenna said to Ortok. "And the women to scatter for their summer homes. Now!" She slapped the horse's rump. Ortok looked back at her as the horse took off at a gallop.

Frantically, Ilyenna and Lanna shoved skeins into the sacks. The sound behind them grew louder. Any moment, Tyrans would round the bend.

"Leave it!" Ilyenna said finally, grabbing Lanna's arm and hauling her to her feet.

They ran hard for the trees. After floundering through a snow drift, they threw themselves on the other side and lay flat. The pounding hooves grew louder. Ilyenna stared at the bright skeins scattered across the snow.

"Why didn't they light a signal fire?" Lanna sounded close to tears.

There wasn't time for Ilyenna to answer. Horses careened around the bend, all bearing men with shields and axes. She tried to count, but they came too fast and there were too many. Hundreds.

Please don't let them notice the wool, she chanted in her mind. Please, please, please don't let them notice the wool.

The group barreled past, their horses tramping the skeins and felt, churning the bright colors with dirt and snow until they lay like broken butterflies. Ilyenna bit her lip. The entire clan had worked so hard on that wool, and the Argons desperately needed it. Now it was ruined.

Before the whole army could pass by, one man stopped and stared down at the ruined skeins, his horse dancing to follow its companions. Ilyenna gripped her knife hilt. The man pulled his horse around, circling the wool. At the footprints in the snow, he stopped. His eyes followed the tracks to Ilyenna and Lanna's hiding place. He shouted an order, and another man broke off from the group.

The first man pointed toward the snow drift, and both riders started forward. Ilyenna inched backward. "Run," she whispered.

Lanna gaped at her, her face frozen with terror. Ilyenna grabbed her arm and heaved. The girl stumbled and nearly went down, but Ilyenna held tight and she managed to keep her feet.

"There!" came the shout from behind them.

Ducking branches, Ilyenna and Lanna struggled through the deep snow. She heard the heavy sound of horses crashing through the undergrowth and glanced behind. Unable to ride farther in the snow, the men tossed their reins around a tree limb and started after them on foot.

"Stop," one of the men shouted. "We won't hurt you!"

Lanna slowed, but Ilyenna grabbed her sleeve. "Just like they didn't hurt the Argons?"

The young woman fell back in beside her, her face grim.

Her lungs burning from exertion and cold, Ilyenna looked back. The Tyrans were gaining on them.

Can't outrun them. Can't hide, she thought.

That only left one option. She stopped and slid her knife from her belt. Lanna noticed and did the same. Ilyenna nodded, and Lanna nodded back. Pivoting, they held out their knives.

The two men slowed, circling the women tentatively. Both had blue eyes, copper beards, and thick builds. Brothers, Ilyenna realized. She'd seen these men before, but she was too frightened to recall when or where. She stood back to back with Lanna. The man facing her rested his hand on his axe hilt. "My name is Hammoth. That's my brother Darrien. We don't want to hurt you. Put down your knives and we'll bind you and take you back to your village."

She instantly recognized the names. They were the sons of the Tyran clan chief. Ilyenna's palm was slippery with sweat against her knife hilt. "Just like you didn't hurt the Argon women?"

The Tyrans exchanged glances. "They fought beside their men. What would you've had us do?" Hammoth said.

"Leave the Argons alone. Leave us alone," she hissed. She felt Lanna trembling behind her. Two small knives against axes. They had as much of a chance as a mouse against a fox.

Very slowly, Hammoth shook his head. "I can't do that."

"And I can't put this knife down," Ilyenna said.

He eased his axe from its loop. "One last chance, Shyle clanwomen."

Ilyenna thought of the Argons she'd tended—her father and brother, the young girl with the broken arm, the old man, and all the others who would be buried when the ground thawed. Then she thought of the babies who'd likely die before tomorrow, and her fury burned hotter than her fear. Steadying herself, she lifted her knife.

In response, Hammoth hefted his metal studded wooden shield and slid forward. Ilyenna's gaze flicked to the bloodstained blade. Was it from the other two boys she'd sent to guard the canyon? Enraged, she lunged toward him, but he blocked her with his shield and clocked her in the side of the head with his axe haft. She stumbled forward dizzily and he caught her, almost gently.

She drew back her knife. He hefted his axe, no doubt planning to kill her, then hesitated. She didn't. She drove in her knife, just under his ribs. It sank easily to the hilt. Blood gushed, pulsing hot over her hand and down her forearm.

His mouth gaping, he stared at her as he sank to his knees. "Darrien!" he gasped as he reached toward the other man.

It was shockingly easy, no harder than killing a goat. Ilyenna felt no sorrow. Nothing. The Balance protect her, what was wrong with her?

"Hammoth!" Darrien cried. "No!"

Ilyenna whirled to see Darrien behind Lanna, his face frozen in horror. She heard a soft flop as Hammoth collapsed into the snow behind her.

With a shriek of rage, Darrien swung at Lanna. She threw herself backward, landing flat on her back. Ilyenna rushed forward, putting her knife between the Tyran and Lanna. He jumped out of range and slammed her hand with his shield.

She felt her bones shatter and pain lance up her arm. The knife slipped out of her useless fingers. Before she could react, the axe sliced toward her. She tried to jump back, as Lanna had, but she wasn't fast enough. Cold metal drew a line of fire through her belly. She smelled the unmistakable scent of bile mixing with blood. She sank to her knees, propped up by one hand, her injured arm wrapped around her belly to keep her bowels from spilling out.

The healer in her understood, even if the rest of her couldn't. She was going to die—a long, agonizingly painful death.

She glanced up as Darrien lifted his axe again. Lanna jumped in front of her and threw her knife. He blocked it with his shield. Redirecting his blow, he slammed his axe into Lanna's shoulder, splitting her from shoulder to belly. With a sickening sucking sound, he pulled it free.

Lanna was dead before she hit the ground. Ilyenna stretched her bloodied hand toward her friend. The movement shot barbs through her belly. She doubled up, wondering why the pain hadn't killed her. "Please," she hissed through clenched teeth. "Please, kill me."

Darrien crouched in front of her, but she couldn't meet his gaze. "You murdered my brother." Without another word, he stepped around her. She heard him heave Hammoth over his shoulder.

"You're no better than a Raider!" she panted.

He didn't answer. Eventually the sound of his footfalls faded, leaving her only the silence, Lanna's body, and the pain that burned until it swallowed her whole.

4. Winter Dance

I lyenna watched as snow twirled and danced delicately on the breeze, gently covering Lanna's bloody body with pure white. It was as stark and disturbing as it was beautiful.

Ilyenna now felt neither cold nor pain, only wonder at the beauty around her. She knew she was dying, her soul slipping away. She waited for darkness to come for her.

One snowflake danced toward her, twirling and spinning like a silver bowl. It hovered above her and spoke in a voice like singing crystal. "I think this one might do."

Other snowflakes danced and twirled, floating above her face. "She may," one of them replied in a tinkling voice. "But then again, she may not."

Strange, Ilyenna thought, that upon my death, I should hear talking snowflakes.

"Shall we choose her?" asked a third snowflake.

Everything grew hazy and out of focus. Ilyenna could no longer see the snowflakes, only hear them speaking as if from far away.

"She's been marked," came the voice of the first. "She's already one of us."

"Well then, that's something else entirely. But if we choose her, it must be quick. She'll not last much longer."

Ilyenna could no longer distinguish one voice from another. Her life was slipping away as softly as a twirling snowflake.

"I shall choose her," said one.

Something small, like a frozen teardrop, touched Ilyenna's mouth. Her body instantly came back to life. The dim, grainy landscape grew clear again. She looked at the snowflakes, but their glamor was gone now. They weren't talking snowflakes at all, but fairies. The one directly above her was the size of her largest finger. She had fluffy white wings that looked like rabbit fur.

Ilyenna's eyes shifted to take in the other fairies. All had high, pointed eyebrows and ears. Their hair hung long and soft as silk down their backs. Their skin varied from bluish white to purplish black, with wings as varied as their faces.

With wings like clear ice, the purple-black fairy flew down and pressed her tiny lips to Ilyenna's. Suddenly, the cold embraced her like an old friend. She felt as if winter's secrets were hidden somewhere deep inside her, waiting to be discovered.

Another fairy, with wings like fans of frost shards, bent down and kissed Ilyenna. In her blood, ice crystals formed, searing her veins. She screamed. The sound was swallowed by an avalanche roaring in her ears. The pain seemed to slowly shred her body one icy knife at a time.

"You drag on her torment unnecessarily, Ursella. Choose her or not, but do so quickly."

The fairy shook out her mane of silver hair. "They are weak, even the strongest of them."

"The Balance requires a queen, Ursella. Choose now or she dies."

Ilyenna felt the truth in the words. Her life ebbed away. The pain still tore at her, but it was as distant as a fading echo.

"Very well."

Faintly, Ilyenna felt the last fairy's lips on hers. Pain and time fled. She'd lived seventeen years, but she'd not lived at all. Her body, previously broken and bleeding, now pulsed with white light. Her wounds no longer existed. She suddenly realized she hadn't breathed in many long minutes. She gasped, taking air into her lungs.

"And so a new winter queen is born," said the fairy with furry white wings.

White streamers, like ribbons of silk, slipped around Ilyenna's body. They shimmered and rippled like water before absorbing into her skin. Light gathered at her fingertips, and crystals sang in her ears. A new awareness grew inside her chest. She let her thoughts go and felt herself fragmenting, her body disintegrating into swirls of snow.

From deep inside Ilyenna, something whispered a warning. Danger and chaos and destruction lay before her.

"No! Not yet," one of the fairies cried.

The warning was drowned out by the chiming of crystals and the wind rushing in Ilyenna's ears. As if in a trance, she continued to fragment. The four fairies pulled and tugged at her hair and clothes, but they were no stronger than hummingbirds.

The one with furry wings planted herself in front of Ilyenna, fists on her slim hips. "You will not enter winter. Not yet. If you do, winter will never let you go."

Shocked, Ilyenna pulled back into her physical form.

Clearly relieved, the fairy bowed. "I am Chriel, my queen."

The fairies circled her, their small hands reverently tracing her temple, neck, hair, her bare back. "The power inside her—so beautiful."

Ilyenna wasn't sure which one of them said it. Once again, she realized she hadn't expelled the air in her lungs. When she did, wind and snow rushed from her lips. Chriel tumbled back, her wings beating hard. Ilyenna clamped her hand over her mouth.

Shaking snow from her hair, Chriel fluttered back to her. "You might want to be a trifle more careful with winter's wind, Queen."

Ilyenna took a deep breath and let it out very slowly, very carefully. As cold as it was, her breath should have misted the air. It didn't. "Winter queen?" she asked.

The fairy with wings like the finest glass fluttered them unhurriedly. "Winter has birthed you, endowing you with its power. You are a force of nature manifest in flesh—hence you are winter queen."

"I'll live forever?"

The fairy's wings quivered. "Not forever. But neither are you a mere mortal." She bowed, her wings dropping low. "I am Tanyis. We would have you as our queen—the conduit of winter's power, if you are willing. But there is a price."

"A price?" Ilyenna echoed.

"There is always a price." The fairy with wings that looked like broken glass flew forward. "You mustn't agree unless you're certain, mortal. The transformation has been set in motion, but you have yet to enter winter. We can still stop it."

The other fairies shot the fourth looks of cold disapproval.

Normally, Ilyenna wouldn't have been so bold, but the ice racing through her veins lent her courage. "If you had doubts, Ursella, you shouldn't have chosen me."

Ursella's eyes narrowed into a tiny glare.

The other three shot her looks of triumph. "I knew she called to me." Chriel clapped her hands in delight.

"What price?" Ilyenna asked again.

"Your humanity," Ursella said, her wings stiff.

Ilyenna tried to speak, but she had no breath in her lungs. She had to remember to keep breathing. She inhaled and spoke carefully. "I don't understand . . ."

The blue fairy with wings like fans of frost smiled. "I am Qari, my queen. You have been reborn into winter, but as Ursella said, the transformation is not complete. You must agree to the price first—your humanity."

Ilyenna looked from one fairy to the next in confusion.

Qari went on. "Humans feel all ranges of emotions. As a queen of winter, the emotions on the light side of the Balance will be alien to you—emotions like passion, protectiveness, trust. Instead, you will naturally gravitate toward indifference, jealousy, and rage. You will no longer belong with mankind. Instead, you will be a force of nature. Your soul will be reborn, as your body has been. In return, the powers of winter shall be yours permanently."

"And if I refuse?"

"Winter will fade and you shall forever return to your human state," Qari said.

"Do not make the decision, lightly," Ursella warned. "The price will cost you everything that makes you Ilyenna—a healer, daughter, sister, friend. All of it will be gone."

Ilyenna tried to concentrate, but the thrill of winter kept luring away her thoughts. It took all her will, but she forced herself to ignore it. "Powers of winter?"

Three of the four fairies laughed. At the sound, the wind picked up.

"A strange question," Qari said. "What is winter if not the power of the blizzard, winter winds, snow, ice, cold. . . the ability to put the world to sleep, to make ice flowers bloom, and to deck the world in thousands of sparkling frost diamonds."

"On the last day of true winter," Chriel sang.

The three shifted on the breeze, their tinkling laughter filling Ilyenna's head with thoughts of flight. Long wings uncurled from her back, shifting and shimmering with the colors of an aurora. The rest of her body was nearly as pale as the driven snow, and as bare as trees in winter. She gestured to the snow. It swirled forward, coating her in a gown of white.

Part of her wanted to stay on the ground, to ask more questions, but the wind called for her to dance. Her wings beat to life. She rose, her arms outstretched as they commanded the storm. She dove in and out of heavy clouds, swam through swirls of snow, sang and danced the dance of the storm.

Other fairies appeared, pressing their lips to hers. As they did, a pleasant awareness of each grew inside Ilyenna. Some of those fairies brought shards of frost and diamonds. After sweeping up her black hair, they placed a headdress upon her head. In its center was a diamond the size of Ilyenna's thumbnail.

The storm slowly shifted. "Come with us," the fairies sang. "We move north for summer."

Her wings ached to follow them, but as she did, she happened to glance down at a small village, nestled in the mountains. Smoke rose up from gutted stone houses. Memories of a past life tugged at her heart. She lifted her bluish white hands. "Who am I?"

Chriel glanced nervously at the storm as it moved further away. She seemed faded somehow, her brilliance melting. "We must follow. We've held on as long as we could, but the last storm of winter has passed. Summer comes."

As winter's power slipped from Ilyenna's body, memories of a people she'd once loved blossomed in her mind. They were in trouble somehow. She must remember why. She shook her head, trying to remember. "Can I not stay, Chriel? Can I not?"

Chriel strained against an invisible current, her arms outstretched and her voice pleading, "My queen, you must come with me! You're not strong enough yet—not yet."

Ilyenna's wings wilted, melting like frost before the sun. She fell back toward the earth. "I can't, Chriel. Not yet."

5. MARKED

Ilyenna lay on the ground, staring into Lanna's clouded eyes, her grayish blue skin. She felt no grief. No pain. Nothing. Perhaps she was dead too. So she stared, waiting for her own eyes to glass over.

Voices floated in and out of her waking dreams. Only when one spoke right next to her could she make sense of the words. "There's two of 'em over here."

She groaned, trying to make her mind work.

"She's still alive!" he gasped.

"Alive? She can't be."

"But she is!"

Hot fingers brushed the snow off her face. "Get her on the horse."

Strong hands gripped her arms and dragged her, then hauled her, belly down, onto a saddle. Why didn't that hurt? Darrien had cut her there. Ilyenna tried to fight, to kick, but only succeeded in wiggling. Her body had no strength. The men tying her down didn't even seem to notice her efforts.

"Look at her clan belt," one of them said.

The other man grunted. "Looks like we found the missing clan mistress, eh?"

She managed to look at the man just finishing up her wrists. He frowned at her before grabbing the reins and leading the horse through the trees and onto the road. There, he mounted another horse and kicked it into a trot, pulling her horse behind.

The jarring ride clouded her brain, and she passed back into oblivion.

Some time later, hands gripped hers. She pushed against unconsciousness, but it was like trying to catch hold of mist. She groaned and shifted. A man pulled her from the saddle and carried her, at one point slinging her over a shoulder before taking her back in his arms. She nestled her head against a strong chest as her thoughts slowly ordered themselves. Fairies. There'd been fairies. Dancing. Kisses. Power. Queen.

She heard a door creak open, and the arms dumped her on a bed.

"By the Balance, what have they done to you?" Bratton cried. When she didn't answer, he shook her so hard that her head hit the bed frame. "Ilyenna! Ilyenna!"

Moaning, she pushed her brother away. The ropes beneath the straw mattress shifted as he sat next to her. She heard a door shut and a wooden bar fall into place. She groaned again and forced her eyes open. She blinked up at her brother. Something was wrong. Bandages wrapped his head. Dark blood had seeped through them and dried on the sides of his face. She pushed all thoughts of fairies far away. "Bratton?"

He tipped a wooden mug to her lips. "Are you all right?"

She swallowed a mouthful of qatcha, nearly gagging at its strength. She pushed it away and glanced around. They were in one of the smaller rooms in the clan house. "Wh–what happened?"

His hands probed her stomach. "You're covered in blood. Where are you hurt?" He shoved his hands through his hair, tugging the bandage awry. "By the Balance, I'm no good with healing. That's your talent."

She reached inside her torn dress and felt skin as smooth and soft as a child's. In wonder, she wiggled the fingers of the hand Darrien had crushed. Her searching fingers found the matted blood on her head. "I'm not hurt."

She remembered Darrien's axe slicing her stomach. Remembered hunching over as the pain burned up her thoughts and hot blood seeped through her shattered fingers. "He gutted me. But the fairies healed me with a kiss."

Still not quite believing it herself, Ilyenna glanced up to see disbelief and worry written across her brother's face.

Suddenly, she felt so tired. "It was real. I saw them. They asked me to be their queen."

Bratton smoothed her hair away from her face. "Listen to me, Ilyenna. In a battle, sometimes a man gets confused. That's all this was. It wasn't real—none of it was. But don't say it again. You'll frighten the others with talk of fairies."

Ilyenna barely heard him. All of yesterday came back in a rush. The wool trampled into the snow. The men. Lanna.

May the Balance protect her, Lanna's death was her fault. She closed her eyes. "Lanna's dead."

Bratton rocked forward and cradled his head in his hands. "You're sure?"

Ilyenna nodded once.

Rage hardened his face. He spoke through gritted teeth. "She isn't the only one."

Ilyenna sat up in the bed, clenching the blankets in her fists. "What are you trying to tell me? Is it Father?"

Bratton pressed his palms into his eyes as if to stave off tears. "He was alive when the Tryans took him a few hours ago."

Ilyenna felt her mouth go suddenly dry. "Otrok?"

Bratton swallowed. "He died trying to avenge his father."

A wave of horror rolled through her. She'd gone to the dead, asking her brother and father's lives be spared, and her request had been granted. In the space of a day, they'd gone from the brink of death to fighting in a battle. And in return, the dead had taken two others whom Ilyenna loved.

"The Balance," she gasped. "Lanna and Otrok for you and father."

Through his haze of grief, Bratton stared up at her.

She scooted back, trying to get away from him. "You need to stay away from me."

Bratton's brows drew together in confusion. "What? Why?"

"Otrok and Lanna—their deaths are my fault."

"You weren't even with Otrok," he said.

She shook her head, desperate to make her brother understand. "Bratton, I—I was so afraid you and father would die. I—I went to the dead. I begged them to spare you. And now, Otrok and Lanna are dead."

Bratton gaped dumbly at her.

"Don't you see? The dead spared you and Father and took two others in your place."

Bratton shot to his feet, his hands fisted at his sides. "No."

"I saw the shadows boiling, saw them crawl up my skin. I'm marked." And will be, until the dead claim me forever as their own.

Horror dawned on Bratton's face just before the doors behind him burst open and several Tyrans entered. Two grabbed Bratton; another two came for Ilyenna. They hauled her out of the bed and to the ladder. "Down. Both of you."

Bratton cast a hard look at her before climbing down. She followed him. The hall was filled with what remained of the Argon and Shyle clans. Most of the men had fresh wounds mixed with old ones. Many of the women and children were gone—perhaps Otrok had come in time for the them to flee to their summer homes.

She reached the bottom of the ladder and stood beside Bratton, who glared toward the main doors.

Ilyenna followed his gaze to see a group of Tyrans, the sunlight streaming behind them and casting their faces in shadows. The guards at their sides took Ilyenna's and Bratton's arms and pushed them through their clan.

As Ilyenna came closer to the Tyrans, she could make out their features. At their center stood a man with twin streaks of white running down his ruddy beard. His gaze bore down on her.

Ilyenna recognized him immediately—Undon, the Tyran clan chief. All along the spectrum of the Balance, men ranged from good to evil. Ilyenna had the distinct impression Undon was on evil's side.

A man flanked his side, a young man with a red beard. His stunned gaze met hers. It was Darrien. Unconsciously, she planted her feet and tried to twist her arms out of the guard's hands. They relentlessly dragged her before Undon and his son.

"Otec's children," one of the men said. Then the guards backed up a few steps.

Ilyenna's gaze flickered to Darrien and away again. If he told his father she'd killed his other son, she'd be dead in a handful of heartbeats.

Darrien opened his mouth to speak but stopped at the sound of a scuffle behind him. Ilyenna strained to see past them. Her father was thrown face first into the room.

She reached forward to help him to his feet. Bratton's hand shot out, holding her back. A knot of anxiety unraveled in her chest. Her father was alive. And after four days, he was awake. The dead had kept their end of the bargain.

Holding himself up with one arm, her father met her gaze. The lines around his face seemed to soften. He glanced at Bratton and nodded slightly. Bratton nodded back. Ilyenna wondered what silent communication had passed between them.

Otec held his arm snug against his belly. Only then did Ilyenna see that it was hanging unnaturally, broken. Blood circled the back of his neck to drip from his chin. Bruises marred his weathered face.

A cry arose in Ilyenna's throat. They'd beaten him. Her brother tightened his grip on her arm. She wanted so badly to help her father, but Bratton wouldn't keep her back without good reason. Tears of helplessness slipped down her face.

Her father pushed himself up with his good arm. His eyes closed and he struggled to take a few deep breaths before slowly turning to face their attackers.

His face twisted with rage, Undon said, "Otec, you banded with my enemy, the Argons, and fought against our clan. In doing so, you became my enemy. Then your men murdered one of my sons."

Ilyenna winced. Undon didn't know she'd killed Hammoth. If he did, she'd already be dead.

"I come to claim the right of reparation for what you've taken," Undon continued. "For the deaths of my men, I claim half your herds, half your wool, half your gold and silver, to be paid faithfully at harvest for the next five years."

A gasp rippled through the clan. Ilyenna blinked in shock. Five years of giving up half of everything? They would starve.

Protests rose from Shyle throats.

Undon caressed his axe hilt. "For my eldest son, who would've been clan chief after my death, I claim tiams to serve five years." He stepped toward Ilyenna's father. "You first and foremost among them, Otec."

Her father—the clan chief—a tiam? Until his debt is paid, a tiam must serve and submit. The Balance demanded it.

Somehow, her father managed to remain standing, though his body swayed. Ilyenna longed to run to his side, to offer him a steadying hand and tend to his wounds. "Undon, the Argon clan has been next to kin to the Shyle for generations." Otec's gravelly voice sounded strong. "We helped defend them and offered aid when you sacked them. This is no crime."

Undon took a menacing step forward. "This was between me and Clan Chief Seneth. You made it between me and you as well."

Her father shrugged away Undon's warning, a dangerous thing to do when his enemy held an axe and he held a broken arm. "You've no claims here."

Undon slowly turned to the men beyond sight of the door. "Seal the clan house. Bar the doors. Bring in the torches. Burn everything." Embers of hatred smoldered in his eyes. "Everything."

Cries and gasps erupted. Ilyenna's eyes widened and her throat went dry. Bratton's grip tightened around her, as if the strength of his arms could shield her from the flames.

"You do this, and the Council will band against you! Your wheat will grow red with Tyran blood," her father cried.

Undon stepped forward. "The Council can't even agree to plant potatoes in dirt. They won't risk a war with my clan. Accept my terms. Only then will I forgive your betrayal."

Ilyenna didn't believe it. The Council would never stand for this treason. But the Council wasn't here. The pounding of hammers rang in Ilyenna's ears. Slowly, the light was being snuffed out. They were boarding up the windows. She gripped a fistful of Bratton's shirt.

They had no choice. "All but the tiams and land," her father finally whispered.

"You can burn." Undon lifted his axe to slice off her father's head.

"No," Ilyenna cried as she tore herself from Bratton's grip. Leaping forward, she threw herself at Undon, her fingers straining to scratch out his eyes. Her father's good arm reached out and jerked her back just as Undon's axe arched toward her skull. Bratton was moments behind, trying to pull her deeper into the crowd. She fought against him, struggling and cursing Undon.

Somehow, she managed to break free. She grabbed Undon's axe handle just as he swung it. He wrenched it back, but she managed to hold on by her fingertips, knowing she'd die if she let go. "Honor to the Shyle! Honor to the Shyle!" she shouted her clan's war cry.

Within moments, her clan surrounded her, bare hands against bare steel. They wrestled Undon's axe from his grip while others took down Darrien. A scream tore through the air—the sound of a soul torn from its body.

Tyrans flooded the room by tens, axes shining with fresh blood. A Shyle woman dropped. And another. They were falling like lambs before wolves.

"Back!" her father cried. "Back!"

With fresh wounds, her clan retreated. It had barely begun, and it was over.

Breathing hard, his glare murderous, Undon gestured for his men to bring Ilyenna to him. Bratton stepped between them. More of her clanmen blocked their path. The Tyrans pushed them back with their shields and bashed them with the butts of their axes.

"Stop," she commanded her clanmen. "Let them through."

Bratton grabbed her arms. "No! I'll not let them harm you!"

She felt the bruises forming under his grip. "The clan needs one of us to live," she whispered. He didn't move. "I'm marked," she reminded him. Unless she somehow managed to elude the dead's attention, she was as good as dead anyway. She gently pried his fingers from her arms.

She looked in her brother's eyes and saw understanding overtake his need to protect her. The clan came first. They both knew this, had known it since childhood. With fists clenched until the sinews stood out, Bratton lowered his hands to his sides.

Iron grips jerked Ilyenna away from him. Refusing to be dragged, she forced herself to keep her feet under her. The Tyrans shoved her into Undon's arms. He jerked her back by her hair and held his axe to the soft skin of her throat. She glared at him, daring him to kill her. The ringing of hammers set her teeth on edge.

Undon's gaze lingered on her face. "I remember your mother, Clan Mistress Ilyenna. Perhaps instead of killing Otec, I'll satisfy myself with you." He pulled back his half-moon axe. Cries erupted from her clan.

So another cost of seeking the dead would be her life. So be it. At least she had saved her brother and father. She shut her eyes and turned away.

"Wait," she heard Darrien say. She opened her eyes to see his hand on his father's arm.

Undon paused. His son stepped forward and probed the slash in Ilyenna's dress. She shuddered as his fingers touched her bare flesh. His brows knit together. "What kind of power is this?" he murmured so softly she was sure no one else heard him.

At some point in the scuffle, her braid had come loose. He took advantage, sifting through her black hair, something only her husband should ever do. He caressed her jaw and throat. "White as milk," he murmured. Leaning in, he whispered, "My brother wouldn't have hurt you. You'd have been better off to kill me. I'll make you pay for your mistake, little one. And I'll enjoy every moment of it."

A shiver of terror ran down her spine.

"Make her the tiam instead, Father," he said loudly.

Undon slowly nodded. "Very good, Darrien. That'll keep the Shyle in line."

"No," her father gasped. "I'd rather you killed her."

Ilyenna saw the desperation on her father's face—desperation that mirrored her brother's. As she understood, her stomach roiled.

More than her life was at stake. Darrien would force her to marry him. That would give him claim to the Shyle.

Undon sneered at her father. "You know the law, Otec. Any clan who trespasses against another is subject to reparation."

Her father spat at his feet. "The Council orders reparation when one clan wrongs another, not you! You're no better than a Raider!"

Undon chuckled darkly before stepping so close to Ilyenna she couldn't focus on his face. She forced herself to stand erect, her shoulders thrown back. "I shall leave the choice with you, Ilyenna. Five years as my tiam. Serve faithfully, submit to my will, and I'll allow the Shyle to live as long as they hold to the rest of the terms."

"No, Ilyenna," the cry was from her brother and was echoed by her clan.

Her head ached. She wanted to vomit. She wanted to scream. Instead, she narrowed her gaze. "You'll leave our lands alone?"

Ondon shrugged. "If your people pay honestly and faithfully, I'll leave their lands intact."

Her shoulders dropped. A tiam—a slave but for the rights she bargained for. But her time wouldn't last. The Council would intervene. They had to. She held onto that candle flame of hope, wavering as it was. "I will submit my sweat, but I will never marry you. You'll not harm me, by violence or neglect."

Undon turned to his son. "Darrien?"

His gaze felt hot against her skin. "I'll not marry her unless she asks for it."

She saw the triumph in Darrien's face. But soon he'd find out just how strong a Shyle clanwoman could be.

Undon nodded. "And I agree not to beat you."

It was better than she could have hoped for, but her words tasted like bile. "I submit. I will serve five years as tiam."

Her clan howled with rage.

Darrien simply crooked his finger, and she had to obey. He eased the knife from her belt, somehow making that simple gesture lewd. He tossed it in the air, then caught it and checked its balance before slipping it into his clan belt.

Ilyenna paused at the door, casting a final glance back at the hall. Her father and Bratton were fighting bare-fisted against the Tyrans, who beat them back with axe hilts. Her clan's cries grated against her ears.

At the front of the clan house, three men waited. Darrien climbed upon a magnificent bay gelding, then kicked a muddy foot out of the stirrup. She looked up at him. She'd exchanged safety with the fairies in the hopes of saving her clan. She'd failed, except to save her father and brother. Perhaps that knowledge would make her fate easier to endure.

Grateful she wore her riding leggings, Ilyenna hiked up her skirts and hauled herself up behind Darrien.

He glanced back at her. "Put your arms around my waist." She ground her teeth and gripped the cantle tighter. "You promised to submit. Shall I tell my clanmen to continue boarding up your clan house?"

Her skin crawling, she pried her grip from the saddle and wrapped her arms around Darrien's waist.

"Now lean your head against my shoulder."

"You swore I wouldn't have to submit my body."

He turned so she could see his profile. "I am not asking you to my bed, Ilyenna. Just your head on my shoulder."

She kept her head erect.

He nodded to one of his men. "Burn it."

Tears smoldering down her cheeks, she laid her cheek against his shoulder.

He laughed dryly. "And so you have learned your first lesson." He dug his heels into his gelding's sides, taking her away from the family and people she loved.

6. TIAM

Darrien and his men kept a pace meant to cover ground quickly without killing one's horse. Dividing the hour into quarters, they galloped, dismounted to walk, remounted to trot, and then slowed back to a walk. Then they began all over again. Her knees chafing, Ilyenna wished for Myst and her own saddle.

You've no horse. You're a tiam now, she silently chided herself. The notion was as bitter as the feel of her body pressed against Darrien's. She had no clan, no possessions—nothing but her name, her honor, and her wits. A lamb at the mercy of wolves.

Her only consolation was the hope that some of her mark might rub off onto Darrien.

He reached into a saddlebag under Ilyenna's leg, pulled out long sticks of cured meat, and began eating. The smoky aroma sent her mouth to watering. It had been a long time since she had eaten Enrid's bread. She forced herself not to listen, not to smell. Instead, as they traveled steadily downward and into warmer country, she concentrated on the shrinking forest and mountains of her homeland. How long before she could see them again?

She watched Darrien drink loudly from his waterskin, the crumbs of an oat cake scattered across the front of his shirt. Her throat nearly cracking for want of moisture, Ilyenna worked her tongue over the roof of her mouth. A warm wind gusted from the south, thawing the chill from her bones. Winter had lost its grip.

She closed her eyes. She should've gone with Chriel. She searched the trees, looking for any signs of fairies, listening for the sound and power of winter. But it was gone and had taken her powers with it. Ilyenna was truly alone.

Darrien pulled his horse to a stop. Ilyenna scrambled down, careful to keep him in front of her. A tiam wasn't supposed to walk before her master. When she was sure he and his men weren't looking, she scooped up a chunk of melting snow and began sucking. With one eye on him and one on her surroundings, she searched for any signs of food.

She saw some green shoots poking through the snow. Wild onions. Bending down, she worked them loose. Darrien turned just as she pulled them free. In two strides, he stood before her. He held out his hand. "I see you found me something besides cured meat." The other men laughed.

Her hands itched to take her knife from his belt. His gaze dared her to do so. She took a shuddering breath. He didn't have to behave like this. She'd treated Otrok as a brother, and now the boy was dead. Tears blurring her vision, she held out the onions.

Darrien jerked them from her, peeled off the outside layer, popped one in his mouth, and wiped the juice from his lips. At the sound of his crunching, Ilyenna remembered the fresh, mild taste and her stomach growled all the louder.

Darrien grinned and strode a little closer. His breath, heavy with onions, blew against her face. She held perfectly still as his fingers combed through her hair again. It was indecent having her hair down like this, but she hadn't had the time to braid it yet.

"For these onions, will you sell but one smile, Ilyenna?" he said.

She fought to keep her eyes from darting to the bulbs dangling from his hand. A smile today, a kiss tomorrow. Where would it end? No, better she never begin to play his games. Obedience. Honor. She kept her voice steady. "Every onion I find, I will deliver to you."

He grunted as he popped another in his mouth. With a jerk of his head, he motioned for the others to mount. He walked to his own horse, and Ilyenna followed. But after Darrien got on the gelding, his leg didn't move from the stirrup "My horse is tired. You'll have to run in front of us until he's recovered."

She stepped back from the saddle, fists clenched at her sides. He'd made himself clear. She was playing the game whether she wished to or not. She began running. Laughter followed her. By the time the sun extinguished itself on the mountains, her lungs were on fire and her legs had no more strength to bear her up than rotted wood. She tried to concentrate on one more step. Just one. She stumbled and fell to her knees. She was vaguely aware of the rocks scraping her palms, of the mud soaking through her dress. More than anything, her whole body ached to stay put. She struggled to haul her feet under her. Her legs buckled, and she went down again.

Someone gripped the collar of her dress and hauled her backwards. The fabric cut into her throat. She choked, her hands clawing at the collar. Darrien yanked her into his saddle, settling her in front of him. Both arms went around her.

Her mind wanted to fight, but she was so tired. She slumped forward. Soon, the rhythmic motion of the saddle began to lull her. Night was coming on, and she'd had so little sleep over the last week. Her eyelids closed and she felt herself leaning into Darrien's arms.

The next morning, she saw the first of the Tyran fields. Here, in the lowlands, green feathers of wheat were already poking through the damp earth. The snow had melted in all but the darkest shadows. Winter was fast becoming a memory. The air hung heavy with the smells of mud and the ripe decay of last year's leaves.

Ilyenna wasn't a winter queen anymore. She wasn't even a clan mistress. She was one small step above a slave. Tears stung her eyes. She tried to focus on something, anything, to take her mind off the arms around her.

With the fields came the familiar river-stone houses with split-shingle roofs. The houses grew in size and frequency the closer they came to the heart of Tyran lands. Darrien leaned forward and whispered, "I have a conundrum, little one. You see, you killed my brother, and for that I want to make you suffer. Yet, by killing him, you've moved me into his place—a place of power. For that, I'm grateful. Nor can I forget your own power to heal yourself. I must admit it fascinates me. Yet you stand helpless before me. Perhaps it's time we tested that power."

Ilyenna leaned away from him. "I don't have any power."

He went on as if she hadn't said anything. "You see my difficulty? But yesterday, I realized all of it could be solved in the same way." Darrien licked his lips as if savoring a lingering sweetness. She tried to drop from the horse, but he held her tight. "When I find what I want, I take it. And I want your power, and claim to your clan through marriage. Time, Ilyenna. I have five years. Has your answer changed?"

She gritted her teeth. "It never will."

He laughed. "The longer we play this game, the higher the stakes. Remember that. All that is required is for you to say the words, and the game ends."

Fear tore at her resolve like wolves clawing a hole under the barn door. She held herself erect, trying to look every bit the part of a clan mistress. He must never see her fear.

Soon, they reached Tyranholm—easily twice the size of Shyleholm. At the clan house stables, Darrien motioned for her to get off before dismounting himself. For the briefest moment, she considered vaulting into his saddle and heeling the horse away. But the Balance demanded she serve five years, regardless of the injustice of it.

Besides, even if she somehow managed to get away, where could she go? The clans didn't tolerate runaway tiams. The last one to run away was sold to distant lands as a slave. Ilyenna would be hauled back to Darrien. He could do anything he liked after that. She'd have no rights and no means of recourse.

No, better to wait until the Council intervened.

A stable boy came for Darrien's horse. Cowering as if expecting a slap, the boy took the reins.

Darrien jerked his thumb toward her. "Boy! Get me the soaked strap."

The boy cringed and ran.

Ilyenna felt her face drain of blood. Soaked strap?

Gripping her arm, Darrien steered her toward a tall pole. At the top, a rope dangled from a metal ring that had been driven into the wood. A beating pole—reserved for punishing thieves, abusers, and drunkards.

She clenched her jaw. "What have I done to deserve a beating?"

Darrien stopped at the base of the pole. "Will you tell me the secret of your power?"

She pursed her lips. "Winter fairies healed me."

He snorted. "I want the truth, not children's fairy tales." He stepped closer. "Will you marry me?"

"You swore," she whispered.

"I swore not to marry you unless you were willing. I'll not force you, Ilyenna. But I'll beat you for refusing to submit to my will. What is your answer?"

"Undon swore I'd not be beaten."

Darrien leaned forward and whispered, "No, Ilyenna. He promised he wouldn't beat you. He said nothing about anyone else."

They'd tricked her. Terror coursed through her body. "No. He couldn't have meant this."

"And you're going to appeal to him, are you? Because then I might just have to remember exactly who killed my father's favorite son."

She shuddered. Darrien had her trapped, and they both knew it. Ghosts of the coming horrors danced in her mind.

He wrapped her wrists with the rope that dangled from the topmost metal ring. "A good tiam submits to her master in all things. It may take time, but I will teach you how to be a good tiam." He finished the knot. "You should've killed me, Ilyenna."

She looked him in the eye. "Give me another chance. I won't make the mistake again."

He chuckled. "You have to decide, are you a healer or a killer?"

"I killed your brother." As soon as Ilyenna said it, she knew she'd made a mistake.

Darrien's eyes shimmered with pain that had twisted into hatred. "So you did. Perhaps we're more alike than you thought."

The stable boy came running, warily holding a strap that dripped what looked like watered-down milk, but the way it made

Ilyenna's nose sting was unmistakable. The strap had been soaked in lye. It would cause tremendous pain and discomfort without leaving scars. She'd be lucky to abide clothes for days.

Tears burned in her eyes. "I'm nothing like you." But as she said it, she wondered if she was really all that different. Hammoth had reached out to keep her from falling, been reluctant to hurt her, and she hadn't even hesitated to shove her knife under his ribs.

A crowd had begun to gather. By the knots on their belts, most were Tyrans. But there were also a good number she recognized as Argons—mostly women who wore despondency like a shroud. So, Undon had taken Argons as tiams too. Ilyenna searched for someone she might recognize. Her gaze landed on Narium, Rone's mother and clan mistress for the Argons.

They'd taken two clan mistresses? It was unthinkable. Her mind tried to make Narium into someone else, but her eyes refused to lie.

Upon recognizing Ilyenna, Narium gasped and whispered to another woman. The woman took off running. Narium straightened and their gazes locked. Sorrow and fear twisted the older woman's features.

Ilyenna tried to keep her emotions from her face, to stop her knees from shaking.

How many feast days have our clans spent together? she silently asked the other clan mistress. How many times have I supped beneath your roof, and you ours? How could it come to this? What about Seneth and Rone? Are they even alive?

Ilyenna's eyes fluttered shut. Rone.

Darrien jerked a knife from its sheath and held it in his teeth. He moved aside her mussed hair, then nicked the back of her dress and jerked it down, baring her back. She felt the cool air against her skin. Bare skin everyone could see. Humiliated, she tried to concentrate on how her flesh felt—whole and hale. She felt no pain. She needed to hold onto that feeling so she didn't cry out when the beating began.

She sensed him pull back the strap. With a slap, it connected with her back. Every muscle in her body clenched in protest. A scream tore at her throat. She forced it down. Only a grunt clawed its way free. She felt lye running down her back like liquid fire.

The strap hit her again. And again. And again. After the fifteenth time, Ilyenna's legs gave out. She would've collapsed to the ground if her hands weren't tied over her head.

With each blow, her flesh swelled and blistered. Too tired to fight, she whimpered softly each time the strap struck her back. Soon, she lost track of the number of hits. Her mouth ached for water.

Then a wonderful thing happened. The strap didn't hurt anymore. Ilyenna floated in a space between consciousness and awareness. Her head dangled like a ripe piece of fruit from a tree.

"You'll kill her!" someone cried.

Darrien didn't even slow.

Somewhere, from far away, she thought she heard a man say, "You want her to live in order to break her?"

The strap stopped. How many times had he hit her? Thirty? Fifty?

Darrien grunted. "You're right. Anymore, and she'll bear scars." He lifted her chin with his finger. She tried in vain to open her eyes. "Perhaps next time I ask, you'll be a bit more obedient." Her chin dropped back to her chest. She felt her tormenter step back and heard him say, "Tiams, clean this up."

Ilyenna was suddenly surrounded by hands—hands that worked the ropes free, hands that guided her gently to the ground. Water sloshed across her back. Her eyes fluttered open. Faces surrounded her, faces she vaguely knew. Narium was there. Three more buckets of water were poured on her back.

The cool water soothed the burning in her skin. Far above the people surrounding her, she saw swirls of color. Colors that shifted and twirled. "It's the fairies," she whispered. "They've come back."

Narium leaned directly over her, blocking her view of the fairies. "How long since he gave you anything to drink?"

Ilyenna tried to focus through the agony. "Not since this morning," she croaked.

Moments later, water met her lips. She gripped the waterskin, chugging greedily. Fingers pried her hands away. "Too much and your stomach will sick up," a female voice said.

The burning from the lye seemed to redouble. Ilyenna cried softly.

Another face suddenly joined the others. Rone.

"No!" he cried. "Not her too!"

His beard had grown a little shaggier than the clan's usual close-cropped style. Dark circles lined his eyes like bruises. But he was alive. Ilyenna gasped in relief.

Rone cursed. "What did he do to her?" He gently took her battered body into his arms. She locked her wrists around his neck as he ran. This was not the first time they'd met this way, not the first time he'd carried her to safety.

"He beat her with a soaked strap," Narium said as she ran at his side. "Deprived her of food and water. By how shaky she is, I think he ran her, too."

I'd hoped to have hidden that, Ilyenna thought miserably.

Rone glanced down at her and managed a tight smile. "Stubborn, were you?"

She shook her head and immediately regretted it. "I refused to marry him."

Rone's eyes widened and he cursed again. They entered the edge of the forest. Ilyenna heard swiftly running water. Splashing in, Rone sank down with her in his arms.

It felt so deliciously cool, soothing the heat and swelling. But only Rone's firm grip kept her from bolting. She couldn't swim, and water any deeper than her knees brought up memories. Memories of the river bouncing her along. Memories of seeing the sky through a window of ice—ice she'd clawed at until each and every one of her fingernails had ripped off.

"I've got you." Rone tightened his hold around her. He understood better than anyone her fear of water. She held on, afraid the river would tear her away from him. He pressed his cheek against her forehead. "I'm not going to let go."

"Take that shirt off," Narium ordered Rone. Even as she said it, she started untying Ilyenna's clan belt.

Rone gently untangled her hands from his neck. "It's only waist deep. See?"

She opened her eyes long enough to discover it was true.

"You'll be all right?"

Too overwhelmed to speak, she nodded again.

He backed away and watched her for a moment, then jerked his shirt off and began scrubbing his already red arms.

"Downstream." Narium pointed.

Rone glanced at Ilyenna, who now wore only her underdress. He turned and hurried away. "If Darrien comes back, call me," he shouted.

Narium shook her head. "And have your pretty little head end up on the sharp end of a halberd? I think not." As she spoke, she kept pouring water over Ilyenna's back.

Several Argon women came running.

"Wash the lye from her dress," Narium said.

The other women went to scrubbing Ilyenna's dress or busied themselves scouring every bit of lye residue from her skin before it could do more damage.

At first, the blissful lack of lye and the coolness of the water had been a balm. But the scrubbing burned her already blistered skin. By the end, she had to grit her teeth to keep from crying out. Finally, the women helped her out of the water. Someone brought a blanket and wrapped it around her.

"Rone," Narium called.

He reappeared, shirtless. His body was muscled from a lifetime of working the land and lean after a long winter. His arms and parts of his chest were a painful, swollen red. She was sorry for the pain he'd taken on for helping her.

Without hesitation, Rone scooped her back into his arms. She couldn't help but blush at the feel of his bare skin next to hers.

"Take her to the women's house," Narium said.

Ilyenna rested her head against the soft hair on his chest, her heart fluttering in her ribs. "You're alive," she said softly.

Rone grunted.

"We didn't know if you were dead."

"Perhaps I should be." His voice was as hard as stone.

Before she could ask what he meant, he shifted her in his arms. She gasped softly, her question forgotten. He glanced apologetically at her. Someone opened the door to a one-room house. Rone helped her lie on her stomach and brushed back her hair. "What happened to the Shyle, Ilyenna?"

She sighed heavily and looked away. "We were still trying to find beds and clothing for all the Argons. Lanna and I went to Volna Plesti's for wool skeins. On our way home, Otrok rushed past, shouting for us to hide." She paused and wiped a trickle of moisture from the bridge of her nose. "Lanna died. For a time, I thought I had, too. But then I saw . . ."

How could Ilyenna explain dying and having fairies bring her back to life? If she told Rone she was marked, would he look at her with repulsion as her brother had? She braced herself. "You should stay away from me, Rone. I think I've been marked."

His brow furrowed. "That's just superstition, Ilyenna. The dead don't do that."

Narium pushed her way between them. "You best get back to work, Rone. If Darrien finds you shirking, he'll have you strapped next. And with you, he'll not care about scars."

Rone tugged on his undershirt and began working the laces. "He'll have me there whether I shirk or not." Soon, he hurried out the door.

Narium peeled back the blanket, leaving only Ilyenna's buttocks covered. The older woman laid some cool, wet rags over Ilyenna's back. Almost immediately, the burning subsided, leaving only the rawness. She sighed in relief. "What's that?"

"Witch hazel," Narium replied. "We keep plenty of it on hand. Tyrans like their straps." She combed through Ilyenna's tangled hair with a wooden comb and began weaving it into a braid. "What of your father and brother?" she asked.

"They were alive when last I saw them," Ilyenna answered.

Nodding, Narium tied a leather strap around the end of Ilyenna's braid. "Seneth didn't live past the first day. I'm glad for him, at least." Narium's voice broke as she said it.

Ilyenna squeezed the woman's hand. "He was a good clan chief."

Narium nodded. "Yes. And Undon took him away from me. If he has his way, he'll take Rone, too." She must have seen Ilyenna's surprise. "You want to know why Rone hasn't died trying to avenge his father, or save the rest of us for that matter?" Narium chuckled bitterly. "Darrien has promised that if Rone or the two men with him so much as touch a weapon, they'll kill us all."

Ilyenna was too shocked to respond.

Narium was silent for a time. "Otec is still alive," she said finally. "The spring feast is in a month. If we can just make it until then, the Council will listen to your father."

Ilyenna understood. If her father and brother still lived, so would the Shyle. They wouldn't abandon her to the Tyrans. The Council of Clan Chiefs would declare that the Tyrans had broken clan law and come against them.

Narium rubbed some of the cloudy water into the angry rash on her hands.

"I'm sorry the lye hurt you," Ilyenna said.

Narium waved the apology away. "I have to leave you now. If I don't finish my work, I'll be punished. And every time they punish me, I'm afraid Rone will interfere. Darrien is expecting him to." Standing, she smoothed her damp skirt. "Rest now. I'll be back as soon as I can."

7. Apples

Slipping behind a tree, Ilyenna held her breath. She pressed herself against the icy bark.

"Ilyenna," Bratton growled. Footsteps started back toward her, crunching through the cold snow. "You might as well come out. We already saw you."

Letting out her breath in a cloud of vapor, she put on her mother's best clan-mistress glare, crossed her arms, and stepped out. "I want to come too."

Rone looked at her with something close to apology in his eyes.

Bratton pointed the tip of his bow at her. "You're too little. You'll slow us down. And you make too much noise."

"Only because you won't teach me," she shouted. Then she dropped her head, trying her best to appear humble. They had to take her. They just had to. She couldn't spend another day stuck at the house while Mother coughed up blood. "Please."

"Come on, Bratton. She could come," Rone said.

Ilyenna glanced up at Rone. He studied her with green eyes framed with lashes like a bird's wings. His mass of wavy golden hair was tied back.

Bratton gave him an exasperated look. "She'll scare away anything we find."

Ilyenna narrowed her gaze at Bratton. "You never catch anything anyway."

Bratton lunged at her, but she slipped out of his grasp. He was bigger and older. She knew he'd wrestle her to the ground and hold her face in the snow until she agreed to go home.

Rone grabbed his shoulder. "Come on, Bratton. Let her be."

She could see Bratton itch to take her down. He jerked out of Rone's grip and took a step toward her. "Go. Home." As he whipped around; his bow smacked her ribs.

She winced and then tried to still her features so neither of them would know he'd hurt her.

"If I catch you behind us again, I'll throttle you good," he called over his shoulder. "Come on, Rone."

Rone studied her, indecision on his face. "Can you make it back all right?"

His kindness seemed to make her side throb harder. She dropped her gaze so he wouldn't see her tears.

Rone pointed back the way they'd come. "Just follow our tracks. Cross the river where we crossed it. Can you do that?"

She nodded quickly.

"Rone!" Bratton called impatiently.

He studied her. "Hurry back. We won't be long."

Ilyenna watched him run after Bratton until she couldn't see them anymore. She turned around, her eyes wide. The trees were huge and ancient, so big it would take ten of her lying head to toe to circle them. It wasn't long after midday, but the canopy blocking out the light made it seem later.

She'd never felt so alone.

Ilyenna felt a hand on her arm and struggled to free herself from the dream. She forced her eyes open to see the shadowy outline of a man standing beside the bed. With a gasp, she clutched the pillow to her chest.

"It's all right, Ilyenna. It's just me—Rone. You were dreaming."

She let out her breath in relief. Still, she didn't feel much better, naked as she was. The witch hazel had dried. Her back burned and itched so badly she wondered why her hair hadn't caught fire. "I dream a lot."

He closed his eyes as if her words pained him. "Me too." He studied her. "Do you want to go back to sleep?"

"No," she said softly.

He looked away. "I'm sorry, but I have to know," he paused, his eyes reflecting the moonlight. "Did—did Darrien hurt you?"

She couldn't meet his gaze. "Not beyond what you already know."

He ran his hands through his wavy hair. "Mother's not back yet. The other women are with her. If you'd like, I could put on some fresh rags." He didn't say anything more, but she knew enough to figure Narium and the others were being punished—punished for helping her.

Normally, she'd never allow a man to see her bare back, but the thought of the cooling witch hazel squashed any protests. "Please."

Rone removed the old rags and replaced them with deliciously damp ones. His hands were sure and strong, and he was careful to keep his calluses away from her bruised and weeping skin. He helped her drink water and some tasteless broth. "I'm going to take care of you, Ilyenna."

She wondered why he said it. Of course he would take care of her. He was a clan chief now—it was his duty. But she was too tired to ask. He began humming a lullaby, one her mother had sung to her as a child. "Two in the rockers, One in the field." Before long, Ilyenna was sound asleep.

At dawn, she awoke to feel fresh rags on her back. Narium was asleep on the floor, dark circles lining her eyes. How many times had she woken in the night to replace the dressings? Glancing around the small home, Ilyenna saw numerous other women sleeping on blankets on the floor. She was the only one in the bed. Their kindness left her feeling a little less forlorn. But she desperately needed to visit the forest.

Ever so carefully, she reached for her underdress. Just as her hand closed around the linen, the door banged open and Darrien stormed in. "Lazy, ungrateful wenches! Up! Up!"

The other women rushed to tug overdresses over their heads. Ilyenna froze, her breasts pressed into the woven horsehair mattress. Darrien's gaze fell on her. In two strides, he reached the bed. Ilyenna snatched the blanket beneath her and held it tight. He wrenched her to her feet. Her bruised back groaned in protest, and she felt her skin crack. She struggled and kicked as he pressed himself against her. "Get dressed. You're to work in the clan house."

His gaze dropped down, his eyes hungry. She struggled to free a hand to slap him. Shoving her back on the bed, he laughed dryly and headed for the door.

Narium rushed to Ilyenna's side. "Vile man. After beating you the way he did, he should let you rest for a week."

She plucked Ilyenna's underdress from her clenched fists and tugged it over her head. Ilyenna gasped as it scraped her back. Narium cast her an apologetic glance.

Utterly humiliated, Ilyenna stood, quivering and wishing everything below her neck and above her waist would simply stop existing.

Narium was a little more careful with her overdress. Ilyenna gritted her teeth and hissed every time it touched her skin. Finally, Narium strapped on Ilyenna's clan belt while the other women hurried from the room. "I can put a running stitch through or leave it open."

Ilyenna grimaced. What was worse? The humiliation of having her back exposed for the entire day, or letting the fabric rub her raw? She shook her head in despair. What use was pride? Hadn't Darrien just hauled her from her bed in nothing but nature's dress? "Leave it."

Narium nodded, then wiped Ilyenna's back with witch hazel. As the Argon clan mistress turned for the door, Ilyenna called, "Thank you for caring for me last night."

Narium shook her head. "Rone did most of it." And then she was gone.

Ilyenna stood for a moment, vaguely remembering someone caring for her while she slept. An unexpected warmth spread outward from her belly.

She walked stiffly from the house, her ripped dress bumping her like a tail. She paused before entering the clan-house kitchen. The smell of bacon, cooking eggs, and porridge assaulted her. Her mouth watering in anticipation, she stepped inside.

Three women froze in the midst of preparing the food. Two girls, about fourteen and ten, bore Undon's reddish hair. Ilyenna guessed they were his daughters. The third looked nothing like the other two. She had glossy blond hair and, even more surprising, generous curves. Ilyenna gaped. She'd never seen such a plump person before—there was never enough food for it.

Ilyenna noted a rolled up blanket in the corner. Someone slept in the kitchen. That meant the woman was either a servant or another tiam. One treated far worse than Otrok ever was.

The plump woman crossed her arms over her ample chest. "My name is Metha." She jerked her thumb at the other two, oldest to youngest. "And this is Bennis and Hanie. You're to obey us as you would Undon or Darrien." Her voice brimmed with an odd combination of affection and distaste when she said Darrien's name. She pointed to the fire, where a heavy pot of porridge burped thin, steaming wisps that smelled of bacon grease.

Ilyenna's mouth watered in earnest. But instead of offering her any, Metha thrust a cloth and wooden spoon into her hands. "You're to serve the men. Spill one drop and I'll count it as your breakfast."

Definitely not a tiam.

Hanie gave Ilyenna a small wave behind Metha's back. Bennis ignored her.

Using the cloth to protect her hands, Ilyenna took the pot and moved through the wide doorway. Speaking in hushed tones, Undon and Darrien sat at the thick table before an immense fireplace. This great hall was much larger than the Shyle's, but it felt so empty with only two men inside it. Ilyenna pursed her lips in disapproval. Besides wasting firewood, the men debased their women by refusing to eat with them. Her father would never force her to sit so dishonorably.

But she wasn't a Shyle anymore. She was a Tyran tiam. With a deep breath, she spooned porridge into Darrien's bowl. Father and son went silent. Ilyenna froze, wondering what she'd done wrong. Then, she suddenly understood. If they were this obstinate about sitting arrangements, what about serving the clan chief first? She hurried to Undon and scooped up a spoonful of porridge.

Darrien gripped her wrist and wrenched it to the side. The porridge-coated spoon flew out of her hand, sticking to the floor like a spear driven into the ground. "Always, always serve my father first. Do you understand?"

She blinked. "I didn't know."

"Didn't know?"

His grip tightened and she felt the bones of her wrist shift. Suddenly, the pain all seemed too much. Lanna and Otrok dead. Five years of her life gone. Her back on fire. Her stomach turned inside out from hunger. She cried out.

Satisfaction crossed Darrien's face. He threw her to the floor. The pot landed with a dull thud, the porridge slowly flowing toward the floor. He raised his fist. Ilyenna held up her arm like a shield.

"Patience, Son," Undon intoned. "She cannot learn if she's dead."

Darrien lowered his fist to his side. "You're right, Father." He sat back in his chair without giving her a backward glance.

The porridge bulged out of the pot like a tongue trying to lick the floor. Ilyenna caught it in her hand and righted the pot. Her hands burned terribly, but she forced herself to scrape it back inside. At least she'd saved her only chance for breakfast. Shakily, she rose to her feet. She pulled the spoon from the floor and tried to still her trembling hands enough to finish filling their bowls.

After she'd served their eggs and cleared away their plates, she went back into the kitchen. Now that the men had been served, the women sat down to breakfast. Ilyenna stood, waiting for Metha to acknowledge her. When the woman was scraping the last of the porridge into her mouth, Ilyenna couldn't stand it anymore. "I'm hungry."

Metha dumped her bowl into a basket full of dirty dishes. "You dropped the spoon."

Ilyenna's shoulders slumped, and her hands seemed to burn all the more. No breakfast today.

"Wash them at the stream," Metha called as she pushed herself up from the table and waddled away.

Resting the basket's weight on her hip, Ilyenna filled it with dirty bowls, plates, and pots. Hanie came from the great hall.

Without pausing, the girl placed a piece of bread on the table and hurried outside.

Ilyenna watched the girl disappear. Before anyone could take the bread, she shoved it in the space between her over and underdress. As soon as she was out of sight on the trail that led to the river, she wolfed it down so fast it made her stomach hurt.

The river wasn't far. The water was clear and clean, as it came straight from the Shyle. The bottom was coated with the river stones etched from the mountains behind Ilyenna's home and carried downriver. Cupping her hands, she drank her fill.

She paused before dunking the dishes in the water. Ridges of porridge lined the bowls, and remnants of eggs stuck to the plates. Her mouth began to water. After only a moment's hesitation, she grabbed the cleanest spoon and scraped the food into her mouth.

As she washed the dishes, she studied her surroundings. Insects darted above the rushing stream. Above her, an apple tree was heavy with dark pink blossoms that were yet to open. There was a swirl of color—a dancing flower that spun and pirouetted, somehow staying airborne while it twirled from one flower to the next. Within moments of its touch, the flowers opened wide.

Ilyenna froze. This wasn't a flower anymore than the snowflakes had been. She squinted at it and saw not petals, but gently curling wings, white at the tips and gradually darkening to a deep pink at the base. And the wings would be attached to a tiny body.

Suddenly, she could see the little fairy's body. Hope making her heart pound, Ilyenna hurried to her feet, shading her eyes with her hand. "Who are you?"

The fairy started and whirled to face Ilyenna. She gave a little yelp of surprise and zipped behind the apple tree.

"Please don't go!" Ilyenna cried. "I didn't mean to frighten you."

A tiny face peeked out at her. But this fairy was different from the ones who had saved Ilyenna. Instead of a harsh, sharp beauty, this creature was soft and rosy. The ends of her hair were white which gradually darkened to pink at the base—like an apple blossom. Her eyes were almond shaped and as golden as pollen.

"You're a summer fairy, aren't you?" Ilyenna asked. In response, the fairy disappeared. "Come out. I promise, I won't hurt you. What's your name?"

The fairy's face peeked out again. She was so small it was hard to read her expression. But Ilyenna noted the hesitant way she stepped onto the branch, the way her wings seemed wilted behind her. "I am Jablana. What does the winter queen wish of me?"

Ilyenna wet her lips with her tongue. "Can you help me?"

The fairy laughed. "The winter queen wishes my help?"

Ilyenna nodded. "Please."

Jablana's wings came up, and Ilyenna wondered if reading a fairy's emotions was as simple as watching her wings. "For how long?"

"For as long as it takes."

The fairy's wings flattened. "You must think me a fool, because only a fool would agree to such an open-ended agreement."

Ilyenna shrugged. "Until I am free then."

The fairy watched her warily. "And the payment?"

Ilyenna sighed. "What do you want?"

Jablana fluttered forward, so close Ilyenna could see her pink lips. "You and your fairies will not freeze my apple blossoms, no matter how pretty the flowers look covered in frost."

Ilyenna blinked in surprise. "Very well."

"You must say 'yes.'"

Ilyenna suppressed a groan. "Yes." A ripple of power flowed through Ilyenna. The fairy's wings spread wide, as if stretching to devour the sun.

"You'd better hurry," said a voice behind her. Ilyenna whirled as an Argon woman with a basket of washing on her hip emerged from the trees. "If you're not back when Metha thinks you should be, she won't let you eat lunch."

Ilyenna pivoted back to the fairy, but she was gone. Ilyenna wanted to call after her, but somehow she knew it wouldn't do any good. The fairy would not come back. And even if she did, the Argon woman wouldn't be able to see her. She'd think Ilyenna mad if she started talking to a flower.

Ilyenna rinsed the last of the sand from the dishes. Then she hurried back to the kitchen and traded the clean basket of dishes for a basket of soiled washing.

When she arrived back at the river, the Argon woman was still there. "I'm Ilyenna," she offered.

The woman's face darkened. "I know. I'm Shia." She turned and searched the forest, as if expecting to find someone watching them. "If we're caught talking, we'll be punished. We'll speak tonight."

Ilyenna nodded. At least she'd have nights in the women's house to look forward to. Perhaps Rone would even be there. With that prospect to lighten her day, the washing didn't seem so bad. Her stomach still felt slightly hollow, but she felt stronger. Her back didn't even hurt as much.

After hanging up the last of the washing behind the clan house, Ilyenna stepped inside the kitchen. The women had just filled the wash basket with dishes from lunch. Metha squared off in front of her.

"You took too long. No lunch, either." She handed Ilyenna a rag and bowl of water with soap shavings floating in the bottom. "Scrub the great hall from top to bottom. Then do the dishes. You take too long or don't do a proper job, and you'll not get supper, either."

Ilyenna scrubbed tables, floors, and walls until her knuckles bled. By the time she finished, she could smell dinner cooking. Metha met her at the door with a scraper. "Clean out the chicken coop. Bring in the eggs."

With a sigh, she took the wooden scraper and left the room. The midday sun added heat to her back. She started to wish she'd let Narium sew her dress after all. When she had finished with the coop, there were more dishes to wash. No matter how fast she worked or how good a job she did, Metha always found something wrong. A scrap of food stuck to a plate cost Ilyenna supper.

It was dark by the time she finished lugging in the last plates. After she'd put them away, she trudged toward the women's house. Footsteps echoed her own.

She turned to see Darrien coming toward her. She crossed her arms over her chest to keep them from shaking, from fear as much as from hunger. As always, he came too close. She squared herself, resisting the urge to lean away from him. His nose wrinkled in disapproval. "You stink like sweat and chicken dung."

Her eyes narrowed. "I swore to give my sweat, and that's what I'm doing."

He stepped closer. "You don't have to. Marry me, and you'll not have to work one day of the five years. You can sleep in my rooms, eat at the clan-house table. I'll give you fine clothes and . . ." His hand shot out, deftly unfastening her clan belt. Before Ilyenna could react, he held her identity in his hand. "You can have this back."

Without her belt, her overdress gaped at the sides. She felt a cool breeze moving against her underdress. Her father had fashioned the leather from one of their sheep. Her mother had sewn in all the knots but the last. That one, the clan-mistress knot, Ilyenna had added days after her mother's burial. She reached for it, but Darrien held her back. "You've no right to take that!"

He smiled in satisfaction. "You don't have a clan anymore. You'll endure what I want you to endure." He stepped so close she could feel the heat from his body. "Unless you wish me to tell my father you killed his favorite son?"

Tears pricked her eyes. Of all the things Darrien had done to her, taking her clan belt cut closest to her heart. Reaching out again, she tried to snatch it back. The movement brought her closer to him.

He pulled her in, his lips inches from hers. "It's a pretty good bargain, Ilyenna."

She squirmed until she felt the skin on her back crack and sting. "What you want is a harlot."

He released her and took a step back. A smile tugged at the corners of his mouth. "You'll come to me. Sooner or later, you'll come. And when you do, I'll make you beg." He turned and started towards the clan house.

She watched him go. Was he right? Could he afflict her until she submitted?

She lifted her head higher. Shyle are stronger than stone, more supple than a sapling. No matter what any of them said, she was still a Shyle, and she wouldn't forget her clan's pride. Ilyenna felt eyes on her back and turned. A dark shadow peered at her from behind the trees—Rone. How much had he seen?

His smoldering eyes said he'd seen enough. "One of these days, I'm going to kill that son of a whore."

Ilyenna rubbed her forehead. "What are you doing here?"

"I've been looking for you."

Suddenly her emotions seemed too much to bear. Starting past him on her way to the women's house, she lashed out, "Why? You've never cared about me. Why start now?"

His hand shot out, gripping her arm. "Don't say that. When we were children, you were like a little sister to me."

She took a deep, shuddering breath. "You're right. I'm sorry." Tears burning her eyes, she turned, her gaze staring after Darrien. It wasn't Rone's fault. Not her being here, or Darrien, or her being marked, or the fact that Rone thought of her as a sister. She relaxed her fists.

His grip loosened. "The other women all came in a long time ago." He handed her something draped in an old rag.

Ilyenna unwrapped it. A piece of crusty bread and a sliver of cheese. Without Metha lording over them, the other tiams must be eating better. Her mouth watering, Ilyenna took a bite, ignoring the crunch of weevils. "Thank you."

Rone stared up at the moon, which reflected dark glints in his green eyes. "I'll kill him if you'd like."

She nearly choked on her cheese. Without asking, she took his waterskin and swallowed. "Kill him?" she whispered with a furtive glance. "If you even touch an axe or knife, they'll kill us all."

"Mother told you." It wasn't a question. The lines around Rone's eyes tightened. "Sometimes I think that might be a relief."

Ilyenna froze, the food in her hands forgotten. "Do you not recall who you are?"

Almost immediately, the hunch in his back straightened. "I am an Argon."

"You are the Argon clan chief," she said sternly.

His gaze looked her up and down. "And you are the Shyle clan mistress."

A wry smile tugged at the corners of her mouth. "A clan mistress who smells of chicken dung and sweat and wears her dresses backless?"

He chuckled. "Well, there's that."

She closed her eyes. It didn't have to be this way. Being a tiam was supposed to teach a lesson, not break a spirit. For instance, with Otrok, Ilyenna had offered a trade. She'd allowed the child's father to stay home and continue to scrape together enough to feed his wife and other children, as long as his youngest son came in his place. In doing so, she'd probably saved the child's life—only to have it taken from him months later.

"We aren't criminals," Rone went on. "We've done nothing wrong. I am the Argon clan chief, and you are the Shyle clan mistress." They arrived at the women's house. "Good night, Ilyenna," he said before walking away.

She watched him go, her eyes heavy. "I suppose it could be worse," she murmured. "I could be alone in this."

8. Strong as Stone

Ilyenna took the bowl of porridge Narium offered. Trying not to notice the black flecks, she spooned some into her mouth and made an effort not to wince when weevils popped between her teeth. Dim light slanted through the small, dirty windows. The women weren't allowed candles and only enough wood for cooking their meals.

Narium hurried over and tied a rag over Ilyenna's hair. "It will keep your hair out of your eyes." She nodded toward the gruel as she wiped Ilyenna's back with a cloth dampened with witch hazel. "Eat it quickly or you won't have time to eat at all."

The other women were shoving spoonfuls in their mouths as fast as they could. Ilyenna increased her pace. After only a few more bites, a man appeared at the door with a strap in hand. He cracked it against his palm. Abandoning their bowls, the women rushed for the door.

Ilyenna hurried after them. "Where will you be working?" she whispered to Narium.

Narium glanced at the man before she whispered back, "In the fields."

"Then where are the men working?"

"They're gathering river stones."

"To build what?" Ilyenna asked.

Before Narium could answer, Ilyenna bumped into one of the other women. All of them had stopped, their mouths set in grim lines. Ilyenna followed their gazes down the long road. A cluster of dirty, ragged women trudged toward them. One woman staggered and fell. A man rode up behind her and whacked her with a switch. She lifted her arms as if to protect her head, then lurched to her feet and scurried forward. Ilyenna's eyes widened as she recognized her—Larina.

Cold fury burned within her. These were her people—her clanwomen. She recognized the others one by one. Jossa, Wenly, Kanni, Parsha, and Bet. Lowering her head like a charging bull, Ilyenna marched forward. A hand clamped down on her wrist.

Narium pulled her back and hissed in her ear, "You want to know what our clanmen have been building for these devils we call Tyrans?" She didn't wait for an answer. "Another tiam house. Did you really think Undon would settle for taking only you?"

Suddenly, Ilyenna couldn't catch her breath. "How long has he been planning this?"

Narium shrugged. "Undon's no fool. He knew the Shyle would aid the Argons."

"From the beginning," Ilyenna finished, answering her own question. Tears of betrayal filled her eyes. The group of Shyle women moved closer. Each was around the same age as Ilyenna. She didn't want to dwell on the reason young women had been chosen. She tried to pull free, but Narium held her firmly.

"They might know about my father, my brother," Ilyenna protested.

Narium's grip only tightened. "Are you sure you want to know?"

Fear blossomed in Ilyenna's breast like a thistle flower. Bratton and her father had been fighting Tyrans when she'd been taken. Had Undon simply waited for her to leave before killing them? Perhaps she hadn't saved anyone. "Do you think"—she cleared her throat— "do you think they're dead?"

The women next to her shifted to let someone through. Rone. He rested a hand on her arm. "Even Undon wouldn't dare kill a surrendered clan chief."

She watched as her clanwomen milled uncertainly near the barn, and suddenly she had a purpose. A clan. Tiams be strapped! She was still their clan mistress. "Make the roof of their house tight."

Warily scrutinizing her, Rone nodded.

Shrieks erupted all around Ilyenna. The Tyran with the strap was using it on any tiam he could reach.

Gripping her skirt, Ilyenna dashed toward her clanwomen. Relief and hope crossed their faces when they saw her. "Ilyenna," some of them cried.

Larina gripped her hand. "What are we to do?"

The other women voiced so many questions that Ilyenna could barely distinguish one from another. "Quiet. There isn't time," she commanded softly. Her eyes met Larina's. The girl had a pained look Ilyenna had seen on the chronically ill. "Are you hurt?"

Crossing her arms over her chest, Larina hugged herself tight. "I'm fine."

"What happened after I left the clan house?"

Larina squeezed her eyes shut.

Bet answered, "They took everything they wanted. Killed or beat anyone who tried to stop them."

"And my father and brother?" Ilyenna forced the words out.

"They were badly beaten, but still alive when we left," Jossa said.

"How many of you are there?" Ilyenna asked as she began counting.

"Eleven," Bet said. Her eyes took in Ilyenna's ripped dress. "What're we to do?"

Ilyenna wet her cracked lips and stepped closer. "For now, do what you're told. If you don't, you'll be beaten." Pain shot through her back. She tried to hold in her cry, but it came anyway. On her knees, she turned to see Darrien standing over her, strap in hand. "You dare keep Undon waiting for his breakfast?"

Casting a warning glance back at her clanwomen, she scampered away from him and ran. Humiliating as it was to flee from Darrien or his strap, she hoped her clanwomen would watch and learn to do as they were told as quickly as they could.

***

Metha kept Ilyenna busy with dishes and scrubbing until long after the plump woman had fallen asleep before the hearth. But at least Ilyenna had managed to find a forgotten, moth-eaten rag she could use in place of a clan belt. Moments after she left the clan house, Rone stepped out from behind a tree. He handed her another wrapped bundle.

"Did they feed you anything today?"

She shrugged. "Metha wasn't pleased with my cleaning of the chamber pots, but at least I had breakfast." She didn't mention it had been a piece of moldy bread.

Opening Rone's offering, she found an oatmeal biscuit and a boiled egg, but she hesitated to take it. "Is this from your own share?" If he gave this to her, he wouldn't have enough for himself.

He kicked at the dirt. "No. It's from the allotment given the tiams."

"Thank you." She took a bite of the egg. She'd give just about anything for a withered old winter apple right now. "How are my clanwomen?"

Rone glanced at her sideways. "The Shyle are a strong people, but they need you to reassure them."

He opened the door to the women's house, and Ilyenna surveyed the sullen faces. An even mixture of Shyle and Argon women.

Why has Undon taken three Argon men but no Shyle men? Ilyenna wondered.

"It isn't right, Clan Mistress," Larina cried. "The Tyrans had no cause to take even one tiam, and they've taken eleven of us."

"To take a clan mistress or clan chief is unheard of," Jossa put in, "and they've taken three and killed the other."

More grumbles rose up. Ilyenna lifted her hands and said firmly, "I know, but there's nothing we can do right now. The clan chiefs meet for the spring feast in a month. They'll hear of our plight and force Undon to release us."

Larina sniffed. "And what are we to do until then?"

Ilyenna looked into the women's faces one at a time, making sure each of them met her gaze. "War and peace—opposite ends of the Balance. Make no mistake about it, we are in a war. Battles will be lost, but only when winning will cost more than can be gained. Keep together as much as possible. Look after each other."

Kanni asked Rone, "What do the Tyrans expect of us?"

He stepped forward. "The men are gathering stones for a new tiam house. The women have been put to work in the fields. The rest of the Tyrans aren't as cruel as Undon and Darrien, but try to avoid them. And Ilyenna's right—it is best to stay in groups." He eyed the women. "Especially you clanwomen. Some of the men have been . . ." He glanced at Ilyenna. "Unruly."

The women lowered their heads. Larina gripped her overdress so tight Ilyenna wondered that it didn't disintegrate beneath her clenched fists.

The door opened and a burly Argon slipped inside. "Men from the clan house are coming this way."

Rone reached for the axe that was no longer there. He grimaced. "You women better get in bed. You'll have less than two minutes." He paused at Ilyenna's shoulder. "I'll not be far. Call out if you need me." He joined the other man out the door.

The women scrambled to wrap up in their blankets. Rone had calculated correctly. No sooner had the last woman tucked the blankets around her than the door opened. Darrien stepped inside, a line of men behind him. His gaze raked across the women. Reaching the nearest one, he yanked off Jossa's blanket. "Sleeping in our overdresses now, are we?"

"If Tyrans are going to barge in here, we certainly won't be sleeping in only our underdresses," Narium shot back as she clambered to her feet. Ilyenna and the other women did the same.

Darrien crossed the room to Narium in three strides. He lifted his fist. Narium didn't flinch. He shook his head and dropped his hand. His eyes searched the room, stopping on Ilyenna. He pulled his axe from the loop at his belt.

Has he come to kill me? she wondered.

She wished Rone hadn't left. The temptation to call for him nearly overwhelmed her, but she knew Narium was right. If Rone interfered, he'd be killed. No matter what happened, Ilyenna had to keep her mouth shut.

Besides, she'd been marked. Death would seek her at every turn. The question was, how many more times could she evade it?

Darrien casually tested the weight of his axe. "I have reports you had a meeting here tonight. What was said?"

Other Tyran men crowded into the room. Big, strong men with axes, against unarmed women. It would be a massacre. Ilyenna felt like she was suffocating. Some of the women exchanged terrified glances.

Darrien wandered through the room, staring the women down. "A good tiam answers when her master asks a question." He paused beside Ilyenna, his shoulder brushing hers. "Shall I show them what happens when a tiam refuses to submit?" She clenched her teeth to keep from making a sound.

He gripped Narium's arm. "Shall I start with you?" He shoved her toward the door. Narium stumbled and hit the floor hard. Darrien reached for her again.

Ilyenna knew Rone would be watching from the barn. If he saw Darrien hauling his mother to the beating pole, he'd interfere. Then they'd all die. Ilyenna jumped between Darrien and Narium. "The Shyle wanted to know what was expected of them."

"And what was your answer?" Darrien growled.

"I told them to obey and keep their honor."

Darrien rotated his axe in his hands. "Perhaps that's so, perhaps not. Either way, tiams do not meet. They do not discuss. They obey!" He glared at each face in turn. He moved so close to Ilyenna that his shirt brushed against her breasts. "Choose one for the beating pole, Ilyenna."

She closed her eyes, willing her tears to stay at bay. "I choose myself."

Darrien looked surprised.

Narium gathered herself up from the floor and straightened to her full height. "I'll go in her place."

Larina jutted out her chin, tears streaming down her cheeks. "No, I will."

Within seconds, the whole house erupted as women volunteered to be strapped.

Ilyenna fought to keep the triumph off her face. The Shyle and Argons had just won a battle.

Darrien glared at the women. "Silence!"

The clatter died like a capped candle. Darrien circled Ilyenna, his axe balanced in his hands—the same axe that had nearly killed her before the fairies' healing. At her back, he stopped. Her skin crawled, but she didn't dare turn. He rested the sharp point on her shoulder. "I wonder," he said as he began drawing it down.

The axe dragged along the length of her back. Ilyenna's still-tender skin flamed. Darrien came around her. His axe probed open the ripped belly of her dress. Fear rose in her throat till she nearly choked on it.

"I wonder if you aren't the cause of such . . . rebellious thoughts." He stroked his jaw as he exchanged glances with his men. "What do you think, clanmen? Shall we keep a closer eye on this one?"

"I'll watch her for you," one of the men jeered.

Ilyenna fought the urge to wrap her arms around herself as Larina had.

Darrien chuckled and began pacing in front of her like a wolf before the barn door. "I'm not sure I would trust you with her, Ondeb. She's as tricky as a mountain goat. No, I think she must stay in the clan house." He paused to watch her reaction.

She clenched her fists at her sides to keep them from shaking. She wouldn't allow him to see her despair. "I am a Shyle," she said softly.

He backhanded her. She fell to the floor, dazed. "No. You are a tiam," he said, "and tiams don't have a clan." He chuckled. "My room will do. I can keep a very close eye on you there."

The men snickered.

Ilyenna lay stark still. She was afraid if she shifted at all, she'd black out. "I am a Shyle," she repeated. "A Shyle is strong as stone and supple as a sapling. You cannot hurt me, Darrien of the Tyran clan."

He stopped laughing and booted her in the stomach. Air fled her lungs, and her stomach cramped. He crouched before her as she coughed up blood. She lifted her face and glared at him.

"I can hurt you plenty, Ilyenna." He moved to his feet, staring down any woman who dared meet his gaze. "There are no Shyle or Argons in this room. Only tiams. And tiams obey. Any who wishes to ease her burdens, has only to . . . keep an eye on things."

Ilyenna knew she should keep her mouth shut, but she said it anyway. "You won't find traitors here."

He kicked her thigh. She felt it all the way to her bone. Her muscle seized up and she grunted, her body straining against the pain.

"You see? Plenty of pain." Thrusting his axe through his belt loop, he headed for the door. "I won't wait, Ilyenna."

Narium was there in an instant to pull her to her feet. "You're a Shyle," she whispered fiercely. "He cannot take that from you. If he did, all honor would be lost. No clanmen can do such a thing."

Ilyenna limped toward the door. She didn't trust Darrien's honor any more than she trusted a pig to stay out of the slop, but she nodded anyway. With her head down, she followed Darrien toward the house, rubbing her thigh as she went. Was Rone watching? She tried to force her steps to fall evenly.

Please stay away, Rone. He'll kill you. He'll kill us all, she begged silently.

In the kitchen, Metha looked up from her blankets before the fire. When she saw Ilyenna with Darrien, she glared so hotly Ilyenna wanted to slap her. Could the woman actually think she wanted to be here? Darrien led her to the second floor and opened a door. Inside was a wide bed covered in furs.

Dread squeezed her heart. The walls were coated with mounted heads, skulls, and antlers of almost every creature she'd ever seen—boar, deer, bear, mountain lion. Above the bed, her clan belt had been nailed to the wall. Another of his trophies. Ilyenna stared at it.

Darrien pointed to a rough-hewn ladder that led to a trapdoor. "You choose. My bed or the attic."

He wasn't going to force her. Despite herself, she gasped in relief. She walked to the ladder and looked back at him. She placed both hands on the rungs and climbed. At the top, she opened the trapdoor and glanced around. The only light came from below, and all she could make out in the attic were cobwebs, dead insects, and dust. She pulled herself up. Even at a crouch, the ceiling brushed her shoulders. She peeked down.

Darrien looked up at her. "You've but to ask, and you can sleep in a real bed with blankets and pillows."

And you, her mind finished for him. She moved away from the hole, circling the cramped room, looking for snakes or mice or any other number of things she could throw at Darrien's head.

"Perhaps you should stay here until you're willing to divulge the secret of your healing." He climbed up the ladder and shut the trapdoor, plunging the attic into total darkness. She heard the ladder scrape as he pulled it away.

But as her eyes began to adjust, she realized it wasn't pitch black after all. A shaft of moonlight filtering through a small chink in the mortar between river stones. Light. It wasn't much, but it was something. Wearily, she curled up under it.

9. Supple as a Sapling

Tears kept blurring the frozen footprints. Ilyenna pushed them off her cheeks as fast as she could, and still they kept coming. She hated being a girl. Hated that Rone and Bratton wouldn't let her go with them because of it. Hated that the tears came whether she wanted them to or not. Hated dresses and being smaller and weaker.

She saw the river like a dark ribbon on the snow. Argonholm was built just beyond its flood plain, past the ridge that was iced with frozen trees, and next to the lake. Ilyenna didn't want her mother and father to see she'd been crying, so she sniffed and wiped her nose on her sleeve, determined to stop.

Sitting on her bottom, she slid down the slippery bank to the riverside. The layers of ice deadened the sound of the rushing water. But Ilyenna saw it below, black and colder than ice. It had taken all her courage to cross it the first time, when Rone and Bratton had been within calling distance.

Now she was alone, and she couldn't swim. Few of her clan could. The lakes of the Shyle were fed by glaciers. They were clear as the finest glass . . . and cold as the ice that bore them.

Ilyenna was a little below where Bratton and Rone had crossed, but not much. It was less steep here. She'd find their path easily on the other side. She eased her foot out and listened for any cracks.

Silence. She took another step, her arms out like a bird in flight. Her hands started sweating inside her mittens. She slid one foot forward and brought the other behind. Slowly, slowly, she shuffled across the river.

When she was three-quarters of the way across, she heard a loud crack, like the sound of an axe chopping a tree. She froze, her heart in her throat. Even slower than before, she eased her foot forward and gingerly put her weight on it. The ice cracked again.

For an agonizing moment, she waited. At the sound of the third crack, she bolted. She felt the ice splinter beneath her feet and fall away.

"Ilyenna. Ilyenna," someone whispered.

Ilyenna struggled to free herself from the dream. She saw someone ease the trapdoor open. After leaving her locked in the attic for an entire night and a day, had Darrien come to break his word? Well, not without her putting up a fight. She lurched to her feet, a scream on her lips.

Rone's head appeared. At the sight of her balled fists, his eyes widened. "You planning on killing me, then?"

All the fight went out of her, and she slumped back onto the dirty boards. She wouldn't admit it, but she was weak from hunger and sore from Darrien's fists and feet. Her head ached for want of water. Though Hannie had snuck her a little food and water, it hadn't been enough, and Ilyenna had been sick with heat during the day.

"How did you get away?" she asked Rone now. He usually watched for her after his day's work was done, but to sneak away in the middle of the day?

"That's the thing about gathering river stones—you're out of sight at the river often as not." Rone finished climbing up and handed her a waterskin. She gulped down the liquid. Almost immediately, she felt the water traveling from her shriveled stomach outward, spreading through her chest and abdomen, to her aching joints and withered brain. She took another drink and another, until she was almost drunk with water. Suddenly drowsy, she lay her head on Rone's lap.

"How did you get in here?" she whispered.

He began to stroke her hair. "Not sure why Darrien thought it a good idea to take so many of us. The more tiams there are, the stronger we become."

"And the weaker our clans," she responded.

He paused for a moment. "How so?"

She took another long drink. "We're hostages. Our clans won't attack when their daughter's lives are at stake."

Rone grimaced. "I hadn't thought of that. You've dried blood on your cheek." He pulled his sleeve over his hand, dribbled a little water on it, and began wiping the corner of her mouth. As he worked, he kept glaring at the attic door, as if he'd like nothing more than to sneak down there, find Darrien, and put a knife in his heart. A part of her longed for him to do just that.

"I didn't even find out you were up here until today. Why didn't you call for me when he took you from the others?" Rone asked.

She heard the accusation in his voice. There was hurt, too, but she didn't understand why. "You know why," she said. She winced at his scrubbing and pressed her hand over his to keep it still. He paused and left his hand on her cheek. It felt good to lie there like this with him. Too good. A sister wouldn't have these kinds of thoughts.

Embarrassed, she pushed back. Rone watched her before looking away. Slowly, she worked her stiff jaw. It was swollen and no doubt bruised.

He handed her a cloth-wrapped package. "Mother worried they weren't letting you eat again."

Ilyenna pulled back the rag to find a few chunks of bread and smoked ham. She shoved some bread into her mouth and chewed as quickly as her sore jaw could bear.

Rone chuckled. "I guess Mother was right."

Ilyenna guzzled more water. "My clanwomen?"

He sighed and looked away. "The Shyle are strong. They'll survive." He surveyed her. "How was your seventh day?"

Her frantic chewing slowed. Had it really only been seven days since Darrien had taken her? It was a sobering thought. She wanted to confide her fears to Rone. But what could she tell him? That

Darrien would push her until she broke? That she could already see fractures in her resolve? That marrying him didn't seem half so bad as starving to death? If she told Rone any of that, he'd do something stupid and get them all killed. She swallowed. "What happens if a tiam runs, Rone?"

His gaze swung to the chink in the river stones. She waited for him to reprimand her lack of honor, to tell her to hold fast to courage. "You know what happens. Every clanman takes to his horse and they bring out the dogs. Then they bring the tiam back. But the Tyrans don't stop there. If it's a man, they've the right to kill them then and there. If it's a woman, she loses all her rights." He paused. "The Tyrans will pass her around before selling her to foreigners as a slave."

The food she'd eaten rose in her throat. Rone passed her the waterskin. She drank noisily and wiped her mouth with the back of her hand. He handed her a hollowed-out knot of wood with a cloth tied over it. "Mother mixed the witch hazel with some lanolin she pilfered from the kitchen. If you like, I could help you put it on."

Ilyenna studied him for a moment before turning and pulling back her hair.

"I'm sorry my hands are so rough," he said as he began rubbing the balm on her back. She clenched her teeth, expecting pain. But everywhere he touched seemed to sigh in relief. She found herself longing for his hands to stray from her back. She held very still, forcing herself not to think about it. They were already in enough danger.

When Rone had finished, he gathered up the rag but left the little bowl. "How long will Darrien make you stay here?"

Ilyenna shrugged helplessly.

Rone looked away. "I'm sorry I didn't think to bring you a blanket. I'll get you one."

"I'm all right," she replied. "I haven't been cold."

He studied her disbelievingly before getting to his feet. "I'll figure out how to bring one before night comes."

She could see it in his eyes. He planned on coming every evening to check on her until Darrien let her go. She understood the risk he was taking. If she were half as honorable as she'd like to think, she'd protest. But she couldn't bring herself to. If she didn't have something or someone to hold onto, she might go insane or worse.

She watched Rone climb down the ladder, the ghost of his touch still thick on her skin. Did he take care of her simply because he had adopted her into the Argon clan, or was there something more? She wanted more. She had for a long time, but he still thought of her as a little sister. And he probably always would.

10. Summer Queen

Footsteps sounded in Darrien's room and up the ladder. Shuddering violently, Ilyenna drew her knees under her and waited. Bennis threw open the attic door and shot her a look of contempt. "Metha has twice the load of dishes for you to wash today." She tromped back down the ladder and left.

Ilyenna nearly collapsed in relief. As brave as she tried to be, whenever she heard Darrien below, terror's cold fingers danced up her spine. Glancing down the ladder, she saw the gray light of dawn touching Darrien's array of hunting trophies. But other than their long-dead corpses and the bed, the room was empty.

With her bruised leg throbbing and cramping, she climbed down the ladder. When she reached the bottom, she slowly stretched to her full height. Her body trembled as she made her legs support her weight. It had been two and a half days since she'd stood straight. But at least her back itched more than it hurt. She limped toward the door and made her way down to the kitchen.

Inside, Metha was kneading the small of her back with her fists. She sighed heavily and lifted the weight of her stomach.

Ilyenna's eyes widened. Metha wasn't just large. She was with child. Oh, she was still plenty plump, but Ilyenna now noted how puffy her face and hands were, no doubt made worse by working in the hot kitchen.

Keeping her gaze averted, Ilyenna strode to the basket of dishes and walked out the door before the woman had a chance to berate her. The movement worked her blood, warming the ache in her leg.

At the stream, she knelt on the mossy bank, the water soaking her knees. Ripping off a bit of the moss, she held it to her jaw, grunting as the pressure made the ache momentarily worse. She cupped her hands and brought water to her mouth. The water slipped through her fingers, wetting the front of her overdress.

She drank until she couldn't hold any more. Then she just sat, not caring about chores or Metha. In the silence, Ilyenna thought she heard a song, the sound soft and gentle. The breeze seemed to carry the song over and around her. Then, strangely, the wind carried bits of leaves that must have been clinging to the trees and swirled them around the branches and across the muddy earth.

Ilyenna stared. Leaves of every shape and size were flying instead of falling. She lurched to her feet and squinted. Only then did she see them—wings attached to lithe bodies. Tiny legs instead of a single stem. Hundreds of summer fairies flitted around Ilyenna. Most were differing shades of green, but some were flowers. A few looked like animals, with furry wings or fangs. Ilyenna even caught site of one with antlers.

Unease pricked her scalp. She looked for the apple blossom fairy, but couldn't make her out. "Jablana?"

The fairies froze, staring at her. Then, moving as one body, they all turned and flew away.

Ilyenna reached for them. "No, don't go! Please." But they were gone, leaving her alone again. An ache reawakened in Ilyenna's soul. She folded her hands across her chest, instinctively trying to curl away from the pain. But it was inside her, and she couldn't get away.

"I am told you are Ilyenna." said a voice as sweet as honey.

Ilyenna whirled around. A shadowy form peered at her from behind a tree. A woman stepped into the light, but the shadow seemed to stick to her skin. She smiled, revealing teeth as white as pure snow. Her short black hair made swirling patterns about her regal head.

Sunlight, warm summer winds, and the smell of damp earth seemed to radiate from her, enveloping Ilyenna. The woman was as beautiful and intoxicating as the spring air filled with the scent of lilacs.

Ilyenna's breath snagged in her throat. Just as she felt the winter fairies even when they were far away, just as she could see through the fairy's glamour, she knew this was the summer queen. Unable to stop herself, Ilyenna reached out and touched the woman. Her skin was as warm as sun-baked rock.

To Ilyenna's surprise, the darkness didn't rub off. She remembered stories her brother had told her as a child—stories she'd long ago stopped believing in—about a race of people with skin as dark as charcoal. They lived far to the south, so far that no one knew if the rumors were real or stories. "You're a Luathan," she breathed.

"You would call me Leto." She slowly circled Ilyenna, her gaze lingering on her bruised, blistered back. "And you are one of the clanwomen of the north. If I'm not mistaken, you also have some of the blood of the Highmen."

Leto drifted around the clearing, stopping now and again to touch a leaf or to press her hands against the rough bark of a tree. Every plant she touched grew fatter. Blossoms opened. "Winter is over now," she said to Ilyenna. "Did you know? Even in your high mountains, buds are forming on the trees, and crocus blossoms peek through the snow."

The queen's clothes were brown and slightly tattered. The bones of her wrists protruded as if she hadn't had much to eat lately. But despite the queen's somewhat ragged appearance, Ilyenna was afraid. She felt very much like they were two lions circling each other. And Ilyenna was too injured and weak for a fight.

As if guessing her thoughts, Leto spread her hands. "I came because Jablana thought you needed my help."

Trying to fight the calming effects of the summer queen, Ilyenna shook her head. "Why would you help me?"

Leto met Ilyenna's gaze. "Two reasons. The winter queen before you was cold and cruel and cunning. She fought me bitterly before retreating every spring, destroying so much tender new growth. So this year, I killed her."

Ilyenna took a step back as she caught sight of a blistering heat in the woman's dark eyes—heat that would suck all the moisture from Ilyenna's bones and leave her as brittle as dead pine needles.

"You are not like her," Leto went on. "You are strong and flexible, like a tree bending before a strong wind instead of standing fast and being broken in two."

"Strong as stone, supple as a sapling," Ilyenna whispered.

Leto nodded. "Yes. That is the saying of your people. And it is true of you."

Ilyenna sucked in a deep breath. "So you wish to choose your enemy."

Leto didn't deny it.

"And the other reason?"

The summer queen turned her searing gaze away. "For their queens, the fairies only take those crossing into death. Those who are strong and clever and beautiful. I was all of that and more before death came for me at the hands of those who should have been my friends."

Their gazes met and Ilyenna saw deep empathy in Leto. Ilyenna felt herself softening, like snow seeping into the waiting ground. She thought of Rone, of her family, and a familiar ache rose up in her throat. "What if in the end, I choose not to become a winter queen? Would you still wish to help me?"

Leto tipped her head. "It is a chance I'm willing to take. But know that even as queens, we cannot upset the Balance. Our subjects are the fairies, not humans. I cannot risk directly interfering, but I will give you what aid I can."

Leto held out her hand. On her palm was a delicate white flower with three petals and three sepals. The center of each petal was ringed with yellow and burgundy. "Only one elice flower blooms each spring. So delicate. And yet, one petal has the strength to heal even the direst injuries. Use them wisely, and they will keep you alive until winter comes again."

Ilyenna's eyes were riveted to the flower. She'd never seen its kind before, though as a healer, she'd assumed she knew almost every plant. She believed it might be some kind of lily. She reached out to take it, but Leto curled her hand around the petals and pulled back.

Ilyenna suddenly understood. "And the price?"

The summer queen smiled. "My people had a saying. 'Trick a stranger and you gain an enemy; treat him fairly and you've gained a friend.' All I ask, Winter Queen, is that you retreat at the appointed time and don't stray into summer lands."

Ilyenna hesitated. There was so much she didn't understand. What if Leto was somehow trying to trick her? "And you will do the same?"

"Yes." The word sent a shudder through the forest.

When Ilyenna still hesitated, Leto went on softly, "You have been marked. I can see the shadow clinging to your skin. You will not survive the summer without my help."

Ilyenna reached for the flower.

"Say the word."

Ilyenna closed her eyes. "Yes."

The forest shuddered again.

A branch snapped behind Ilyenna and her gaze darted to the path leading to the clan house. Had Darrien followed her? Would he beat her again? She backed up, seeking the shadows the woman had emerged from. She turned to Leto. The woman had vanished. But in Ilyenna's palm was the elice blossom. Entranced, Ilyenna studied it. She considered using it now, taking a petal and putting it in her mouth to heal herself, but she held the power to save three lives in her hands. She wouldn't waste it on a bruised back.

"Ilyenna?"

She jumped at the voice, her hand straying to her belt knife before she realized Darrien had taken it, along with her belt. But it was Rone who came through the trees. She let out her breath in a gasp. She remembered her brother's warning that she tell no one of the fairies. Quickly, she tucked the flower in her pocket. "You frightened me."

"Sorry." He glanced around cautiously before approaching her. He handed her a needle and thread. "Mother thought you might be tired of exposing your back."

Ilyenna took the needle and fastened it to her dress. She hadn't missed the disapproving way he looked at her bare skin. Always the protective brother. "Yes, your mother is very thoughtful."

Rone's brow furrowed as he studied her. "Very well. I don't like having your back exposed, lovely as it is."

She knelt next to the stream and shoved a bowl into the water. The water was so icy it should've made her arms ache all the way to her elbows, but the cold didn't bother her. With a start, she realized she hadn't felt cold since the first fairy kiss.

"So, will you sew it up?" Rone asked her.

Ilyenna pushed a bowl into the water and watched it fill. "I'll have to do it tonight. Metha won't let me have breakfast if I'm late."

Waiting for the sound of his footsteps to announce his departure, she scooped up a handful of sand and began scouring the dishes. Finally, she said, "Shouldn't you get back to building the new tiam house?"

"That's the thing about gathering river stones—you have to find them at the river." When she didn't laugh, he sighed and squatted next to her. "I am the clan chief, Ilyenna. I'm responsible for my clan. I can't help but feel responsible for the Shyle as well."

Always the clan! Could he really be so blind? She scrubbed harder.

Rone rubbed his temples. "The others are getting by, but what about you? If you don't submit, he'll kill you. If you do submit, you'll die inside. I don't see another option. I have to kill him."

Her chest heaving, Ilyenna shot to her feet, water dripping down her shins. Rone stood as well. She drew back her hand and slapped his face. "Don't you dare! Don't you dare, Rone. You've no right to give up and blame it on me!"

Clearly stunned, he rubbed his check. "I didn't mean—"

She jabbed her finger into his chest. "If I can bear it, you can bear it." Her voice broke as she realized what she was saying, but the image of Rone dead burned her far worse than the thought of Darrien's bed. "If you lay one hand on Darrien, I'll kill you myself."

Rone's eyes wide, he stepped back, his expression a mix of hurt and anger. "Whenever you're upset, you lash out at me. The one person who's risking everything to help you." He spun around and strode away.

By the Balance, he was right. "I'm sorry," she called after him, but he didn't turn or slow. Biting the inside of her cheek so hard she tasted blood, she watched him go. She shoved the rest of the dishes into the stream and scrubbed without really caring if she got them clean or not. By the time she'd finished, she'd spent all her tears.

With the basket of clean dishes on her hip, she approached the clan house in time to see five riders gallop up and halt in front of the doors. Ilyenna inched closer. Just as the stable boy arrived to take the men's horses, she caught sight of the knots on their belts—the Resien clan, whose lands lay to the south of the shyle. The two clans were close—almost as close as the Shyle and the Argons.

One of the Resien spotted her. "Ilyenna?"

Her breath caught in her throat. Could it be their clan chief? "Gen?"

He strode forward, his men following closely. His eyes lingered on her stained, tattered dress and bruised face. He pulled her around. "You're back is bare, and beaten! What've they done to you?"

Undon burst out of the clan house. Gen squared his shoulders and marched over to him. "Undon, the Council has sent me to investigate your reparation."

Undon glanced suspiciously at Ilyenna before resting his hand on Gen's shoulder. "You're welcome, Gen of the Resien. Come, have lamb and beer. You and your clanmen must be tired after your hard ride."

Gen jerked out of Undon's grasp. "I'm not here to observe the formalities. You've attacked two clans. We want to know why." Gen's expression said what his words didn't. He didn't think for a moment that Undon had a good reason.

Ilyenna's heart raced with hope. Maybe she wouldn't have to wait the full month. This could all be over today.

Undon's gaze narrowed. "You come to my clan, Gen, making accusations and insulting my hospitality. But I excuse your anger and hold no grudge. If you'll listen, you'll understand."

"Stop circling the cattle and put them in the pen!" Gen practically shouted.

Undon's nostrils flared as he took a deep breath. "Around the time of the first thaw, Seneth and his Argons attacked Tyran families living along the border between our lands. They stole everything, killed my people, and burned all the buildings."

Ilyenna gaped. She didn't believe a word of it.

"And what proof do you have that the Argons did this and not some roving band of thieves?" Gen asked.

Undon nodded to Bennis, who was peeking around the front door. She hurried out and handed her father a charred clan belt and a bundle of blackened arrows, then disappeared back inside. Undon handed them to Gen. The Resien clan chief's eyes widened.

"My clanmen found them among the charred remains of the houses," Undon said, triumph glazing his bitter words. "That belt was on a man's body. The arrows bear the Argon Fletcher's marks. We followed the tracks into Argon lands. Would you like me to go on?"

Gen turned the clan belt and arrows over in his hands before handing them to the men behind him. "Why would the Argons attack you?"

Undon shrugged. "I'd tell you to ask Seneth, but since he's dead, you'll have to settle for his son. But don't count on Rone's honesty. He denied it when I asked him. I have him here to make sure he doesn't cause more trouble."

Gen's eyebrows rose even higher. "He's the Argon clan chief!"

"You think I should've let him roam free?" Undon's voice slowly rose in volume. "He would've rounded up his clanmen and attacked more of my farms!"

Gen seemed to struggle to hold his tongue. His gaze flicked to Ilyenna. "The Shyle? What gave you the right to attack them?"

Not thinking, Ilyenna stepped forward, silently daring Undon to defend his actions.

Undon grimaced. "The Shyle interfered in the battle, killing many of my men. I retaliated."

"How does that give you the right to take tiams?"

Undon took a threatening step forward. "The Shyle killed my men!"

"And you killed theirs. No tiams are granted for a battle death. That's reserved for carelessness that leads to a death."

Undon pointed toward the Shyle lands. "One of their clanmen pretended to surrender and then murdered my son!"

Ilyenna knew the truth, but fear stopped her tongue.

Gen glanced at Ilyenna again. "Why the clan mistress, Undon? What do you have to gain by stealing Otec's daughter?"

Undon took a step back. "His men killed my son, so I took his daughter."

"So it's revenge, is it?" Gen's voice went dangerously soft.

For the first time, Undon looked nervous. "She's alive. That's more than I can say of my son."

"She's beaten and half starved. What else have you done to her? To the other girls?" Gen's face had acquired the look of deadly calculation she'd seen on men's faces before they killed.

"She was punished for disobedience."

Gen's gaze narrowed. "Your account doesn't match what the Shyle claims. And even if it did, the Council decides matters between clans. We don't take up arms against one another. You'd no right to take Ilyenna or to attack the Shyle. At the spring feast, the Council will decide what to do about your attack of the Argons."

Gen tugged Ilyenna behind him, always keeping Undon in his line of sight. "Ilyenna, get on my horse. We're taking you and the other women back to your father."

Undon laughed. The Riesen men tightened their grips on their axes. Ilyenna held the basket of dishes so tightly that she felt the weave imprinting on her hands.

Undon stroked his axe haft. "You've no right to interfere with my tiams, Gen. Come to me with the Council's verdict, not your own. Then we'll see what course to take."

Ilyenna knew a verdict from the Council would have to wait another few weeks. She didn't think she'd last that long.

Gen suddenly changed tactics. "Why, Undon? You know the Council will send the girls home in a month. What do you have to gain by keeping them here until then? Let them go."

Ilyenna felt a flicker of hope. Undon could have gone to the Council and demanded tiams for the crimes against his clan. Instead, he'd crippled both the Shyle and Argon, taking tiams who would ensure his clan remained untouched until the Council returned them in a month's time.

"I'm afraid I must insist on taking Ilyenna," Gen said. "You agreed not to let harm come to her by violence or neglect, yet I can clearly see she has been beaten. And any fool can see she's half starved."

Undon snorted. "And who can trust the word of a fool?"

Gen's hand flew to his axe hilt.

Undon held out his hands and took a deep breath. "We agreed not to harm her so long as she fully submitted. She hasn't, and so we must teach her.

"I tire of you, Gen of the Resien. Ilyenna is my concern now. You may speak with Rone. Then I'll send a man to lead you to the burned-out farms. But thereafter, I suggest you leave Tyran lands. The hunt is on, I would hate for someone to mistake you for a boar."

The men around Gen pulled their axes free. The Resien clan chief took a menacing step forward. "Don't threaten me, Undon of the Tyran clan."

Undon slipped his axe from its loop and ran his thumb along the edge—an edge sharp enough to peel a mushroom. "The truth is, the Tyran is one of the largest clans. You can no more stand against us than the Argons or Shyle could."

Gen gripped Ilyenna's arm. "We're leaving with the clan mistress."

Undon rested his axe hilt on the ground and leaned against it. "Clanmen!" he roared.

Dozens of men bearing axes and shields slowly began filtering out of the clan house. Undon must have guessed how this meeting would go, and he'd been prepared. Ilyenna's hope shattered like glass.

Undon smiled congenially, but his eyes held a threat. "We're off on the hunt, Gen of the Resien. Care to join us?"

Gen exchanged a tight glance with Ilyenna. He'd lost, and they both knew it. "This isn't over." She thought he said it as much for her own benefit as for Undon's.

The Tyran clan chief slowly shook his head. "I certainly hope not. I look forward to meeting you again."

Gen stared at Ilyenna, his eyes seeming to try to convey the words he couldn't say. He and his men mounted their horses. "I'll come back," he said to Undon. "If I don't find Ilyenna well, I promise you, the entire Council will descend on you." He leaned forward in his saddle. "And if they don't, I will."

Ilyenna's heart sank. The Council's power lay in the clan chiefs' willingness to send their men to war—men needed to plant crops and protect their own lands. Dead men meant years of hunger and fatherless children. It wouldn't be easy to convince them, not when the attacked clans had already been defeated.

Undon gave a mocking bow. "I look forward to such a day."

After one last look at Ilyenna, Gen kicked his horse. He and his men galloped down the streets, scattering Tyrans as they went.

Undon watched until the Resien were out of sight, then turned to Ilyenna. Beads of sweat dotted his brow. Perhaps Undon realized just how sharp a knife he was playing with after all. "I trust you know better than to hope, Ilyenna. The Tyran clan is one of the largest. It'll take more than two defeated clans to raise the Council's axes. By the time they convene, tempers will have faded, allowances will have been made. Especially when they learn you could've ended your suffering simply by becoming a Tyran clan mistress."

Ilyenna kept her expression blank. "I've washing to do."

Undon smiled. "I'm glad you're learning."

For the rest of the day, it seemed no matter how fast Ilyenna worked, Metha always found something wrong with the chore she'd just finished, and she was forced to do it over.

Ilyenna had just headed out the door with a pilfered bit of soap when Darrien's voice stopped her from behind. "Where're you going?"

She didn't turn. "My work's done. I'm going to bathe."

"Until you agree to marry me, your smell doesn't distress me." He circled her, an evil smile on his lips. "I could, however, be persuaded."

She glared up at him, trying not to notice how big and strong he was. "No."

"Let her go, Darrien." She startled at the voice and turned to look behind Darrien. Undon stood in the kitchen doorway. "Her smell might not bother you, but it does me."

Darrien's jaw flexed in anger before he bent forward and sniffed loudly. "Perhaps you're right, Father."

He turned and both men disappeared back inside the kitchen.

Trying to keep from running, Ilyenna started up the path to the river.

"What exactly do you think you're doing?"

Nearly jumping out of her dress, she turned to see Rone hurrying to catch up. "I asked what you're doing."

She studied him askance. He had a very handsome chin—strong and square—and the brightest, spring green eyes she'd ever seen. And she'd never felt less attractive. Much as she wanted to be near Rone, she didn't want him near her. "I'm going to clean myself up."

He chuckled softly. "Bit spoiled, are you?"

Suddenly he was the old Rone, the Rone of her childhood. The one who teased her mercilessly. "Spoiled?" She shoved him, so glad he'd forgiven her earlier outburst. "I haven't bathed in a week."

He sniffed and wrinkled his nose. "Yes, I noticed."

She glared at him. "I just finished cleaning the chicken coop." She knew full well it was more than just the coop that made her smell.

He shook his head and pulled out a nutty wedge of bread, wagging it at her like a finger. "I'll wager you this piece of bread Metha hasn't had a bath in four times that."

She snatched the bread from his hands. He gave it up easily, adding a couple boiled eggs. "Did you eat today?"

She nodded. "Metha let me have some lunch."

"She's a real apple, that one."

Ilyenna sputtered, nearly choking on her bread. "Round and rosy?"

Rone grinned mischievously. "No. More like a smelly, rotten, mushy old apple."

Oh, an apple sounded lovely right now. She adored apples. She took a bite of the egg, and he handed her some water. She took it gratefully. "Metha's expecting a baby."

He froze, his mouth hanging open. "Someone stuck around long enough to get her with child?"

Ilyenna laughed; it had been such a long time her cheeks felt stretched and stiff. But suddenly she wanted to know why Rone was helping her. As a clan chief? Her brother's best friend? "Thank you for the food—for everything. But Rone, why are you watching out for me? I'm not an Argon."

He folded his arms. "No, but you need someone as badly as anyone here. Besides, after what your clan did for mine, how could I not offer help?"

"Oh." Her food suddenly tasted like sawdust. Didn't he find her pretty? Now she was smelly and skinny and pale as birch bark, but she hadn't always been. What she wouldn't give for Rone to feel ardor for her like Darrien did. She shivered deliciously at the thought.

"You're quiet. My answer didn't settle?" Rone said.

She handed him the waterskin, glad she could hear the rushing water and have an excuse to end this embarrassing encounter. "Honor is a fine reason to help a woman. Sleep well, Rone."

She found a full bush and began undressing behind it. When she turned, she was surprised to see him still there, though his back was turned away, his eyes riveted to a tree. "You can go back now," she said.

He shook his head. "I don't think I'd better. What if Darrien comes?"

"Then you'd better be as far away from me as possible." Checking to make sure he didn't peek, though a part of her wished he would, Ilyenna tested the water. It was as cold as ever, yet that cold felt comforting to her aching body.

"One day, I'll kill him for you." A hardness had crept into Rone's voice.

"Go back, Rone. I'll be fine."

He shook his head. "I brought more ointment. I'll rub it in once you're finished."

"Stubborn man," she mumbled. But secretly, she was pleased. The thought of Rone's hands on her made her tremble with excitement.

Soap in hand, Ilyenna washed her dress, wrung it out, and hung it over the bush. Then she went in as deep as she dared and splashed water on herself. She began lathering up. She sighed at the sight of her body, a mass of bruises in various degrees of healing. She could feel the ridges of each rib.

Soon, she stepped out of the water and pulled on her damp dress. She tried to adjust it, but the water made it hard to shift. With her dress twisted and heavy, she made her way to Rone.

"You must be freezing."

She shrugged. "Not really."

He took out the ointment, and she turned and pulled her hair over her shoulder. His hands were rough as cracked leather, but so gentle on her skin. She shivered.

"See, you are cold."

Not trusting herself to speak, she bit her lip. His hands seemed to linger as he rubbed in the ointment.

"Your skin is as pale as moonlight," he said.

"So was my mother's," she said without thinking. She was usually careful not to speak of her mother. Memories always dropped a smoldering coal of guilt in her chest. After all, it was her fault Matka was dead. But now Ilyenna had started, she couldn't seem to stop. "Do you remember her? She had hair the color of a midnight sky and eyes as dark as earth."

"So do you."

Ilyenna turned to face him. "If only I were half so beautiful."

Rone's brow furrowed. "I don't see how she could be any more beautiful than you."

"You shouldn't say things like that."

Rone threw his hands up. "I'm sorry. I never know what to say to you." He turned to leave.

She snatched his hand. "I'm sorry. It's just . . . do you really think that? That I'm beautiful?"

He stepped closer, the intensity of his gaze surprising her. "Yes."

Her eyes shifted to his arms, the bulge of his muscles visible beneath his undershirt. How would it feel to have those strong arms around her? She couldn't help herself. Her gaze rested on his lips. Her heart pounded so loud she was sure he could hear it.

He cocked his head to the side, studying her. Unable to bear it, she looked away.

Rone took a small step forward, still watching her. Was he mocking her?

If he starts tickling me, he'll have more to fear than Darrien's axe, she thought.

Calling up her courage, she matched his step, her eyes trained upon his lips. He leaned toward her, so close they breathed the same air. She closed her eyes.

"What are you two doing?"

They jumped back like thieves caught stealing spring lambs. Ilyenna's heart thudded painfully in her chest. If Darrien found out . . .

But it was Narium who appeared through the trees, her expression twisted in disapproval. Crossing her arms, she glared at the two of them. Ilyenna dropped her gaze and stared at the ground in a mixture of embarrassment and shame.

"Do you have any idea what would happen if anyone else saw what I just did? They'd kill him, Ilyenna. They'd kill my son."

"They'll kill me regardless, Mother. The slightest slip—"

"And you think to leave your death on her hands?" Narium interrupted. Her gaze softened, and she stepped forward and placed her small hand on his shoulder. "Don't be selfish. You're not the selfish kind. I still need you. Our clan still needs you. Ilyenna still needs you." She dropped her hand. "From now on, I'll see she receives food, but not from you." Narium's face was hard as flint. "Not anymore."

Rone took a deep breath. "I am clan chief. I've the right to—"

"Silence!" Narium said with all the power of a clan mistress. She turned to Ilyenna. "Please understand, he'll die."

Ilyenna dropped her head as tears blurred her vision. "I'm sorry. I'm so sorry!" She turned and ran.

11. HEALER

Though her blankets were spread before the hearth, Metha was nowhere in sight. Ilyenna was glad to have the kitchen to herself so she could stitch up her overdress—her underdress would have to wait until she had both light and privacy. With fingers accustomed to a needle and thread, she worked quickly, not wanting Darrien to catch her in the kitchen in nothing but her underdress.

She sighed when she pulled the mended overdress over her head. It was such a relief to have her back covered. Suddenly, she heard voices beyond the door—a man and a woman arguing.

"Why are you doing this?" the woman asked, and Ilyenna recognized Metha's voice.

"Shh! Do you want to wake my father?"

That was Darrien. Ilyenna cringed. The voices moved toward her. As fast as she could, she ducked outside and pressed her back against the cool river-stone wall. She heard the kitchen door creak open.

"I will not 'shh!'" Metha said loudly, "You told me you loved me. You told me we'd marry! Now everyone knows I'm with child. My family has thrown me out, and still you won't give our child a father!"

Ilyenna braced herself against the river stones to keep from falling over. Darrien was the father to Metha's child? She wanted to marry him? It seemed so preposterous. Ilyenna couldn't help herself; she peeked through the door, which was slightly ajar.

Darrien shoved Metha into a chair and pressed his palms into the table behind her, boxing her in. "If you weren't carrying a child, I'd beat you for speaking to me that way. I will be clan chief. The daughter of a wheat farmer will never do."

"Not just a child, your child." Metha's voice came out half strangled. "You helped create it, so why am I the only one being treated like a whore?"

Darrien shrugged. "Because you're a woman."

Metha's chest heaved on a silent sob. "And I suppose that scrawny little witch from the Shyle would make a better breeder?"

Darrien pulled back his hand and slapped her full in the face.

Ilyenna covered her mouth with her hand to keep from crying out.

Metha screeched and raised her hand to slap him back. Darrien grabbed it. With his other hand, he roughly grasped her face. "Don't you ever, ever speak to me that way again. I got you work out of pity, but if you'd rather, I can take it away and you can live as the harlot outcast you are."

He released her face and gently stroked the red marks he'd left there. "As for Ilyenna, yes, she'll make a fine breeder. I'll enjoy every moment of breaking her. After fathering a few whelps with her, you and I will be free to meet in the woods, as we once did."

Metha slowly shook her head. "There won't be any more of that. Ever."

Darrien chuckled. "We'll see about that. I like my women with a bit of flesh on them."

Metha spit in his face. The thin line of spittle ran down his cheek. He wiped it off with his fingers and gazed at it in shock. He threw her to the floor, drew back his foot, and slammed it into her stomach. She gasped in shock and pain, curling protectively around her swollen belly. He kicked her again and again and again.

Ilyenna couldn't process what she saw. She remembered the Argon babies—the ones she'd tended. The ones who might even now be dead, like Metha's would soon be. Ilyenna threw open the door and screamed, "No!" Ducking her shoulder, she barreled into Darrien.

He barely had to shift his weight to absorb the blow. Without taking his eyes from Metha, he backhanded Ilyenna. She hit the floor hard. Blackness curled in from the outside of her vision. Shaking her head to clear it, she saw Metha, her face screwed up in agony as Darrien pounded her, his features contorted with rage.

Ilyenna threw herself over Metha, screaming as loud and long as she could, "Rone!" A kick to her already bruised ribs stole her breath. Her whole body clenched in protest. Darrien kicked her over and over, and a scream of pain tore from her throat. Ilyenna realized her folly too late. She hadn't saved anyone. He was going to kill all three of them.

Something cracked. It sounded like lightning. The kicks finally stopped.

Ilyenna rolled off Metha and vomited. When her retching finally stopped, she managed to look up.

Rone had Darrien underneath him, his fist working the other man into a pulp. Undon must have come down while she'd been sick. He was trying, unsuccessfully, to pull Rone off. Ilyenna tried to shout, but her words came out as little more than a hoarse whisper, "No. Don't kill him, Rone. They'll execute you."

The opposite door flung open. A Tyran barreled into the room, shouting for help. But others were already coming. They must have heard Ilyenna's screams. It took four Tyrans to pull Rone off. Even then, he struggled to reach Darrien.

Ilyenna realized her hand was wet and looked down. Bright blood pooled beneath her. For a moment, she thought it was hers. But then she remembered Metha. Barely holding on to consciousness, she leaned over the woman. Ilyenna had to help her, but she couldn't reach through her own pain to think straight. Every time she moved, she wanted to cry out.

Rone. Would they kill him for saving her and Metha? Would they kill them all?

Undon's daughters hurried to Metha. They grabbed the woman and dragged her out of the kitchen, leaving nothing but a trail of blood as testament to what Darrien had done. Ilyenna watched them go, trying to force herself to get up and help.

A face appeared before her. It took a moment for Ilyenna to recognize Narium. "The Balance protect me, what've they done to you?"

Ilyenna tried to shake her head. "It's not my blood." But she tasted blood in her mouth and spit it onto the already stained floor.

Narium glanced up. "Get her to the women's house," she said. Then she was gone.

Shyle and Argon women surrounded Ilyenna and carried her between them. She tensed with every step they took, and the pain grew so intense she blacked out.

Dreams took her. Dreams of Darrien's axe slicing fire through her stomach. Dreams of fairies and winter and dancing. Of a woman with skin as dark as the richest soil and a laugh that sounded like wind through aspens. In her hand was a tiny white blossom. "Eating this will heal even the direst injuries," she said, her voice like a song.

"No you will not!"

Ilyenna woke with a start. A deep ache radiated from her abdomen, and she knew something was broken inside her. Her abdomen was swollen and tender. She was on the only bed in the women's house, naked but for a blanket tucked around her. Her body had been washed. The voices were coming from outside.

"You will get back to work." Ilyenna recognized Undon's voice.

"I won't! Your sorry excuse for a son nearly beat her to death. She still might die. Isn't his child and the child's mother enough?"

Metha was dead? Ilyenna closed her eyes, hoping Narium's mouth didn't land her a visit to the beating pole.

A long pause. "He lost his temper. If Ilyenna hadn't interfered, he would've stopped on his own."

"If my son hadn't interfered, your son would have killed them both. You think you have me beaten, Undon, but you'd be wise not to forget who I am. Who Ilyenna and Rone are. If Ilyenna dies, if my son dies, you'll have the deaths of more clan mistresses and clan chiefs on your hands—and before the Council can even decide if your reparation was just. They won't wait for the summer feast. They'll come now and cleanse the clan lands of Tyrans."

Another long pause. "Fine. Today you tend her, but tomorrow you will work."

Ilyenna heard retreating footsteps. After a lengthy pause, Narium let out a long, shaky sigh.

Wincing, Ilyenna lifted the blanket to reveal arnica leaves covering her broken flesh. From the top of her breasts to the bottom of her abdomen, she was black with bruises. Just moving the blanket hurt so much she had to lie back, her energy spent. She felt death waiting for her.

The flower. The one the summer queen had given her. Ilyenna looked for her overdress. It lay nearby, freshly laundered and mended. On top of it was the elice flower.

Ilyenna strained toward it, her battered flesh screaming in protest. Black spots danced before her vision, and tears sprang to her eyes. Her fingers brushed against the soft petals. She picked up the flower. The three petals looked as fresh as when Leto had handed it to her.

Ilyenna plucked one of the petals and laid it on her tongue. It dissolved as though made of spun sugar. Warmth blossomed in her mouth before taking her far away, high in the mountains. She lay in a meadow. The air was thick with the sweet scent of freshly cut hay and clover blossoms. The early summer sun warmed Ilyenna's skin. The melody of bird song and scurrying animals filled the air. This was the promise of spring. Renewal. Reawakening. Rebirth. For a long time, she lay in the grass, relishing the warm sun and invigorating smells.

Then the Luathan woman was there, smiling down at her. The sun seemed to have absorbed into her skin, condensing until it shone out of her. "'Tis a fair thing, when summer comes."

Ilyenna tentatively laid her hand over her ribs. Her pain had vanished. "I don't know how you did it, but thank you."

Leto inclined her head and sat beside her. "In times past, other queens have been enemies. Such a shame. We should be sisters, two ends of the same loaf. I awaken the world, you put it to rest."

"Opposite sides of the Balance," Ilyenna said softly. She had so many questions, but the warm sun made her too drowsy to ask them. "I would be your sister," she managed.

The summer queen smiled broadly. "Well then, go back. Survive the summer, and all will be well."

Ilyenna opened her eyes to stare up at the roof beams. In her hand, she felt the softness of flower petals. Daring to hope, she lifted the blanket. The black bruises had faded to a greenish yellow. Holding the blanket to her bare chest, she carefully sat up. She was stiff and sore, but it was the soreness from a hard day's work rather than the agony of nearly being kicked to death. Her hunger raged far stronger than any pain.

Moving carefully, she grabbed her underdress—someone had mended it. She tugged it over her head and tightened the laces at her throat. Next came her felt overdress. She tied the rag around her waist to keep it from hanging open at the sides. With the movement, her body was slowly warming up and the stiffness working out. She was tying the laces of her boots when the door opened.

Sunshine streaming in behind him, Rone gaped at her. "What're you doing up?"

Ilyenna couldn't help but smile in delight. She'd expected Narium. "Rone? But . . . how long have I been here?"

He came in, shutting the door behind him. "This is the second day."

A whole day since she'd last been conscious. That explained Narium's absence.

Rone looked her up and down before moving to Narium's makeshift bed on the floor and pulling out a knotted bit of cloth. "Mother said you might die. How're you even out of bed?"

Noting the stiff way he moved, she waved his question away. "What did they do to you?"

"I'll tell you all about my *ordeal* after you've eaten something." He untied the cloth and handed it to her. Dried apple slices, cheese, and a bit of bread. "Sorry there's not more of it."

Ilyenna's mouth watered at the sight of the apples. Her hands trembling from hunger, she picked out the apple slices, saving them for last. "Don't be sorry. I know you take the food from your own share." She took a bite of the bread.

Rone sat beside her on the bed and watched her eat most of the bread before he spoke, "They beat me with a soaked strap."

Ilyenna's breath snagged in her throat. Fingering an apple slice, she wondered why his punishment hadn't been worse. She hesitated before asking, "Is that all they're going to do?"

"For now. I think Undon's afraid if he kills me before the Council makes their decision, they'll come against him. Which they will."

"And he let you care for me?"

Rone grinned. "Undon and Darrien are too busy to keep track of me today."

Ilyenna finished the last of the cheese and tucked the remaining apple slices in her pocket. "Metha?" She undid her loose braid and combed through her hair with her fingers.

Rone watched her, a soft look around his eyes. "She's dying."

Ilyenna sagged as she rebraided her hair. Metha hadn't shown her anything but cruelty, yet Ilyenna felt sorry for the woman, for what Darrien had done. Metha's story and hers were more alike than Ilyenna would've ever guessed.

"Has anyone been to see her?" She tied off her braid with a cord.

"Apparently Undon's daughters didn't learn much of healing before their mother's death. My mother did the best she could for her."

Ilyenna was on her feet before she could even think it through. Wincing, Rone moved to block her. "Where are you going?"

She tried to sidestep him. He mimicked her movement. She felt the heat from his body and hated that her stomach twisted in a delicious knot. "Rone, let me past. I might be able to help her."

He gripped her forearms. "She's beyond anyone's helping, Ilyenna. You need to rest. And you need to stay away from Darrien."

She jerked out of his grasp and glared at him. "The Balance protect you, Rone of the Argons, if you don't let me pass!"

He folded his arms across his chest. "Don't you look at me that way—like I'm Darrien, because I'm not. I'd never hurt a woman, and you know it!"

She couldn't help but notice how thin Rone had become—partially from sharing his food with her. He was right. She always lashed out at him when she was angry. "No, you'd never hurt me, but you're still treating me like I can't make a rational decision. I can help Metha. I know you think of me like a little sister, but I'm not little, Rone. I'm a woman now."

He snorted. "Oh, don't I know it."

She stomped her foot. "Rone!"

He studied her for a moment, his pale brows gathered, before he stepped out of her way. "Fine, but I'm going with you. Everyone knows your rational thoughts blow away at the first sign of an injury."

She couldn't argue with that. Walking as quickly as she could, she crossed the distance from the women's house to the clan house. She pushed open the kitchen door. Undon's daughters gaped at her.

"Where is she?" Ilyenna demanded.

The oldest, Bennis, couldn't have been more than fourteen, but she squared herself like a clan mistress anyway. "She's with her son."

"Where?"

Hanie, a girl of ten or so, nodded toward the ladders. "In our room."

Bennis shot her a murderous glare. Hanie ducked her head and mumbled, "Maybe she can help them."

"Narium showed you how to make qatcha?" Ilyenna asked.

Bennis's chin jutted out. "Yes."

"Good. Make some more with some knitbone, bethroat, and cocklebur, if you've got it, and bring it up" Ilyenna started past them.

Bennis planted herself firmly in front of Rone. "He doesn't come into the clan house."

Ilyenna looked back when Rone said, "I'm not letting her be alone in this house with him."

Bennis dropped her head and swallowed. "He's not here."

"Wait for me outside?" Ilyenna said to Rone.

He pressed his lips together in disapproval, but she was gone before he could argue. She climbed the ladders and entered the room shared by Undon's two daughters. Metha lay on the bed, her skin the color of ash. In her arms, she held a shriveled, nearly translucent baby who was even grayer than his mother. Ilyenna had delivered enough children to know this one was far too early, but the fact that he was alive meant he was a fighter.

Ilyenna sat on the side of the bed and placed her hand on Metha's forehead. She was cold. Her breathing quick and shallow. Neither were good signs. Trying not to disturb her, Ilyenna lifted the blanket. At least the bleeding had stopped.

She touched the baby. He was breathing, though not nearly often enough. She tapped his forehead with her fingertips. No reaction. She pinched his arm. He didn't even clench his eyelids. She sighed. He wouldn't make it another hour. But his mother had a chance if she didn't start bleeding again or develop a fever.

Ilyenna pressed her hand against the flower, still tucked beneath her overdress. If she used it on this child, that would only leave one petal. She had no doubts Darrien would kill more of her clan before winter, perhaps even in the next month. She and Rone were at the top of that list. Leto had given Ilyenna the flower to keep her alive until winter returned.

Ilyenna glanced at the baby. He was Darrien's son, yet as innocent and deserving of life as any other child. Gently, she shifted Metha's arms and lifted him. Such a small thing. Barely any weight at all in her hands. She felt a stirring in her breast, an instinctive protectiveness. "Yes, little one," she breathed, "I will save you."

Reaching inside her overdress, she plucked a petal. Then she lay the child across her lap, opened his tiny mouth, and slipped the petal inside. For a moment, nothing happened. Then he gasped, his arms flailing to the side. Warmth surged from his tiny body into her hands. His face pinked up. With a contented sigh, he settled into normal breathing.

"Don't touch my son."

Startled, Ilyenna looked at Metha. The woman reached for her child, and Ilyenna laid him back in his mother's arms. "Lie still. You don't want to start the bleeding again."

"What did you do to him?" Metha rasped, hatred glowing in her eyes.

"You blame me for what Darrien did? I was trying to save your life."

Metha's cheeks went red and she looked away. "Before you came, he loved me. You stole him away from me."

Ilyenna laid a hand over her ribs, ghosts of pain echoing in her bones. "Let him go, Metha. It wasn't real—it never was. Hold on to your son. That love is real."

"As if you know what real love is!" Panting, Metha lay back in the bed. "Get out!"

The door pushed open. Bennis came in, a steaming cup in her hand. One look at Metha and she glared at Ilyenna. "What did you do?"

Metha groaned. Bennis lifted the blanket and threw it back. Bright blood stained the rags. The young girl stared at it, her face turning white. "Metha, you have to stop moving," she said. "You have to calm down."

Metha shifted in her bed. "You get out too. You know whose baby Harraw is. You know he should be the next clan chief, but still you deny it!"

Ilyenna pushed Bennis to the side. "You're right, Metha. They know who your son is. But if you want to live to raise him, you have to keep still."

Metha lay back, clearly exhausted. "It doesn't matter. I'm dying."

Ilyenna glanced at the crimson sheets and thought of the last petal she had left. A petal she could use to save someone she loved. To save herself. But that would mean she would have to watch Metha die, knowing she could've stopped it.

She bent over the woman. Metha's eyes had grown heavy. Not much longer and she'd slip into unconsciousness. "Yes, Metha," she whispered. "You're dying. But I can help you." She held out the flower with its last remaining petal. "If you trust me."

Metha glanced from the flower to Ilyenna. "Why would you help me?"

Ilyenna felt a pang course through her. She thought of what Darrien had said days before. Was she a healer or a killer? "I am a healer," she said steadily. "It's what I am."

Metha hesitated before nodding. Ilyenna plucked the last petal and slipped it onto her tongue. As quickly as it had worked on Harraw, Ilyenna saw the changes begin in Metha. She clutched the stripped flower head to her chest and left the room.

12. DARK OF NIGHT

Waiting for morning, Ilyenna sat in Darrien's attic. In her palm lay the flower head. Her fingertips circled it over and over again. Exhausted as she was, she hadn't been able to sleep. Darrien was going to kill her or one of the others, and now she couldn't save any of them.

She glanced up at the sound of horses. Peeking through the chink in the mortar, she saw three riders come to a stop outside the clan house. Two dismounted, leaving the third to hold the reins of their horses. Ilyenna wondered who would ride here this early. She put the flower away and pressed her face against the wall. They were strange men, wearing long, hooded cloaks instead of coats.

One of them rapped at the kitchen door and waited before rapping again. Finally, the door opened, spilling lantern light across the stranger's face. He and one of his companions came inside. Ilyenna heard voices, and soon footsteps sounded beneath her. Darrien was up. Why were the Tyrans meeting with strangers in the middle of the night?

Something was wrong—evilly, wickedly wrong—and she had to know what. Quietly as she could, she lifted the trapdoor. Darrien's room was empty. Lying on her stomach, she strained to reach the ladder, but it was too far. She groaned in frustration. Below her were Darrien's hunting trophies—antlers, skulls, and skins—stretched across his walls. What if she could use them like vertical stepping stones?

Swinging her feet over the edge, she lowered herself from the attic. Her feet dangled above a bear skull. She pointed her toes, her feet barely grazed the bear's forehead. Would it support her weight?

Holding her breath, she let herself drop. The skull held to the wall, but something clattered out of its mouth. Ilyenna dropped to the floor. She found a large, heavy piece of onyx, which she now remembered seeing before in the bear's mouth. She quickly shoved it under a sheepskin rug and rushed to the door. Glancing up and down the hall, she hurried down the ladders. At the bottom, she paused, her pulse racing as she stared at the light glowing from beneath the kitchen door. If anyone came into the great hall, she'd have nowhere to hide.

Her whole body tensed to flee, she tiptoed to the kitchen door and pressed her ear to the wood. She heard whispered voices, mumbles, but no matter how hard she strained to make out words, she couldn't.

Ilyenna dared not linger. She raced back up the ladders. In Darrien's room, she gripped the back of the skull and climbed up. Stretching, her fingertips found the wooden lip around the trapdoor. She heaved with all her strength, scrambling with her bare feet, but she slipped down. Footsteps echoed down the hall. He was coming! She tried again. Her foot brushed against a knot of wood. Digging her toes into it, she heaved herself up.

She eased the trapdoor down just as Darrien came into the room. Completely drained, she collapsed on the floor. She pressed her palms into her forehead as thoughts of the foreigners meeting secretly in the clan house reverberated inside her head.

Hours later, Ilyenna startled when she heard the ladder scrape along the floor of Darrien's room. "Get up and get down here!" he hollered.

She crawled to the door and lifted it. Darrien stared up at her, his face an unreadable mask. Her gut twisting into knots, she stepped down the rungs. Once her feet were on the floor, she forced herself to meet his gaze.

He was so close that she instinctively took a step back. Still, he said nothing. She started walking away, but his voice halted her.

"You healed Metha, her baby, and yourself. How?"

She turned to face him. "Fairies."

He thumbed his nose. "Unfortunately, I am no longer allowed to lay a hand on either you or Metha." He circled Ilyenna, close enough that his shoulder brushed across her chest. "Not unless you ask for it, that is."

Her hands ached to slap him, so she clenched them to keep herself in check. Not trusting herself to speak, she clenched her jaw as well.

Drawing even with her, Darrien whispered, his lips brushing against her hair. "You'll ask."

Ilyenna rushed from the room. She had to find Rone, to tell him about Darrien and Undon meeting with strangers in the dead of night. Downstairs, she stopped short at the sight of Metha sitting at the kitchen table, Harraw nuzzling at her breast.

It was the first time she'd seen the other woman since she'd given her one of the elice blossoms. Already, some of her swelling had gone down, revealing her jaw line and the joints of her fingers. Metha met her questioning gaze with an unreadable expression. "Come here."

Ilyenna hesitated before moving to obey. Metha gazed down at her son. "What did you do to him, to us?"

"I healed you. Isn't that enough?"

Metha shook her head. "Yesterday, I was dying. My son was dying. Today, I am stronger than I've been in months."

Ilyenna started past them, toward the serving spoon and the pot of porridge. "You're stronger than you think."

Metha's hand shot out and grabbed Ilyenna's arm. She used it as leverage to pull herself to her feet. She gestured to a bowl of porridge circled with thick, rich cream. "First, eat your breakfast. Then you can get to the dishes."

Without another word, Metha left the kitchen to serve the men.

Dumbfounded, Ilyenna stared at the porridge. She glanced around to make sure no one would backhand her before she slipped in the chair. Without bothering to stir the porridge, she ate every single bite as quickly as she could. Metha came back and put the pot in the basket. Apparently the girls had already eaten.

Her belly warm and full for the first time in days, Ilyenna took the basket of dishes and headed toward the house Rone was building. But as soon as she stepped out, Narium joined her. Shooting a wary glance back at the clan house, Ilyenna took Narium's arm and steered her toward the forest.

"Last night, three foreigners came to the clan house. Two entered and met with Undon and Darrien. I sneaked downstairs, but I couldn't make out what was said."

The older woman rubbed her forehead between chapped fingers. "I'll tell Rone."

Ilyenna's heart dropped. "Shouldn't you be in the fields?"

"Shouldn't you have finished the dishes by now?" Narium asked testily.

Ilyenna drew a deep breath. "I didn't realize you were waiting for me."

"I wasn't waiting," Narium growled.

"Narium, stop circling the sheep and put them in the pen."

The woman sighed. "I'll have one of the girls bring you the dishes, the washing, and your noon meal. Stay at the river." She turned on her heel and headed back.

Ilyenna plunked down the basket of dishes. "Narium, wait!"

She turned. "If you trust me at all, Ilyenna, you'll do this."

Ilyenna shook her head. "Not until you tell me why."

"Do as I say!" Narium took off at a swift walk.

Bewildered, Ilyenna watched her go. Whatever was going on, the other clan mistress didn't want her to know about it until it was over. By then, Ilyenna would be too late to interfere. She glanced at the dishes and then toward the clan house. Slowly, she shook her head. "You aren't the only clan mistress, Narium."

After stashing the dishes inside the forest, Ilyenna eased through the woods. Hidden behind the trees, she searched the village. Nothing seemed out of place. Cautiously, she stepped out and ran to the barn.

It was then she heard it. The rhythmic slap, slap, slap of the strap. Someone was being beaten. Cautiously, she peered out. She recognized Darrien immediately. But who was he beating? Long, blond hair. A Shyle dress. Ilyenna stepped closer.

Larina.

The strap connected again. Ilyenna shut her eyes and winced with each blow. Why was Darrien beating her? And why didn't Narium want her to see this? Did she think Ilyenna would try to stop it? She wasn't a fool. Interfering would only make it worse.

Knowing there was nothing she could do, Ilyenna hurried back to the river and washed the dishes as fast as she could. She was so distracted she didn't notice the apple blossom until it was hovering over the water directly in front of her. She smiled. "Thank you for bringing Leto."

Jablana tipped her head to the side. "You asked for my help." The fairy's tiny wings beat faster, and she zipped back to the apple tree. But just before she flew out of sight, she paused and held her hands over the apple blossom. The petals fell off. The area behind the pollen-coated tips grew fat and green then red.

Jablana pulled her hands away. Her wings beat tiredly, but she was smiling. "They don't taste as sweet without a touch of frost."

Ilyenna felt her mouth hanging open and closed it. "Apples are my favorite."

The fairy's wings perked up and Ilyenna could see the wide smile over her pale pink skin. "Apples like winter's kiss. Perhaps this is why I am drawn to you." Her wings darkened with what Ilyenna could only guess was a blush. Jablana darted away.

Ilyenna reached up and plucked the apple from the tree. It was warm beneath her hands. She bit into it. Jablana may have been right about it not being as sweet, but after a winter of withered fruits and vegetables and days of half-rotten, infested food, it was the best apple she'd ever eaten.

Long before midday, Jossa arrived with a basket of washing and Ilyenna's noon meal. "Metha's actually feeding you now?"

Unwrapping her food, Ilyenna found a handful of fresh peas, a chunk of ham, and a piece of fresh bread. She palmed the whole lot of peas into her mouth. "I'll be sure to stay on Metha's good side from now on."

Jossa had already scooped up the clean breakfast dishes and headed back to the clan house.

"Jossa?" Ilyenna called after her. The girl paused but didn't turn. "I know something's going on. What is it?"

Jossa hung her head. "Nothing, mistress."

Carefully setting down her food, Ilyenna stood. "Jossa, I am your clan mistress, not Narium. Now tell me what's going on."

Jossa slowly turned, tears forming in her eyes. "Nothing's going on, mistress."

Ilyenna blinked in surprise. Jossa was lying. This was much worse than Ilyenna had thought. She placed her hand on Jossa's shoulders, and the girl gasped in pain.

Ilyenna turned her around and pulled her hair to the side. Angry red welts stretched up her neck into her hairline. She'd been beaten with a soaked strap. "Darrien did this? Why?"

Jossa's started backing away. "Please, mistress. Please don't. I promised I wouldn't say anything."

"Stay here and finish the washing," Ilyenna ordered.

Without waiting for the girl's reply, she ran all the way to the women's house and yanked open the door. What she saw stopped her cold. All of the women, even Narium, lay on the floor, strips of rags soaked in witch hazel across their backs. "By the Balance . . ."

Wincing, Narium sat up. "What're you doing here? You've work to do."

Ilyenna stepped into the room. "I want to know what's going on, and I want to know now! Why did Darrien beat all of you?"

No one answered. Ilyenna looked at each of her clanwomen in turn—Wenly, Kanni, Parsha, Bet, Larina—then at Narium and her clanwomen. None but Larina would meet her gaze. The young woman was glaring at her like she'd stolen all her spring lambs.

Cold fear shot through Ilyenna. "Larina, you want to tell me what this is about?"

Narium shot Larina a look that would've singed the bristles off a pig. "You say anything, and you'll have me to deal with."

Larina opened her mouth to argue.

"Think what you're doing, Larina," Narium said. "He won't touch us again till we're healed. And by then the Council will have freed us."

Larina glared at Narium before turning away.

Looking between the two, Ilyenna felt a sob on the edge of her throat. They'd all turned against her. Her own clanwomen! After everything that had happened, she didn't think she could bear that too. Tears burned her eyes. "Fine. Don't tell me," she said, her voice trembling. "I'll ask Darrien." She stormed out.

"Get Rone," she heard Narium shout.

Ilyenna was halfway to the clan house before Rone grabbed her arm. She whirled, pushing the tears off her cheeks. "Are you going to tell me what's going on?"

Rone dropped her arm and stared at the ground. "They won't tell me either, only that it's best I not know. I believe them, and you should too."

Ilyenna threw her hands in the air. "Isn't that for me to decide?"

He shook his head. "Not this time. Leave it alone, Ilyenna. Just leave it alone." He turned on his heel. She watched him head back to where the men were laying the foundation for a house. A large house, much larger than even the clan house. This couldn't be a tiam house.

She hurried into the kitchen. Metha was standing at the table, changing her son's bottom. She looked up when Ilyenna stormed in. "Where's my laundry?"

Ilyenna stopped short. "I left Jossa to do it."

Metha frowned. "The girl was just beaten with a soaked strap, and you're making her do your work?"

"I—"

Metha pointed at the door. "Get back to that river and do your job. Now."

"I want to speak to Darrien."

Metha's finger jabbed the air. "Now!"

Ilyenna stormed back to the river, determined to get something out of Jossa. But as soon as the girl saw her coming, she fled as if Darrien himself chased her.

Helplessly, Ilyenna watched her go. What secret was so dangerous Jossa would run from her, injured as she was? She didn't get a chance to find out. Hanie brought her supper and the last of the dishes. Ilyenna tried to get information out of the girl, but she claimed not to know anything, though her pained face spoke otherwise.

By the time Ilyenna was finished, her hands were wrinkled and raw, and deep night had come on. Balancing the basket on her hip, she went back to the kitchen. Metha was at the table, patting Harrow's tiny back. "Darrien's already gone to bed. You're to sleep in the hallway."

Ilyenna stared at the woman's back, trying to will Metha to tell her something. As if sensing her, Metha half turned. "Don't, Ilyenna."

Fine. She'd ask Darrien herself. Up the stairs, she eased into his room. Drawing her courage, she shut the door. Instantly, she was plunged into darkness. Her heart lurched into her throat.

"Hello, Ilyenna." It sounded like he was in bed after all.

She breathed a little easier that he wasn't lying in wait for her. "Why did you beat all the tiams?"

"Come closer and I'll tell you."

Her eyes had begun to adjust to the dark. He was in his bed. A warning pounded in her head. Narium, Rone, and Metha had all told her to leave it alone. But she couldn't. He was hurting her clanwomen. If she could do anything to stop it, she would. She came to the side of the bed, making sure to stay out of arms' reach. "Why?"

"Why, Ilyenna?" She smelled whiskey on his breath. Cringing, she stepped back, suddenly full of terror. "Because they disobeyed. Just as you continue to do."

Faster than she thought possible, his hand snaked out and grabbed her wrist. She twisted and strained. He surprised her then, lunging out of the bed and knocking her to the floor. He pinned her beneath him. She cried out, shoving and beating against his chest.

He grabbed her arms and held them above her head. He pressed against her, his hungry fingers working her dress up. No matter how hard she fought, she couldn't stop him. He was so much stronger. "Please, no! Please!" she cried out.

He worked faster.

"You swore you wouldn't!"

He paused.

Tears streamed down Ilyenna's face and soaked into her hair.

Twisting, she strained to get as far away from him as she could.

Releasing her hands, Darrien lowered his head, his breath coming hard and fast against her neck. "You were smart to bargain for that right. Very smart. But you aren't the only one I can hurt."

All the blood in Ilyenna's body went cold. "No," she gasped.

He leaned in and whispered into her ear. "I told you I'd make you pay, Ilyenna. And pay you will. I will beat each and every one of them until you marry me or tell me the secret of your healings."

"I told you. The fairies did it. They gave me a flower, but I used it all."

Her searching fingers found something smooth and hard under the skin rug. The onyx. She fumbled to pull it out without Darrien noticing. "I'll kill you," she said through clenched teeth.

He laughed. "You proved it with Metha. You're a healer, a clan mistress. Not a murderer." He took her earlobe between his teeth. "Not like me."

She clenched her eyes shut, not wanting to see what was coming. "Why? Why are you doing this?"

She felt him smile against her neck. "All my life my mother spoke of the Balance. But she was always so weak compared to my father. I realized the truth when she died. It's the strong side of the Balance that survives—that leads, that rules. I'm stronger and smarter than anyone else in the lands. And one day they'll all be mine. Let me hear the words, Ilyenna"

He'd given her no choice. They both knew it. He'd won. Unless . . .

Her finger tightened around the onyx stone. It would cost her life, but so would agreeing to what he wanted. She slammed the stone against his head. His weight collapsed on top of her, his breath hot on her throat. Wiggling, she managed to get out from under him. Already, he was starting to moan.

Dropping the bloodied stone, she ran.

13. FALLING

The clan-house door cracked against the river-stone wall as Ilyenna streaked through. Metha cried after her, but she didn't stop or slow. She flew down the path, the trees shadowed blurs as she passed. At the river, she paused to catch her breath and listen. Nothing. But he would come.

She ran until the path disappeared. Not much deeper, the forest grew too dense to move through, forcing her to run parallel to the river. Dodging a boulder, she splashed in, soaking herself to her knees. A little farther down, the trees crowded so close to the bank she had no choice but wade in the water up to her waist. Water that terrified her. But Darrien terrified her more.

Suddenly, she felt the slippery stones shift beneath her. She slid and went under. Immediately, she was ten again, drowning under the ice. She clawed at the water. Her braid came loose and her hair flared around her like a dark sheaf of wheat.

Fighting the current, she finally managed to get her feet back under her. The river had carried her downstream to where the bank wasn't as steep. She scrambled out and ran.

The water grew swifter and the crashing sound louder. Just as she was starting to wonder what it was, she leaped over a log and her ankle gave way. With a cry, she crumpled to the ground. She was soaking wet, her dress clinging to her. Now her ankle throbbed. But over her frantic panting, she could hear them. Dogs barking. She lurched to her feet and began hobbling as fast as she could.

The river narrowed and deepened. The air was thick and heavy with the smell of moss. With a sense of foreboding, she climbed up the bald expanse of a flat boulder and looked down.

A waterfall crashed down a cliff, hurtling into a deep pool. Rocks and boulders ringed the pool like the teeth of a hungry maw. An updraft blew against her. For leagues in either direction, the cliff went on. She had nowhere to go. The dogs were very close now. She was trapped.

She stared at the pool, her whole body screaming to live.

The dogs crashed through the trees, baying happily when they found her. She turned. Darrien was astride his gelding. What would he do to her?

He rubbed the back of his head. "That'll cost you."

He was going to take everything she held dear. By the time he finished, she wouldn't be Ilyenna anymore. Yet if she didn't bend to him, he'd destroy her clanwomen. Only one choice remained for her now. She peeked over the edge and looked down.

"Come here now," Darrien said softly.

She turned. From the look on his face, it was clear he knew she planned to jump. She closed her eyes. Drawing every ounce of courage, she inched backward. She was the clan mistress. She protected her clan, no matter the cost. With each step, she expected to feel nothing but open air beneath her.

"Ilyenna, no!" Rone came crashing through the trees, his face white with fear and exertion.

She gasped out the breath she'd been holding. Her heart leaped within her. Why couldn't he have loved her?

Darrien made no move to stop Rone as he cautiously approached her, his hand outstretched. "Come with me, Ilyenna."

She shook her head violently, tendrils of her damp hair swaying. "I can't. I have to protect them. Protect myself."

Rone's eyes were filled with pain, taking her back to when she'd teetered on the edge of the ice. "We'll find another way."

She smiled at him, trying to ease his pain. "There is no other way." She stepped back, and this time, her foot caught nothing but empty air. She pushed off. Rone reached for her, his face twisting in despair. She heard his scream as she fell. Her heart plunged in her throat as she watched the ground rush up to meet her.

Suddenly a blast of hot wind slammed into her body, tossing her end over end. Instead of crashing into the rocks, she plummeted into the pool. The impact drove all thought of duty and honor from her mind, consuming her instead with pain. All the air burst from her lungs. She desperately wanted to live, but no matter how frantically she clawed at the water, she still sank.

Against her will, her aching lungs drew in water. Her throat spasmed. She coughed and gagged. Her lungs screamed for air. Her eyes lost their ability to focus. She concentrated on a grainy point of light as the water grew dark and deep.

The last thing she saw before slipping into unconsciousness was the moon exploding.

***

The water was so cold it drove the breath from Ilyenna, sending her whole body into a cramp. Her lungs burned with fire. Trapped beneath the layer of ice, she slammed into the riverbed before hurtling into the ice. The water dragged her along its jagged surface—so close she could see the pale winter sky, the dark trees framing it like lace. She clawed at the ice, numbly aware of the sting as one by one, her fingernails were ripped off.

Then, by some miracle, the ice broke above her. She bobbed along in the water, too weak and cold to fight the current. She bumped against another sheet of ice, and the water started sucking her down. Clawing at the icy snow, she bent herself in half over the ice. She couldn't pull her legs from the river. She dug into the crystallized snow with her blue hands, trying to call for help. Her voice refused to work.

This is how I'm going to die, she thought.

***

Over and over again, Ilyenna coughed up water. Finally, her

throat and lungs opened and she struggled to draw a deep breath. Her body devoured the air greedily, screaming for more. Ever so slowly, her mind cleared. She lay stomach first over Rone's legs, his hand pounding her back.

"How could you?" She heard the tears in his voice.

She remembered the blast of hot wind slamming into her body. Somehow, the summer queen had saved her.

"How could you do that to me again?" he asked.

Again. Rone must have jumped into the water after her. They were lucky he hadn't been killed.

She stared at the waterfall without really seeing it. Memories as painful as frostbite swelled in her mind. The first time Rone had pulled her half-frozen body from the river, he and Bratton had covered her in their clothes. Bratton had held her skin to skin and practically in the fire while Rone went for help.

Over the following week, Ilyenna's sick mother had nursed her back to health—at the cost of her own life.

Ilyenna dug her palms into her eyes, wishing she could darken her memories as easily as her vision. In seventeen years, she'd nearly died three times. But someone always brought her back. With the exception of Rone, her rescuers had perished. Perhaps she really was marked. Perhaps she wasn't meant for this world. And anyone who tried to cheat death only ended up dying in Ilyenna's place.

Suddenly, she was afraid for Rone. "You should've let me die."

He didn't answer for a moment. "I'm going to pretend you never said that."

Weakly, she rolled to her back, her head on his lap. She couldn't meet his gaze. "He was going to beat my clanwomen until I agreed to marry him. How else could I protect them—protect myself?"

Rone's face darkened. "I told you we'd find another way."

"He's going to kill us all, body and soul."

"He'll be coming for us, with more of his clanmen." Rone gently lifted Ilyenna's head and upper body until she was sitting on the ground. "Can you run?"

She surveyed herself. Her ankle throbbed dully. "I think so."

He stood, then grabbed her under her arms and heaved. Once on her feet, she collapsed against him, her legs as weak as a newborn lamb's. Her ankle stung when she put weight on it. Already she could feel her boot digging into the swelling skin. But after a few wobbly steps, her muscles seemed to remember what they were for.

Rone watched her until she steadied. "We have to put as much distance between ourselves and Darrien as we can before the dogs catch our scent. It's one of the only hopes we'll have of losing them."

Limping, Ilyenna followed him. "One of the only?"

Rone grunted. "Oh, there's lots of ways. None a sure thing."

With that, they started running. They followed the river, neither speaking. Trying to ignore her throbbing ankle, Ilyenna listened for the baying of dogs.

As streaks of morning light strangled the last of the stars, Rone stopped and said between gasps, "That'll have to do. They'll have horses. From now on, we'll have to outsmart them." He pointed across the river. "It's rocky and shallow here. Run across. Touch things, leave your scent. Run until you find a barren place—somewhere that would hide tracks. Then double back. Step in your own footprints or on a rock. Don't leave any backtracks. When you return to the river, wait for me. Understand?"

She nodded. Rone turned and disappeared inside the trees, leaving Ilyenna alone. It was terrifying.

Squaring her shoulders, she forced herself to do as Rone asked. She stepped into the trees and crossed the river, then kept walking. She kept her arms out, touching things and hoping she'd find a rocky place soon. Every moment she spent searching gave time to Darrien and his pursuit. Finally, she found a rocky knoll. But she didn't relax. She still had to find her way back to the river, and she was no woodsman.

She tried to keep to the rocks or step in her own footprints. It was time consuming and difficult. Day deepened, bringing with it heat and insects. Sweat ran into her eyes, while midges feasted on her blood. Ilyenna nearly cried out in relief when she heard the river.

She stumbled out of the trees and looked about. Rone was nowhere in sight. What if Darrien found him? Other unwelcome thoughts assaulted her. Determinedly pushing them away, she examined her ankle. It was worse from all the running, swollen tight inside her boot. She ate some wild rhubarb, swallowing the sour stuff as quickly as she could.

Something white caught her eye. A patch of snow. She suddenly remembered the winter fairies. Were they coming back for her? She stepped toward the snow, but instead of frozen granules, her fingers brushed the soft petals of a small cluster of white flowers. Her breath coming fast, she shook herself.

The winter fairies are gone, she reminded herself.

She looked around for Jablana or the others. There was no sign of them, and still no sign of Rone. Ilyenna sighed. Her skin itched where the midges had bitten her. She listened, but all she could hear was the river.

She smelled of sweat and fear. With nothing better to do, she stripped off her clothing and scrubbed it clean. After laying it out over a bush, she scoured herself with a patch of soapwort and sand.

The water should have been cold, but it felt oddly warm. Not daring to wade any deeper than her knees, she lay down, letting the current take the rest of the sand from her hair. But she'd never liked this much water—more so after last night. She burst up, water running in rivulets down her skin, and froze.

Rone stood at the edge of the river, his eyes burning bright and his chest rising and falling hard. He took a long, ragged breath. "We have to hurry," he said.

Feeling shy under his penetrating gaze, she kept her head down as she walked past him. Just before she drew even with him, he reached out, the backs of his fingers moving down the curve of her hip. He pinched his eyes shut as if in pain. "You're beautiful." He said it with a regret and finality that sent an inexplicable sadness through her veins. He gently pushed her away. "Hurry."

She shivered as a feeling of loneliness overtook her. Quickly, she tugged her damp clothes over her head. Rone led her downstream.

"We're downwind of the trail I created," he said. "I'm hoping the dogs will get confused and lose our spoor. We need to put some distance between our false trail and our real one to ensure they don't find it."

Then they were running again.

14. TRUTH

Rone glanced up and down the road before he and Ilyenna cautiously moved out of the forest. Her arm was around his shoulders for support. They'd been traveling through forest thick as winter wool all day and long into the night.

She had gone beyond exhaustion and hunger into a kind of numb acceptance. Her ankle could barely take any weight now. "We shouldn't be out in the open like this. Morning is coming."

"We can't stay in the forest. We have to find food and a horse or we won't make it another day." Rone looked around. "I've been on this road before. We're somewhere between Tyranholm and Kebholm. If we haven't already crossed the border between the two, we will soon."

He pointed to a lone house and barn alongside the road. "See? Food and a horse. Come on." His grip firm on her waist, he pulled her forward.

From the house, a dog started barking. They slipped in the barn and stood in the darkness, waiting for their eyes to adjust. The barn was like any other, smelling of damp animal hair, manure, urine, and moldering hay. Ilyenna heard the heavy breathing of a cow or a horse, and the sounds of numerous small hooves and warm bodies. Goats. Her mouth watered at the thought of fresh milk.

Rone ducked out from under her arm and started down the center of the animal pens. "You watch the house," Rone said. "I'll get the horse."

Ilyenna's heart sank when she hobbled past the stall. The animal might've been a sturdy plow horse a few years ago, but he was old now, his skin hanging from sharp hips. A still-full winter coat hinted of belly worms, which she would have treated with wormwood. She limped to the barn door and peered out. The dog was still barking, but the house was quiet.

Behind her, Rone searched the barn. "There isn't a saddle."

Ilyenna hadn't really expected one for a draft horse. She glanced back to see Rone ease a bit into the horse's mouth. The animal tiredly started chewing the cold metal.

"He won't carry us far or fast," she said worriedly.

Rone led the horse out. "We'll find something better at a roadside inn."

Ilyenna cringed. Darrien wouldn't need hounds. All he'd have to do was follow their thievery.

Movement caught her eye—someone was outside. Moonlight glinted off an axe blade. With a sharp intake of breath, Ilyenna backed away from the door. "Someone's coming."

In two steps, Rone reached her and threw her belly-first over the horse. Grabbing a handful of mane, she pulled her leg over to straddle his broad back. Rone pulled the door open wide. A young man stood defensively in front of the house, his shield like a barrier between them and the front door. Rone and the man sized each other up, but Rone didn't have a weapon.

Ilyenna thought she saw a flutter of movement at the window. The man's wife? His children? Ilyenna didn't want to do this. "Our need is great," she called, hoping to calm the man.

He shifted behind his shield. "You could've asked."

"You wouldn't have given us the horse," she replied.

The man's eyes widened. "You're the tiams."

Ilyenna and Rone exchanged tight glances. So Darrien had already spread the word.

Rone called out, "I'll do what I can to get the horse back to you."

The man's gaze shifted between them. "Most Kebs don't agree with what the Tyrans have done, but our clan chief has ordered us to hand you over anyway."

Rone backed toward Ilyenna. "Is that a warning or a threat?"

The man dropped his axe and shield to his side. "They've set traps on all the roads. If you go that way, you'll be captured."

Ilyenna looked at Rone. What could they do now? she wondered.

The man looked back at the house. "If you go back to the forest, you could skirt him."

Rone slowly shook his head. "She's hurt. She can't go much farther on foot."

She opened her mouth to argue then shut it again. He was right. Without a horse to carry her, she wouldn't make it another mile. And a horse was too big to move through tangled forest. Plus they had no food and nothing to hunt with, let alone protect themselves.

The Keb looked back at Ilyenna. "How bad is it?"

"A turned ankle," she said.

"We need food," Rone added.

The man looked at his house and back at them. "You can spend the day here. Just the day. Then you have to be off."

"How do I know you won't run to the Tyrans?" Rone asked tensely.

The Keb glanced pointedly at Ilyenna. "Seems to me, you don't have a choice. But if nothing else, know that living on the Tyran border hasn't made me their friend." The Keb slowly moved forward and handed his axe to Rone. "And if I was going to run to the Tyrans, I wouldn't give you this. I am Zezrom of the Kebs."

Rone's fingers closed around the axe hilt. "I'll never be parted with an axe again."

Ilyenna's breath caught in her throat. Rone's words could only mean one thing. He wouldn't be taken prisoner ever again—he'd die first. Well, she wouldn't be taken either. She'd learned there were things worse than death. Much worse.

Zezrom nodded as if he understood all too well. "Go back into the barn and don't come out again." He glanced up at Ilyenna. "You can sleep in the hay pen."

Rone backed toward her and helped her off the horse. She stood, her knee cocked so her foot was off the ground. "Can we really trust him?"

Rone put the horse back in his stall. "We don't have a choice."

Bracing herself against the corrals, Ilyenna hopped toward a pen, which held a scattering of hay left over from winter. She opened the gate and hobbled inside then eased herself down with a groan of exhaustion. The hay smelled like dry mold and it poked her through her clothing, but it cushioned her from the hard ground. For that she was grateful.

Moments later, a woman came from the house, her hair wrapped in a cloth. In her hands, she had a bucket of cold water. "I'm Zezrom's wife, Mally. Drink as much as you need, and then put your foot inside."

Ilyenna obeyed. Mally gave them some cheese, plus bread spread thickly with butter and topped with meat that tasted of damp cellar. Ilyenna and Rone wolfed down the food. After the woman left, Ilyenna lay back, her foot propped in the bucket.

"What do we do next?"

Rone looked at her for a few moments. "We'll be harder to track and move faster if we find a couple of horses."

"Move faster to where?"

"To Gen of the Riesen."

Ilyenna had to admit the plan made sense. Their own clans were in no position to help them, but Gen could offer shelter and hiding until the spring feast. "If Darrien guesses we're headed to Riesenholm," she said, "he'll have more traps waiting for us."

Rone nodded slowly. "After he spreads word through Keb about two escaped tiams, yes."

"Even if we do reach the Council, will they allow us an audience?" Ilyenna asked, but he didn't answer. She knew the Council didn't lean towards mercy when it came to escaped tiams. They didn't like to appear weak. "They don't know why Undon faked an attack on his clan."

"Oh, they were attacked all right."

She cringed. "But not by you?"

"Of course not."

Ashamed for even thinking such a thing, she looked away. "Who then?"

"My guess" —Rone paused and took a deep breath— "my guess is they did it themselves."

Her hand flew to her mouth. "They killed their own clanmen?" Ilyenna whispered between her fingers.

"And women and children."

A wave of nausea washed over her. "By the Balance! Why?"

"Follow the events. Undon staged an attack on his clan, which gave him an excuse to attack the Argons. He knew the Shyle would come to our aid. So he must have planned on attacking them as well. Then foreigners appear at his clan house in the middle of the night. Where does that lead you?"

"He's in league with the foreigners."

"And what foreigners have been our enemies since before our grandparents' grandparents' time?"

"The Raiders."

Rone closed his eyes for a moment, then said, "The Raiders."

"But I don't understand why he attacked our clans and not someone else's."

"The Raiders have attacked the clans by sea many times. They've failed in every attempt. But what if they circled around the mountains and came down Shyle Pass? And what if the Shyle and the Argons were in no shape to hold the passes or spread the alarm?"

Ilyenna swallowed hard. "They'd cut the clan lands nearly in half and have a firm foothold from the highly defensible mountains."

"And if they attacked from the mountains and the seas, it would be like putting the clan lands between a hammer and anvil." Rone stroked his jaw. "But all this is just a guess, and there are flaws in my theory. An alliance with the Raiders doesn't mesh with Darrien's pursuit of you. A marriage would give him claim to the Shyle. But if he's in league with the Raiders, why bother? Nor do I understand his cruelty. It's like he both desires and detests you."

"I know why he hates me." She looked away, unable to meet Rone's gaze. "I killed Hammoth."

Rone's mouth fell open. "You what?"

She couldn't repeat it.

He sank down next to Ilyenna. "Then why didn't Darrien kill you?"

He did, she thought. She kept her face averted so Rone wouldn't see the truth.

After a moment, he lay down beside her and pulled her head onto his shoulder. "It's all right. We'll figure this out together."

Feeling safe for the first time in ages, she fell asleep quickly. She vaguely remembered the woman switching out the bucket of lukewarm water with cold river water throughout the day. Eventually, Ilyenna woke to a steaming bowl of thick stew beside her. She picked it up and ate it so quickly she burned her tongue.

When she finished, she lifted her foot out of the bucket. The skin on her ankle was dark purple and stretched tight. It would take days, perhaps even weeks, to fully heal.

Rone must have heard her stirring. He came in with a leather bag. "We have a few hours until full dark. Do you want to go back to sleep until it's time to leave?"

"No. I don't think I could sleep." She tried to smile.

He sat next to her and handed her strips of rags, and a bunch of slightly wilted mountain daisies. "Mally said these help with swelling."

Ilyenna shredded the daisies, then used the rags to wrap her ankle, with the daisies between her skin and the bindings. "Where are they?"

One by one, Rone showed her the supplies—flint and striker, a dagger, a wheel of cheese, dried strips of meat, travel bread, blankets, potatoes. Zezrom and Mally had given them enough to last a week if they were careful. "Zezrom went to scout ahead. Mally took the children and left. She doesn't want them here if the Tyrans show up."

Ilyenna shivered. "That's wise of her."

She inspected her wrapping. Satisfied, she rubbed her sore, stiff muscles. "You'd be better off without me. I'm slowing you down."

Rone took her hand. "We're together on this, Ilyenna. I won't leave you."

Together? Ilyenna looked into his eyes. Did she really hear tenderness in his voice? Her blood surged hot through her. Then she remembered Darrien, his roving hands and wet mouth. Why couldn't it have been Rone? Tears sprang to her eyes.

"What's wrong?" he asked.

Shaking her head, she glanced away. He squeezed her hand. "Tell me?"

She sighed. Chances were she and Rone would be dead in a few hours. If not, a worse fate awaited her. If she didn't tell him now, she might never have the chance. "The first kiss I ever had to give was taken from me . . . by Darrien. I—I can't bear to think he'll take more." She saw Rone stiffen and forced herself to meet his furious gaze. Softly, she said, "I wish it had been you."

His eyes widened, and Ilyenna wanted to suck the words back into her mouth. Humiliated, she pushed herself to her knees. Rone shot up and locked his arms around her but said nothing.

"I know you've always thought of me as your little sister, but I'm not, Rone, I—"

At the look on his face, the words died in her throat. She was suddenly aware that he held her in his arms. Both of them were on their knees, their bodies only a few inches apart. He'd made no effort to move away. "Ilyenna, I haven't thought of you as a little sister for a long time. I–I love you."

She gasped. Unable to help herself, she pressed her fingertips to Rone's lips as if to feel the words he'd just spoken. Her love for him swelled within her.

He leaned toward her. Trapped in his arms with no desire to escape, Ilyenna felt her lips pound in the rhythm of her heart. She felt his breath against her mouth—she could almost taste him. She leaned into him, and he cradled her head in his hand. His mouth met hers, his lips gentle at first. Then the kiss grew deeper.

Rone pulled back, kissing her eyelids, her cheeks, her nose. He traced her jaw with his lips, then brushed them against her neck and her exposed shoulder. It surprised her that such gentleness could light a fire within her. They kissed again. Ilyenna gripped his shirt in her fists and opened her mouth. Rone responded, pulling her to him until she could feel his heart beating through their clothes. She splayed her fingers over his broad back, exploring his sinewy muscles.

And suddenly his tunic was too thick. She slipped her fingers under the fabric, touching the skin just above his navel. He shuddered. She felt his warm skin prickle with gooseflesh. He tightened his hold, pressing her against him as if they'd both die if he let go. His mouth went to her neck, and he gently took her skin between his teeth. She craved his every touch, demanding more. He pressed her back into the soft hay.

She had this one gift left to give—and by the dead, she'd give her first time to Rone. Then Darrien could never take it from her.

15. Raiders

On the outskirts of Kebholm, Ilyenna lay flat in a field of hay, her belly pressed against the grass, grit etching outlines on her palms. Her neck hurt from constantly peering at the barn where Rone had disappeared. And after a few hours of a horseback ride that had rattled the rabbits in their burrows, her behind ached mercilessly.

She kept her breathing shallow as she listened for the sounds of mirth inside the inn to change to sounds of alarm. If the Kebs inside discovered Rone, there was no way he could fight them all off. It was why he'd insisted she stay hidden instead of going inside with him. That way, at least one of them stood a chance of making it.

Ilyenna's stomach growled again. Silently, she cursed its noises—and the warm smell of food that had set it off. Rich gravies, baked bread, and ham.

Behind her, the plow horse nickered. She'd thought she'd tied him far enough away from the other horses to keep him quiet, but close enough she could use him if she needed. Obviously she'd been wrong.

He nickered again. She turned toward the sound. If he made much more noise, she'd have to abandon her hiding place and move him farther away. She waited, sweat prickling her skin. Silence. With a sigh of relief, she turned back to the barn and muttered, "Rone, what is taking you so—"

Suddenly, she heard a boot against the ground. She pressed herself flat, hoping an inn patron had just gone to water a tree. He would pass her by without seeing her, if she just held still enough.

She strained to listen. Sounds from the inn. The singing of grasshoppers. The breeze through the grass. No footsteps. Had she imagined it?

No.

The hair on the back of her neck stood up. Someone was behind her. She could feel them. Sweat broke out on her brow. Had they seen her?

Keeping her movements slow and even, she glanced back. There was a blur of movement. Darrien must have found her! She tried to lunge to her feet, but he was already on top of her, slamming her into the ground. Should she scream? But that would rouse the inn. They would find Rone. Darrien would find Rone!

She reached for her borrowed knife. Another man gripped her hand, squeezing it so hard she almost cried out. He jerked the knife from her. They began dragging her away. She twisted and squirmed, digging her heels into the ground. Her ankle screamed in pain. They hauled her back to the cluster of trees where she'd tied the plow horse. The animal must have nickered a greeting to their horses when they came in. She should've known.

The first one hauled her around. It wasn't Darrien. What she saw terrified her even more.

Raiders. A scream tore from her lips. The larger Raider's hand clamped her mouth and nose shut, holding her jaw closed so she couldn't bite. But she couldn't breathe, either. The dead help her, she was drowning again!

"No move. I let you go." His heavy accent sounded like a death march to her ears.

Terrified, she froze. He removed his hand. She gulped cool air as the two of them bound her hands. "The men in the inn, they'll notice I'm gone. They'll come looking for me."

The smaller Raider's skull tattoos were making her dizzy. "This why you hide? So they find you? This clan game?"

He was mocking her. But at least they didn't know Rone was with her.

The two men conversed in their guttural-sounding language. Then they lifted her onto the plow horse and started leading her away. She distinctly heard Undon's name. Her heart seized within her. "What do you want with me?"

The small Raider grinned lustily at her. Her whole body crawled with revulsion. She had to buy more time so Rone would come out. "I know who you are and why you're here! You're scouts for the Raiders coming down Shyle Pass." Both men froze and stared at her incredulously. No doubt they were here to count clanmen, find weaknesses, and assess strengths. "Thought to have a little fun while you were out, is that it?"

They exchanged glances. "How you know?" the large man demanded.

"Undon isn't the ally you think he is." Ilyenna tried to say it confidently, but she trembled despite herself.

Moving a few paces off, they leaned toward each other, talking low. Idiots. She didn't speak Raider anyway. They grew louder and motioned with their hands, seeming panicked. For the moment, they seemed to have forgotten her. She considered booting the plow horse, but they still had a firm hold on the reins and her hands were tied.

She eased one leg over the horse and dropped silently down, ignoring the pain shooting through her ankle. Hunched over and using the plow horse's wide body to shield her, she hurried through the field and headed for Kebholm.

One of the men let out a surprised shout. Despite the pain in her ankle, she burst into an all-out sprint. But she knew they'd overtake her long before she reached Kebholm. She had to hide. She veered toward the thick trees clustered around the river.

If they caught her, she'd scream. They'd kill her, but it might raise the inn. If the men found the Raiders, at least they'd know something was wrong.

She heard them behind her, nearly silent despite their bulk. They were experts at this game—a game to which there were no rules—and she was a novice. Fresh terror surged through her. She felt one of the men dive for her, gripping her legs and bringing her down. She filled her lungs to scream when something spun above her, hitting the Raider in the torso and knocking him back. A black mass hurtled above her, a shining axe catching the moonlight.

The large raider only had time to widen his eyes before Rone lopped his head off, spraying Ilyenna with warm blood. With a thud, the head hit the ground, followed shortly by the limp body. Digging her heels into the ground, she scrambled to get as far away from the body as she could.

The other Raider took off in the opposite direction.

Rone snatched the shield he must have thrown. "How many are there?" he cried as his axe nicked the cords around Ilyenna's hands.

She lighted to her feet. "That's the only one left."

"The horses are back there." Rone pointed. "Get them and wait for me by the river." He took off after the other man.

Trying not to look at the dead Raider, Ilyenna retrieved her borrowed knife from where it was tucked in the man's belt. She ran back through the forest and out into the open. Terrifed, she struggled to breathe, hurrying in the dark toward the place Rone had indicated.

She found the horses. They shied when she barreled toward them, but Rone had tied them to a tree. Ilyenna stopped and spoke softly, stroking their necks. She knew they could smell the blood on her clothes, but eventually the animals calmed enough that she was able to mount one of them. She held tightly to the reins of the second.

She nudged her horse forward, but the second horse balked. The reins seared her hand, but she held on, determined not to let it pull free. Just as she was at the end of the rein, the horse finally gave up and grudgingly followed. Ilyenna wrapped the second horse's reins around the horn and moved the horses into an awkward trot.

She fought the sickness in her stomach. Rone was fine. He had to be. But when she reached the river, he was nowhere to be seen. Though it was a cool night, sweat ran down her back. Then it started to rain, washing the Raider's sticky blood from her clothes and hair. Ilyenna searched the darkness and listened. Then she saw a man running toward her through the field, axe in one hand, shield in the other.

"Rone?" she cried, her body tensed to flee.

"It's me, Ilyenna," he said between breaths.

All the tension went out of her, leaving her weak and shaky. "Thank the dead. The Raider?"

"Escaped."

She noticed Rone held something that looked like a wet piece of cloth that was a bit bigger than her hand. He shoved it in his saddlebags before she could get a good look. Then, in one fluid motion, he leapt into the saddle of the second horse. The animal pinned his ears flat against his head and arched his back.

"Couldn't you find a better horse?" Ilyenna asked nervously.

"No complaints from you!" He kicked the horse, his weapon held awkwardly in his other hand. She held her breath, hoping the horse wouldn't buck. She imagined Rone slamming into the earth with nothing but the axe to break his fall.

He kicked the horse again. This time the animal moved forward, though it still looked ready to throw its rider. "I did your owner a favor," Rone muttered as they galloped into the night.

16. RYE WHISKEY

The horses' breathing sounded like a raw stutter. Ilyenna and Rone slowed them to a walk. She was soaking wet and miserable. Rummaging in his pack, Rone tossed something her way. "Put it on."

She started when she realized what it was. A Keb clan belt. "Where'd you get this?"

He smiled mischievously. "I borrowed it."

"You think it will help?"

"There'll be no doubt that we're the runaway Argon clan chief and Shyle clan mistress if anyone sees the knots in my belt and notices that your belt is missing."

"My black hair will give me away anyway," Ilyenna said softly, wondering again if Rone wouldn't be better off without her. She fixed her gaze ahead. "How much longer?"

He motioned to the horses. "Ornery though this one is" —he glanced at his mare as if warning her—"I chose them both for their condition. If we push them, we should be able to make the journey by tomorrow morning."

Ilyenna kept glancing behind them, trying to see through the damp darkness. Her ears strained to hear the racing hoof beats of the Raider above the rain and thunder. But Rone kept a sharp lookout ahead of them, watching for Darrien's traps. Imminent attack might come from any side, by Tyrans or Raiders.

She gritted her teeth as the lightning cast everything in sharp white clarity. "I hate this."

In answer, Rone pushed his horse back into a trot. They rode hard through the night. Ilyenna's head ached from lack of sleep, and her body burned with weariness that intensified with every stride the horses took. If not for Rone, she'd have found a secluded spot and gone to sleep. But he pressed on, seemingly tireless, and her pride wouldn't let her be outdone.

When morning came, he led her off the road through a field of winter rye to a stand of trees lining a stream bed. While he tended their animals, she ate quickly and scrubbed her teeth with a bit of wool. She washed at the river before curling up under some blankets Rone had taken along with their horses.

She was surprised when instead of lying with her, Rone dropped down a few paces away. She stared at his turned back. Since that magical night, he hadn't touched her. In fact, he rarely even looked at her. She had made excuses, but looking at his turned back, she couldn't hide from the truth. He regretted what had happened between them. His sudden passion and declaration of love had simply been a result of their dire situation. It was the only explanation Ilyenna could come up with. Despite her exhaustion, it was a long time before sleep finally took her to the place of dreams.

Rone's hand on her shoulder woke her. "We need to hurry." He turned his back to her as he saddled his horse.

Already, night was coming on. She'd slept through the whole day. Her body was drenched with rain and her mouth tasted like she'd sucked on the wool all night instead of just cleaning her teeth with it. Both thirsty and hungry, she hurriedly consumed her allotment of food before mounting her horse. The pace they forced on the animals was grueling. She felt sorry for them, but Rone insisted they make the Riesen village by morning—even if it killed both horses.

By the time night had gone from black to grainy gray, Riesenholm was a smoky smudge in the distance. At the sight, Ilyenna went from a kind of numb rote to full wakefulness. She glanced at Rone, suddenly very glad she wasn't alone in this, that she had him to protect her.

As they neared the village, he pulled the horses off the road and into a stand of trees. When they were fully concealed, he stared at her. It was the first time he'd actually focused on her since their run-in with the Raiders. It made her hurt deep inside her soul—so deep only he had ever touched her there.

Absently, he stroked his axe hilt. "The Riesen clan house is in the center of the village. But we're not going in there until I can scout a bit."

Ilyenna's hands itched to grip her knife. "Couldn't we just ride in hard, head straight for the clan house?" she asked hopefully.

"Never walk blind into anything, Ilyenna. Not if you can help it." He continued his silent assessment of her. "We'll leave the horses tied inside the field, close to the village. That way we can use them if we have to."

She didn't say anything. They both knew their horses were too tired to outrun even a swaybacked nag.

"Stay with me until we reach the outskirts. I'll find someplace for you to hide. Then we'll figure out what to do." His breath was white in the cold air. He handed her a blanket. "Waiting could be chilly."

She took it, though she didn't feel cold. She rubbed her temples with her fingertips, her weariness suddenly overwhelming her. "Can't we wait until tomorrow?"

He shook his head. "Undon could be patrolling the area. I'm not willing to take the risk of being found."

Rone gripped her arm and led her to the outskirts of Riesenholm, where he searched until he found a berry bush beside a house. "Stay here until I come back for you. If you don't see me by morning, get back to the horses and try on your own tomorrow."

Her hands started trembling. "Rone, I–I'm sorry." She knew she'd been tense and snappish.

He smiled halfheartedly. "I know. So am I."

He turned and trotted away. She stared after him, her mouth full of the words she wanted to say. But he was gone. She tucked herself behind the bush and set in to wait. The rain had slowed to a steady drizzle. Hidden as she was, the only useful sense left for her was sound. It was both a relief and a torture when she continued to hear nothing.

After a time, Ilyenna felt something tiny and warm touch her temple. She pivoted to find Jablana crouched in the bush beside her. For the first time, Ilyenna immediately saw through the fairy's glamour.

Jablana looked around cautiously before whispering, "Be careful, Winter Queen. There are many enemies searching for you here." Her wings fanned out to catch the air, and Ilyenna knew she would soon fly away.

"Wait, please. Can you help us through?"

The fairy paused, her wings trembling. "You humans always believe you can change things, that if you chip away long enough at a mountain, it will become a valley. But there are some things that just are. The sun in the sky. The earth beneath your feet. And the Balance. We are natural enemies, you and I—no more compatible than ice in high summer." The fairy darted past Ilyenna, toward the open air.

She felt tears building up behind her eyes. "Even in high summer, there are glaciers in the mountains!"

The fairy paused before Ilyenna's face, her wings a soft blur behind her. She looked around once more, as if afraid someone might see her, before flitting away.

Ilyenna huddled inside her blanket, wondering if Tyrans slept in the house her back rested against.

The gray of morning was starting to turn to silver when Rone came back for her. She nearly cried out in alarm when he suddenly appeared from the other side of the house.

He didn't seem to notice how close she'd come to giving them away. "I didn't see anything. Let's go."

She pressed her back up against the house. "There are Tyrans everywhere."

Rone squatted beside her. "How do you know?"

She opened her mouth before shutting it again. She couldn't tell Rone about Jablana. He'd never believe her. "I heard people in the house talking about them."

"Why would Gen let the Tyrans stay?"

She gripped her knife handle. "He couldn't turn them out. Not without a good reason."

Rone pressed his lips together. "Idiotic politics."

Terror filled Ilyenna's heart. "What're we going to do?"

He glanced around. "We don't have enough supplies to last another couple days, let alone until the spring feast. Even if we did, I don't think we could avoid being found for that long."

Despite the cold, Ilyenna's palms began to sweat. "So we go in?"

He nodded. "Most everybody's still asleep." He must have seen the despair in her face, for he added, "If the Tyrans catch us, Gen can't do much to help. But if you can just get to the clan house, he'll be able to claim you're his responsibility."

She felt bile rising in her throat. "You mean for me to go in alone?"

"They're looking for us together," Rone said reassuringly. "It'll be less conspicuous if we split up." He glanced at her hair, then gently lifted the blanket from her shoulders and settled it over her head.

His movements were so tender that she wondered if she'd been wrong. Perhaps he didn't regret what had happened between them. But then he pressed his lips to her forehead, as a brother might do, and her heart pounded with longing. He rubbed her arms. "Don't draw attention to yourself. Smile at anyone who smiles at you. Find your way to the clan house and get inside. After that, Gen will protect you. Remember, you're just a Riesen woman getting an early start on her chores."

Before she could think up a protest, Rone pulled her to her feet and pushed her around the house. She was suddenly alone. Trying to hide her limp, she started into Riesenholm. He was right, the streets were nearly empty. The village looked so peaceful. Chickens wandered around, pecking at insects. A cow lowed from a barn. Ilyenna was tempted to feel ridiculous for being so terrified.

She walked past shuttered windows and wondered where the Tyran men were. How closely they were watching for her? She saw movement to the side and spun around, but she saw nothing unusual. For a moment, she stood frozen. Then, remembering Rone's warning, she steadied herself, trying to keep her gait steady but purposeful, her traitorous brown eyes fastened to the ground.

Something darted between the houses again. Ilyenna focused and this time saw Jablana peeking around a corner, desperately motioning her forward. Thank the Balance, Ilyenna thought.

A hand came down on her shoulder. "Are you all right?" a woman asked.

Ilyenna jumped. Her heart pounding in her throat, she forced herself to calm down. "I'm fine."

She pulled away and followed Jablana between the houses. Coming onto the uneven street, she saw nothing. She started toward the center again, her gaze searching for the sudden movement of a fairy.

But as she turned to look back, something caught her eye. A glimpse of a man behind her. She quickly looked away. He might just be a Riesen clanman, out on business. She glared at the ground. She'd drawn unnecessary attention to herself by looking for fairies. Trying to keep her movements inconspicuous, Ilyenna followed Jablana between another set of houses. Just before she rounded the corner, she looked back just in time to see the man turning after her.

He was following her.

Forgetting Rone's warning, she rushed forward, ignoring anyone who called a greeting and desperately trying to keep from running full out. Jablana motioned for her between another set of houses, but that would bring her closer to the man following her, the man Jablana obviously couldn't see.

Ilyenna darted across the street and between another set of houses. She turned back to see if the man was still following her. She was so busy looking over her shoulder that she ran straight into someone. Sidestepping the clanmen, she mumbled an apology and kept moving.

But the man's hand shot out, gripping her arm. In surprise, she glanced at him. His eyes widened with both shock and pleasure. Ilyenna's eyes darted to his clan belt.

A Tyran.

She snatched her knife and thrust it forward. The man twisted to the side. Her knife missed his guts and sliced his arm. He cursed and jumped back, grabbing for his axe. He swung it, the flat side aimed at her. She tried to drop, but he adjusted his swing and caught her on the side of her head. Light was extinguished to blackness before returning in maddening sparks that melted into colors and shapes. There was pain, but it was at an arm's length. Ilyenna struggled to make her mind work. Her head felt as heavy as a river stone. Somehow, she managed to open her eyes.

The blurry Tyran stood above her, satisfaction on his face. "Hello, little clan mistress."

Suddenly, hands appeared. One snatched the Tyran's jaw; another jerked a knife through his throat. The Tyran panicked, trying to grip his axe, but then his face relaxed and he sagged. Ilyenna made out the hazy shape of a man as he caught the dead Tyran under his arms and dragged him into a barn. The man rushed back to her, his bloody hands hauling her up. She struggled, trying to pull away from him.

"Why were you running? I told you not to run."

She knew that voice. Suddenly, everything clicked into place. Rone had been following her, making sure she was all right. Like an idiot, she'd tried to escape him and had run right into a Tyran. But though her thoughts had grown a great deal clearer, her body didn't seem to be working right. Her feet were sluggish and incredibly heavy. Rone half supported, half dragged her toward the clan house.

A man leaning against a house jumped to his feet at the sight of them. Rone hefted his axe, his face cold as ice. Indecision overwhelmed the Tyran's face before he took off at a run. Abandoning all pretenses, Rone scooped her into his arms and ran toward the kitchen door. He tried the handle. It was barred. He kicked it repeatedly. "I have need of a healer," he shouted.

Moments stretched on as they waited. Finally, a disheveled-looking tiam opened the door. Rone shoved past her, kicking the door shut with his heel. "Bar it!" he shouted.

As the tiam hurried to obey, a middle-aged woman appeared, tugging on her overdress. Ilyenna recognized her—the Riesen clan mistress. The older woman froze, her face veiled with shock at the sight of Ilyenna. "Bar all the doors," she said to the tiam, "and get Gen!" Her quick eyes assessed Ilyenna, stopping where the side of the axe had met her head. She directed Rone to lay her on the table. "I'll take her. You make sure no one gets through the front door."

Adusting the shield on his arm, Rone cast Ilyenna a worried glance before darting from the room.

"Curse these men and their politics!" the clan mistress muttered as she searched her shelves. "Why can't we live in peace without these idiotic games?" She dampened a rag with a tincture and pressed it to Ilyenna's forehead.

Ilyenna sucked air through her teeth as the alcohol stung her skin.

"I'm Ressa, in case you've forgotten. I remember you, though." She poured spirits into a wooden mug, then helped Ilyenna sit up and drink. Ilyenna's eyes watered at the strength of the liquid. She hesitated to take another swallow, but the woman tipped up the mug. "You'll be feeling a whole lot better in a few minutes."

The spirits burned like fire. She coughed. Ressa waited until the fit subsided before pouring more down Ilyenna's throat. The herbs inside were strong as well. Her belly warmed.

Her hands as quick as her eyes, Ressa wiped Ilyenna's wound and smeared her head with a familiar-smelling salve before pressing a damp, cool cloth over it.

Someone pounded so hard on the door to the great hall that Ilyenna wondered if it would vibrate off its hinges. Ressa paused, anxiety writing deep lines in her face. There were shuffling footsteps, and then the door creaked open.

Ilyenna desperately wanted to see what was going on. But then she heard his voice and instantly changed her mind. She cringed.

"Gen, one of my men saw my tiams," Darrien growled. "I want them turned over. Now."

There was a long pause before Gen answered, "They're in my clanhouse. That makes them a Riesen concern now."

Darrien swore. "You've no right to interfere with my tiams! The law demands that you hand them over!"

"I will," Gen said calmly, "if the Council orders me to do so. Until then, your rudeness offends both me and my clan. Get out of my lands."

"You dare throw me out? You dare insult my clan?" Darrien roared.

Ilyenna heard slow steps and imagined Gen moving forward. His voice dropped so low she could barely make out his words. "I know exactly how many clanmen you have in my lands. I have twenty times that, all of them ready to kill any Tyran in sight at the sound of the warning bell." Gen chuckled. "You didn't think I'd trust you after what you've done? No, my clan is fully prepared for war. And as stretched as the Tyrans are, you know as well as I that we'd win. Get out. We'll see who the Council sides with."

Darrien started to sputter a reply, but Ilyenna heard the door shut in his face. Gen spoke again. "Arm our clanmen and escort the Tyrans to the border. I want spies watching their every move. Bring in those foolish enough to stay on the outlying farms, by force if you have to. Every clanman is to be ready for war." Footsteps confirmed that the clan chief's orders were being obeyed.

Ressa sighed in relief. "Well, I'm glad he finally had cause to kick them out. Gen's been sleeping with his axe for a week. I'm always afraid I'll roll into it. Anything else hurt?"

Ilyenna pointed to her ankle. Ressa eased the boot from the foot, her lips pressed in a disapproving line. She retrieved a salve, coated Ilyenna's ankle with it, and wrapped the ankle in clean cloths. Then Ressa helped her sit on a chair.

Ilyenna's head still hurt something awful, and the room spun. She gripped the table to keep from swaying in her seat. Gen came into the room and set his shield on a chair. He knelt next to her and studied her head wound. "Ressa?"

"She'll be all right, dear. I've whiskeyed her up a bit. Shortly, she'll be feeling pretty good about things."

With that, she handed Ilyenna a piece of buttered rye bread and a cup of willow bark tea that was half milk with a generous dash of whiskey. Ilyenna began eating carefully, but hungrily.

Rone came in, an anxious look on his face. "You all right?"

Not daring to nod, Ilyenna smiled softly. "We made it."

He didn't return her smile.

"What happened?" Gen asked.

As Rone related their story, leaving out the amorous parts, Gen's face flooded with rage. "The Council will have Undon's clan for this!" he roared just as Ilyenna polished off her second cup of tea. The whiskey was working wonders, and her aching head was nearly a distant memory.

"And you just had to kill a Tyran right in the middle of Reisenholm, did you?" Gen fumed at Rone.

Rone's eyes flicked toward Ilyenna. "It couldn't be helped."

"Well, I suppose it couldn't. I'll send someone to deal with it. Anything else?"

Rone shook his head. "That's all."

"Rone, pick that girl up and follow me to my daughter's old room," Ressa ordered.

Ilyenna snuggled into Rone's embrace, her arms around his neck. He smelled so wonderful.

"Lay her down there," Ressa said as she pointed to a door.

He opened the door to the room and placed her on the bed, but she didn't release him. "You know," she teased, "you could stay with me."

He gently pried her arms from around his neck. "You're drunk, Ilyenna."

She snorted. "And what do you care? I wasn't drunk the other night."

Pain crossed his face, pain that redoubled inside her.

"Get out," she said flatly. Rolling away from him, she covered her head with the blankets. "You can join the dead and I won't care."

After a few moments she heard the door shut, and then she was asleep.

17. Regrets

"Up, child. You'll be needing some more medicine." Ilyenna forced her eyelids open. She squinted at the light, her eyes smarting. She tried to roll over, but pain shot through her skull. "Oh," she moaned.

Ressa plopped down on the side of the bed. "You'll be wanting to drink two mugs of this tea and eat your breakfast. I'll tend to your head."

Ilyenna squinted up at her, her mind hazily trying to put yesterday's events in order. "Can I have more whiskey?"

The clan mistress chuckled. "Whiskey's powerful medicine. But a little willow bark will work wonders."

"Darrien?" Ilyenna said hesitantly.

"Gone, along with the other Tyrans. Gen's making sure they don't double back." She filled the mug half full of tea and topped it with cream. "This will settle your stomach."

Ilyenna took the drink gratefully. Ressa had sweetened it with sugar and powdered raspberries to mask the bitter willow bark. She drank more as Ressa pulled the cloth away from her wound. Determined to be a good patient, Ilyenna stayed still, refusing to flinch while Ressa wiped off the excess ointment with the back of the cloth.

"I'm having my tiams bring up the bath. I'll be helping you scrub yourself and then we'll redress this, hmm?"

Ilyenna had a hazy recollection of Rone bringing her to bed earlier, and judging by the pit in her stomach, she'd said something bad. She took a bite of a biscuit and froze as the memory worked free. "By the Balance," she breathed.

Ressa leaned forward. "What's the matter?"

Ilyenna turned her wide eyes to the woman. "Where's Rone?"

She patted Ilyenna's arm consolingly. "He went with Gen."

Ilyenna wasn't sure how her heart could keep beating through the pain. "No."

Ressa smiled understandingly. "The drink often loosens our tongues."

"He told you what I said?"

The clan mistress shook her head. "No, but I've five children. It wasn't hard to guess that you two had a fight."

"How could you let him go? He needed rest and food and . . ."

Ressa cocked an eyebrow. "It's best that men keep busy when they've a lot to think on. And Rone had many things on his mind. He wanted to speak with my husband about a good deal of them. Rone is a strong man. He's fared better than you, but of course men are more used to traipsing over half the clan lands. I sent him with enough food to put the meat back on his bones. Don't you worry."

Ilyenna's hands fell helplessly to her sides. "I said things to him. Awful things."

Ressa lifted the biscuit and raised a warning eyebrow. "No more talking unless you're eating."

Ilyenna took a grudging bite.

Ressa gave a satisfied little nod. "Well, there are two weeks before the Council meets. That should be plenty of time to make it right." She stood and headed for the door."Two weeks?" Ilyenna managed around her mouthful of biscuit. "I thought it was three."

"They moved it up in order to deal with the situation with Undon."

Ilyenna began counting the nights since she'd escaped with Rone and realized it had been almost a week. "Where is it this time?"

"We'll be leaving for Cardell in nine days," Ressa said from the doorway.

"Cardell," Ilyenna repeated. Just below the Riesen. Lost in thought, she started when she reached for another biscuit only to realize she'd eaten them all.

Two women came in, bearing a beaten copper tub between them. It was as high as Ilyenna's thighs and probably twice as long. More tiams appeared—two young boys carrying a steaming pot between them. The women and boys kept reappearing until the tub was filled with hot water.

As soon as they shut the door behind them, Ilyenna sank into the water up to her chin and let the heat draw the soreness from her muscles. Ressa came in shortly thereafter and washed her hair, carefully avoiding her swollen bruise. Then the older woman worked over Ilyenna's back with a woven horsehair rag. Her skin was still peeling from the lye-soaked strap.

When every inch of her was scrubbed white and the water had lost its heat, Ressa produced a nearly new underdress and overdress. "I couldn't scrub all the stains out of your old one, and really, the thing was hardly worth saving. I made it into rags. This belonged to one of my daughters, Varris. She's around the same size."

Ilyenna sighed. Material was expensive, but the time it took to sew each miniscule stitch was just as costly. "I haven't the money to pay for it."

Ressa waved her protest away. "Bah. Nothing lost. Varris just married the richest rye farmer in the Riesen. And she has two tiams for a month because they got drunk and broke a couple barrels of her husband's whiskey."

Ressa helped Ilyenna out of the tub and started scrubbing her dry. She paused when she noticed Ilyenna's missing toes. "What happened to your feet?"

"Frostbite," she replied softly.

Ressa fingered the stumps. "The healer did good work."

Ilyenna bit the inside of her cheek. Having her toes cut off hadn't been pleasant. Waking up from her fevered dreams to discover her mother was dead had been much worse.

Ressa studied Ilyenna's naked body, frowning. She sighed and tugged the underdress over Ilyenna's head. Then she braided Ilyenna's hair and rubbed more ointment into her wound.

"There now. Why don't you rest, hmm? When you're ready, come down and I'll feed you a hearty meal."

"I won't be able to sleep," Ilyenna replied, but the older clan mistress was already out the door. Ilyenna lay back on the bed and suddenly couldn't keep her eyes open. "Ressa must have put something in that tea," she mumbled just before she fell asleep.

***

It was early in the morning. Ilyenna stood at the clan-house doors, watching and waiting. Ressa had indeed fed her, and fed her, and fed her again, until Ilyenna was sure she'd burst. But she couldn't seem to get enough food, and if she went too long between meals, she became ill. Most of the time, she felt exhausted. Ressa had said recovering from Darrien's treatment might take a year or more. Still, clean, fed, and with a new clan belt around her waist, Ilyenna felt more herself than she had since Undon had attacked the Argons. But she was miserable inside. Rone and the other men had been gone for over a week, and she was leaving for the spring feast as soon as Ressa finished her packing. When the Riesen clan mistress hadn't been fussing over Ilyenna, the two of them had been filling wagonload after wagonload with goods to sell.

The village was in a similar uproar. The Riesen grew rye by the bushel and made rye whiskey by the barrel. They also raised cattle and grew hay. At the spring feast, they'd trade the excess for things like Tyran flour, baskets, and beer; Bassen linen, underdresses, dye, rope, and paper; and Shyle sheep, wool, yarn, blankets, felt, vellum, and overdresses. The other clans would also trade for goods not available in their own lands. There were three feasts a year—spring, high summer, and autumn.

At each feast, the clan chiefs and clan mistresses would meet together as the High Council. They dictated clan law and settled disputes between clans. This year Ilyenna would've sat as one of them. But now, as a tiam, she wouldn't have a place. In fact, she could lose her title altogether. It was infuriating. And she missed Rone. She wanted to face him and apologize, and so she waited, her eyes straining for any glimpse of riders.

Ressa bustled behind her, shooing Ilyenna out the door and closing it after her. "Watching for him won't make him appear any sooner," she chided as she took Ilyenna's arm and steered her toward one of the wagons. "Come, child. He'll catch up."

Ilyenna let herself be led to the wagon, where three Riesen men waited on horseback. Her own personal guard. They weren't the only men who had come back. Gen had ordered them to return to guard either the village or the wagons. "How long will our journey take?" Ilyenna asked.

Ressa pulled her wild hair out of her eyes. "I already told you, child, we'll be there in three days."

More than two weeks after Ilyenna and Rone had escaped from Undon, she would finally bring her grievances to the Council. Unable to help herself, she spent most of the morning straining to look behind them. The Riesen were an animated group, singing songs about rye, harvesting, and whiskey. Staring at the rippling grasses all around them, Ilyenna couldn't help but compare the rolling hills of grain and the bright sunshine to the cool mountains and shady forests of the Shyle.

She missed the bleating of the sheep, Enrid's mutton stew, and the mountain breezes on her face. She missed her father and her brother and the yelps of the sheep dogs. She kept searching for the mountains to use as a compass point, and the constant straining made her eyes tired.

Occasionally, Ilyenna caught sight of a summer fairy. Usually, they blended in with nature, appearing as a butterfly, a bird, or a leaf on the wind. Most of the fairies darted away as if they felt her gaze on them, but a few stared back at her.

When the travelers stopped at a stream for lunch, Ilyenna noticed a slate gray fairy with mossy wings, dancing on the rocks. As they'd passed beneath a stand of trees, a fairy with orange eyes and the wings of a maple leaf watched her from inside an empty bird's nest. The group camped for the night beside a small pond, and Ilyenna saw a fairy with iridescent skin and dragonfly wings perched atop a water lily. And nearly every butterfly drinking nectar was actually a fairy. Ilyenna tried to catch sight of Jablana, but there was no sign of the little pink fairy. Ilyenna hoped the summer queen wouldn't punish Jablana for helping her. She didn't want to get the fairy into trouble.

After dinner, the Reisen began dancing. Ilyenna went to her blankets under the wagon, determined to watch for Rone. Instead, she immediately fell asleep.

She could see the mountains in the distance, could almost taste the glacier-fed streams, the cold water numbing her throat. Lifting her skirts, she hurried forward. But the ground under her gave way, and her home kept moving farther from her no matter how fast she ran. Frustrated, she stopped. The land stilled.

In the distance, she saw her father and brother laughing as they rode from the forest into the lower meadows. She shouted for them, calling for them to come for her. But they couldn't seem to hear her and never once looked her way.

Rone galloped up from behind them. The smile on his face made Ilyenna's chest ache. She shouted at him, begging him to come to her. He looked at her sadly as if he wished he could.

Gasping, Ilyenna jerked upright, smacking her head on the underside of the wagon. She rubbed the sore spot, her gaze darting around. It was dark, and Ressa slept soundly next to her. The guards were positioned around the wagon, also asleep. Flushed with heat, Ilyenna tugged the woolen blankets off. Her underdress was heavy with sweat. The cool air felt wonderful against her skin.

She couldn't shake the feeling she'd never see her home again, never be a part of her family again. And she worried that no matter how much Rone might want to, he'd never see her as anything but a sister.

Unable to sit still, she wrapped up in one of her blankets, tiptoed past the guards, and began walking the perimeter of the camp. A sentinel nodded to her. Embarrassed for not putting on her overdress, she nervously tried to smooth down the hair that had escaped from her unruly braid.

In the light of a dying fire, Ilyenna saw something move. She froze, her breathing coming up short. Rone's glittering eyes watched her from beneath one of the wagons.

Her hand fluttered to her chest. Not thinking, she took a step forward and opened her mouth to speak. Rone shook his head, his finger pressed to his lips as he glanced at the sleeping men around him. He eased out of his blankets, grabbed his axe, and walked toward her.

Without a word, he took her hand and led her away from the wagons.

The guard nodded to them as they passed him, a teasing smile on his face.

"When did you get in?" Ilyenna whispered.

The muscles in Rone's jaw bulged. "Just before supper."

She was still awake then. Why hadn't he found her?

Rone pulled her to a stop out of the guard's hearing, but not out of his line of sight. Before Rone could say a word, she blurted, "I'm sorry. I didn't mean it. I don't know what I'd do if something happened to you!"

He wouldn't meet her gaze. "You were pretty drunk."

She watched him stare back at the wagons as if he'd give anything to be back there. By the Balance, his indifference was killing her. "So-so you forgive me?"

"Of course." He took a step toward the camp. "Is that all you wanted to say, because we shouldn't be seen together like this."

Ilyenna folded her arms protectively over her chest and tried to sound indifferent. "Like what?"

He finally glanced at her briefly. "I don't want to start any rumors."

She dropped her head, unable to look at him. But she had to ask the question. "Do you regret that night?" She shifted her weight from one foot to the other before forcing herself to meet his gaze. "I have to know."

He jammed his thumbs in his clan belt and looked away from her, the muscles in his jaw working. "Of course I regret it."

For a moment, her mind refused to accept his answer. But when it did, she wasn't sure her legs would hold her. Fat tears spilled down her cheeks. Not trusting herself to speak, she hurried past him, toward camp.

Rone grabbed her wrist. "Ilyenna, please. I'm sorry. I thought you'd understand."

She understood perfectly. Tears coursed steadily down her face, and she could barely hold back her sobs. "There's nothing more to say, Rone, so let me go."

He hesitated, then released her. She went from him like a dove freed from its cage. He called something after her, but she didn't stop. She went back under the wagon to sob silently until morning came.

18. New Life

Ressa kept glancing at Ilyenna's red, puffy eyes. "We'll be seeing Cardenholm soon."

At least the Riesen clan mistress seemed to know better than to pry. For that, Ilyenna was grateful. But if she continued to remain silent, the older woman might feel it necessary to ask questions, so Ilyenna said, "It's been years since I've been to Cardenholm." Even this far away, she could smell the briny water and the village—fish and smoke. The smoke she could stand. It was the fish that turned her stomach. She tried to take shallow breaths. How could people eat something that smelled so bad?

Long before they saw the village, the ocean came into view. On and on it stretched. Used to the comforting embrace of the mountains, Ilyenna's mind shied away from such vastness. Water so deep you couldn't see the bottom . . . water she couldn't swim in. She could almost feel the water's arms close around her, wrapping her in their deadly embrace. She shivered. Then she shook off the memories and focused on the sunshine on her back and the sight of steady ground beneath her.

When Cardenholm finally came into sight, Ilyenna stood in the wagon, her hand shading her eyes. With the constant threat of Raiders, Cardenholm had been built to withstand sea attacks. The town sat on a high knoll and was surrounded by a rock and mortar wall. The houses inside were made of rough wood planks and moss-covered wood shingles. The wood had weathered to a dull gray to match the sharp-cut stones of the wall. Ilyenna didn't like the wall. It made her feel trapped.

"Do you see the Shyle clanmen?" she asked.

"No." Looking uneasy, Ressa adjusted her grip on the reins. "Don't plan on seeing any of them, Ilyenna. Rumor is Undon forbad it."

Ilyenna sat down hard, her fists clenched at her sides. If her clan couldn't sell their goods, how would they survive the winter? "What right does he have?"

Ressa pulled the team up just outside the earthen walls. "He doesn't."

The Riesen brought out high-poled canvas tents from some of the wagons. Ilyenna spent the remainder of the day helping set them up. From now until the end of the Council, the men and women would remain separate, with the exception of suckling babies. Ilyenna shared a tent with Ressa and three of her four daughters, including the newlywed Varris, all of them full of prodding questions Ressa managed to fend off with an exceptionally fierce clanmistress glare.

After the tents were up, the women set about making supper—with plenty extra to sell. When the men had finally finished with their side of camp and came in for their food, Ilyenna caught sight of Rone. He didn't glance at her as he took a wooden bowl of beef stew and rye bread from a Riesen girl.

Ilyenna watched him, her hatred suddenly seeming as strong as her love ever had. Abandoning her ladle, she stormed into the tent. Once inside, she paced back and forth. She couldn't decide which emotion was stronger—hate, love, hurt, or betrayal. She only knew she was drowning in them all.

Ressa came inside and lowered the tent door behind her. "Ilyenna?"

"I can't do it anymore. I can't," she huffed.

Ressa looked at her sadly. "You mean the baby?"

Baby? What does a baby have to do with anything? Ilyenna studied the clan mistress in bewilderment.

The older woman blushed furiously, then said gently, "Oh. You haven't realized yet, have you?" She sighed. "You're a healer, yes?"

Ilyenna nodded dumbly.

Ressa took a deep breath. "If a clan woman came to you complaining of tiredness and stomach upset, and she had a faint line traveling down from her navel, along with a flushed face and palms, would you say she was ill? Or would you think—"

Ilyenna's blood froze in her veins. "A baby?" she gasped.

Her arms out, Ressa stepped forward, as if afraid Ilyenna might faint. "When was the last time you bled?"

"A few days before the Argons were attacked." Nearly five weeks ago. Suddenly, she knew without any doubt.

She was with child.

She collapsed. Ressa broke most of her fall. Ilyenna sat, numb and unfeeling. She wasn't sure how long she stayed that way, but finally, everything she'd experienced over the last weeks came crashing down on her. She folded in on herself, silent sobs wracking her body.

Ressa tucked Ilyenna's head on her lap and rocked her back and forth like she was a child. "Let it go. Let all of it go."

"I can't do it. I can't!" Her words came in lurching gasps. She wept until no more tears would come. Then she sat up, exhausted. Ressa gave her a scrap of linen, which Ilyenna used to wipe her eyes and blow her nose.

When she tried to hand the cloth back, Ressa shook her head. "Keep it. I have a feeling you're going to need it more than me." She cocked her head to the side. "Who's the father?"

"Rone." Even to her own ears, Ilyenna's voice sounded dead.

Ressa raised her eyebrows. "Not Darrien?"

Ilyenna couldn't answer. Couldn't tell Ressa that this baby was not forced upon her, that she chose to lay with Rone. She chose this dishonor.

Ressa rubbed Ilyenna's back in small circles. "When?"

"The night we escaped. We thought we were going to die." Ilyenna hiccupped on a sob. "I've loved him since I was a child." From some deep reserve that never seemed to run dry, tears started coming again.

"And Rone?"

She wiped her cheeks. "He's always thought of me as a little sister. He told me last night he regretted it."

"Ah, that explains your red eyes this morning." Ressa continued softly, "You're his responsibility now. He's an honorable man. He'll do the right thing."

Ilyenna jumped to her feet. "No!" She refused to spend the rest of her life with a man she yearned for who didn't return her love. She'd rather go back to her father and live in ignominy and disgrace. She glared at Ressa fiercely. "You will keep this to yourself."

With that, Ilyenna stormed from the tent. She didn't know where she was going, only that she couldn't bear to spend another minute within shouting distance of Rone Argon! More than one Riesen watched her barrel out of camp, but Ressa must have called off the guards, for they didn't follow Ilyenna.

Her mind reeled with the consequences of what she'd done. If by some miracle the Council released her as a tiam, she'd return home to disgrace and dishonor. If her father chose, he could throw her out. Either way, she'd lose her title as clan mistress. She could even lose her place in her clan.

But if the Council sided with Undon and Darrien, the consequences were much worse. Ilyenna's child would be born a tiam, with no rights. Her hand unconsciously strayed to her belly. Was there really a child growing there? For a moment, she hated it as much as she hated Rone. She immediately felt guilty.

It's not your fault, her lips formed the words, but no sound came. It's no one's fault but my own.

She started when she realized she'd walked to the sea. She stepped into it. The water breathed in and out around her ankles. Could she throw herself into the ocean, let it swallow her deep inside its belly and hide her forever from sight?

She stepped out of the water as if waking from a nightmare. She collapsed on the sandy shore, listening to the rhythmic waves and praying for the dead to come and take her with them.

"Hello, Ilyenna."

She darted to her feet, her heart pounding in her throat. Darrien stood behind her, a wicked grin on his face. Wiping the tears from her cheeks, she backed away from him until she stood shin deep in the water.

"Now, this looks familiar. But this time, there's no cliff to jump off. Don't worry, I'll catch you if you fall."

Fear strangled her voice. She stared at him like a sheep stares at a mountain lion. Slowly, Darrien walked toward her. She tried to dart to the side, but he caught her around the wrist. Painful memories raced through her mind. Her legs trembled so badly she could barely stand.

"Good," he whispered. "It's about time you were afraid of me."

His words finally seemed to awaken some long-dead courage inside her. She brought up her knee, trying to catch him between his legs. He twisted, neatly avoiding her, then shoved her. She landed in the water with a splash. For a moment, she was back in the river. Then the waterfall. Drowning.

The sand shifted beneath her hands. She tasted the salt in her mouth and remembered where she was. She managed to get to her knees, away from the water's embrace. Not wanting to let her go, fingers of it clung to her, making her clothes and hair swirl around her. She coughed and gasped for breath.

Darrien stood above her, his laughter fading. "Good to see you still have some embers of your former fire. This wouldn't be any fun otherwise."

To her disbelief, he turned and began walking away. He wasn't going to claim her as his tiam, force her to come back with him? She gaped, letting the waves rock her. Finally, she came out of the water and looked down at herself. She very much resembled a drowned sheep. She shook some of the water from her hands before crossing them over her stomach and hurrying back toward the Riesen encampment.

When she'd first come down this path, she'd been blind to everything but the need to escape. Now, she noted the wild roses, heavy with bloom, their fruity scent crowding the damp air. Her mouth still tasted of briny water. A breeze danced across her clammy skin, and she shivered. When she was about halfway to the camp, Rone came running toward her, his axe at the ready, his face the one she'd seen him wear before he killed a man.

He was the father of her child.

She hugged herself tighter.

"Ilyenna! What happened?"

Tears stung her eyes. By the Balance, she was tired of crying. She planted her feet and glared at him. "What do you think happened?" His gaze darted around, panic plain on his face. Her heart softened a little, the tenderness she'd so firmly tamped down tempering her voice. "Darrien found me by the sea."

"So he tried to drown you!" Rone roared.

Ilyenna shook her head. "No. He shoved me when I tried to hurt him."

She finally allowed herself to look at Rone, really look at him. He was a good man. He might not love her, but he didn't deserve her hatred. Neither did her baby. With that thought, the newborn flames of hate Ilyenna had nurtured toward him sputtered and died. She could only hope those same flames hadn't charred part of her soul.

She hadn't quite forgiven him. But somehow she knew she would.

"He let you go?" Rone asked, his brow furrowed.

Had he? Ilyenna got the feeling Darrien would never let her go. That she'd never be strong enough to completely free herself of him. Unable to stop herself, she reached up and cupped Rone's face in her hand. "For now."

He took her hand in his. "I'll get you back. From now on, you stay inside the encampment until the Council meets." He began pulling her toward camp.

19. The Link

Ressa stumbled into the tent. Behind her, Varris came in, holding a small tub of water. After she'd set it down, Ressa motioned for her daughter to leave them. The younger woman glanced at Ilyenna before moving to obey. Ressa inspected Ilyenna as if doubting her eyes. "He really let you go?"

"Yes." Ilyenna stripped off her clothes and dropped them into the water Varris had brought. She pushed the clothes down to release the air, then began wringing out the salt.

Ressa crossed her arms. "I'm sorry. Rone was right. I shouldn't have let you go anywhere alone." Her lips pulled down into a severe frown. "I just wanted to give you a moment's peace. I'm so sorry."

"Rone didn't want me to go?"

Ressa shook her head. "He started after you and I stopped him. When word came that the Tyrans had come, he took off after you."

Ilyenna tried to smile, but her lips seemed to have forgotten how. "No harm done."

Ressa nodded shortly. "Otec is here."

"My father?"

"He's asked to see you." The older clan mistress seemed to be gauging Ilyenna's reaction.

Ilyenna crumpled, her hands slipping to her lap. She watched the soapy water run down her naked thighs. "See me?" she said in a daze. "I can't see him."

Ressa lifted the tent flap and called for Varris to bring more water. "Your father has every right to see you. You can't deny him that."

Ilyenna swallowed to keep from crying again. "I can't. I'd have to tell him I've shamed him. I can't bear it."

Ressa took over washing the dress, her hands sure and strong. "Under the circumstances, I think it best only you and I know your secret, at least until things settle."

Ilyenna gaped at her. A clan mistress suggesting she break clan law? Varris brought in more water and left again. Ressa tugged the dress out of the soapy water and rinsed it in the fresh tub. "One thing about being a clan mistress as long as I have, I've learned that laws are created to protect people. If the law doesn't protect anyone, it can be bent—or broken all together."

She handed Ilyenna the soap. "Now clean yourself up. I've heard salt water is about as irritating as a dress full of hay."

Using the cleaner water, Ilyenna reluctantly obeyed, moving in numb routine. When she'd finished braiding her hair, Ressa pulled out another of Varris's dresses—this one much finer than the last, with embroidery around the hems—and pulled it over Ilyenna's head. Then she stepped back, inspecting Ilyenna. "Well, I wish we'd had more time to fatten you up, but considering how you looked when you came to us, I suppose it'll have to do."

Ressa gripped Ilyenna's hand and pulled her out of the tent, through the women's side of the camp, and right up to Gen's tent. "Husband," she called. "I've come with Ilyenna to see her father."

"Come inside," Gen called back.

Casting Ilyenna a look that said she'd better follow, Ressa went in. Ilyenna shifted her weight nervously and glanced around, searching for some kind of escape. Her eyes locked with Rone's, who was watching her from beside one of the men's tents with a grim expression.

He might not know about his child, but he knew about their shared shame. He rose to his feet and came to her side. "We'll face your father together," he said. He took a step closer and whispered so softly she barely heard him, "But there's no need to tell him yet. We'll see what the Council's verdict is first."

Both Rone and Ressa were telling her to lie, and Ilyenna didn't have the courage to tell either of them no, to face the consequences of what she'd done. Nodding, she followed him inside. Ressa raised an eyebrow when she saw them together.

Steeling herself, she forced herself to meet her father's gaze. She barely recognized him. He'd aged fifteen years since she'd seen him last, the lines on his face cut deeper. Dark circles under his eyes made them appear sunken. His hair and beard were dull and in need of a cut.

He rose shakily from his chair beside the large table. "You look like your mother did after I brought her home," he choked.

Did she really look as bad as a Raider's slave?

Like he'd never done before, he gathered Ilyenna in his arms. "I'm sorry for what they've done to you, child. I'm sorry I couldn't stop them. A father—a father should be able to protect his children."

She shook her head, her face buried in his shoulder. "You tried."

"But it wasn't enough, was it?" He squeezed her and pulled her back. His shoulder was damp—her tears had come back and she hadn't even noticed. "I want to know what they've done to you."

She shared a glance with Rone before dropping her gaze to the crushed grass that made up the tent floor. "No, you don't."

"It can't be worse than what I've imagined," he replied dully.

Ilyenna closed her eyes. "I can't, Father. I can't."

Rone rested his hand on Otec's shoulder. "We'll speak later."

Ilyenna glanced at Rone in surprise, silently begging him not to tell her father what they'd done. Rone fidgeted under her gaze.

Her father patted her arm awkwardly. "You're not a soldier. I shouldn't ask you to act like one."

Though she doubted he'd meant his words to sting, they hurt all the same. Clearly, he assumed she was too weak. Well, maybe she was.

"The other clanwomen?" he said.

"They're all alive." It was the best answer Ilyenna could give. "The Shyle, Father. Why didn't anyone come to the spring feast?"

He wouldn't look at her. "We've nothing to trade and no one to spare." He seemed to shrink in on himself. "For five generations our family has kept the Shyle safe. And during my watch, we fall into chaos and despair."

"Father, I—" she began.

He waved her to silence "Words, Ilyenna—they hold no comfort." He turned to Gen. "How many clan chiefs have arrived?"

"We're waiting for four more. Rumor is they'll be here tomorrow or the day after."

Otec nodded. "Have you spoken with Rim of the Cardell?"

Gen gestured for them to sit. Ilyenna settled herself next to her father. Before them was an enormous platter of cheese, early strawberries, and crackers. She couldn't resist taking some. As she ate, she could hear the night's festivities beginning. The air was already heavy with music, laughter, and the smell of beer.

Gen took a sip of his foamy ale. "He listened, but it's clear he won't commit one way or the other without speaking with the other clan chiefs."

Otec rubbed his face tiredly, his scruff making a scratching noise against his callused palms. "First, the Tyrans will claim that Rone and I have no rights to sit with the Council."

Gen set his mug down and leaned forward. "The Council will reinstate you. The real worry is how to right Undon's wrongs without bringing on retribution."

"Won't they see their way to war?" Rone asked a little too eagerly.

Gen shook his head. "The Council is full of old men—High Chief Burdin the oldest of us all. And old men don't like war. They'll try to avoid it at all costs."

Rone grumbled an unintelligible reply. Ilyenna suddenly realized she'd eaten every single one of the strawberries. Embarrassed, she clasped her hands to keep from eating everything else. "So what do you think they'll do?"

Her father sighed.

Gen shrugged. "Try to right things without either side losing more face than they're willing to give."

Ilyenna rubbed her eyes tiredly. "And what of the people dead by Tyran hands?"

Gen and her father exchanged glances. "There will be an accounting." Her father's words hung heavy with promise.

"What accounting? Nothing's going to bring them back." Her throat burned with tears. She took a sip of beer to clear them out.

Ressa came to Ilyenna and gently tugged at her arm. "You men can work out your battle plans without us. Ilyenna and I are going to bed."

Ilyenna wanted to argue, to stay and figure this out, but she was so exhausted she could barely keep her head up. Was this what pregnancy was like? Ressa helped her to her feet and steered her toward the tent. People had been leading her around like a little child a lot lately. But right now, she didn't have the energy to care.

***

Ilyenna woke with a groan and sat up, her hand over her mouth. She swallowed several times, trying to decide whether she needed to run from the tent to empty her stomach. As a healer, she knew food should settle her nausea, though she couldn't see how. She crawled to a basket by the door, opened the lid, and pulled out a piece of yesterday's bread. She nibbled on the crust.

Varris eased quietly in and smiled. "Glad to see you're finally up." She went to her sleeping pallet and started searching through her knapsack.

"What's the time?" Ilyenna asked, her voice still thick with sleep.

Varris held a blanket up, shook her head, and rummaged around some more. "After midday."

Ilyenna started out of a stretch and rolled to her knees. Then she realized she was still in Varris's best underdress. "Would you mind fetching the other dress you gave me? It was drying outside"

Varris paused, another blanket in her hands. She glanced at Ilyenna before quickly looking away. "Keep that one for now."

"No, no," Ilyenna said. "This is your best one."

Varris smiled gently. "I know, Ilyenna." She hesitated. "The last of the clan chiefs is due today. They're meeting about the Tyrans as soon as he arrives."

Ilyenna's fate would be decided by nightfall. Suddenly, she couldn't move, could hardly breathe.

Varris set down a blanket and came to kneel behind Ilyenna. Deftly, she unbraided Ilyenna's hair, shook it out, and set to rebraiding it tightly.

"What if they send me back?" Ilyenna asked in horror.

Varris's quick fingers slowed. "I don't think it'll come to that."

"But what if it does?"

Varris tied off the end of the braid with a sheepskin cord. "It won't. That would start a war."

Her heart seizing onto that hope, Ilyenna gripped Varris's hand. "You're sure?"

Glancing at the tent flap as if worried her mother might hear, Varris leaned in and whispered, "The clans are in an uproar over what Undon has done. And they're furious the Shyle couldn't come to the feast." She nodded toward the blanket she'd been searching for. "The lack of Shyle blankets to trade for is an upsetting reminder."

Ilyenna really looked at the blanket in Varris's hand. Shyle wool, no doubt woven by a Shyle woman. "You're going to sell it?"

Varris smiled shyly. "I've a dozen more at home. The price this one will fetch should more than buy the things you need. Then you won't always feel beholden to others."

Ilyenna swallowed her tears. "Thank you," she finally managed.

Varris gathered up the blanket. "You're welcome. Now, come eat with us. You're still such a dreadfully skinny thing."

Ilyenna didn't even think to protest. At least until she saw what looked like rocks floating in the stew pot. "What are those?"

Varris glanced into the pot and smiled. "Clams. The Carden cook them in their shells and pull them out with their fingers. Mother traded for them this morning."

Ilyenna crinkled her nose. "I don't think—"

"Just eat," Varris said with a laugh, then filled a bowl and handed it to Ilyenna.

Ilyenna sniffed dubiously, but her stomach was roaring for food. Finally, she gave in. By the fifth bite, she'd decided the stew wasn't too bad. Not nearly as good as mutton stew, but not bad. As she ate, she noted the Riesen had been busily trading. Sacks of rye, rye flour, and whiskey had been replaced with barrels of salt cod, wheat flour, beer, crates of linen, and numerous other supplies.

As she was studying the wagons, Rone came to sit beside her. He didn't speak. Watching him as she pried a clam free of its shell, she noticed his tense movements, shallow breathing, and the moisture at his brow. "Are you ill?" she asked.

He barked a harsh, humorless laugh. "I—" he paused "—I always get this way before a battle."

Ilyenna tossed the last shell onto a large pile by the pot, no doubt being collected to scrape the hair off hides. "Battle? You mean the meeting with the Council?"

He really looked at her, and for a moment, he was the old Rone, the carefree, gentle boy she'd always loved. "Yes. I mean the Council." He took her hand, pulling her to her feet. "Come with me."

Ressa would be angry if she knew Ilyenna was leaving the safety of the camp, but she didn't care. Rone had her hand in his. For the first time in days, he wanted to be with her. She wanted to savor this moment, draw it into herself and keep it safe in her memory. Breathless, she allowed him to lead her through the clustered camps, away from the people.

He took her down a path similar to the one she'd traveled yesterday. Roses as tall as she lined the trail, their branches sagging with the weight of the blooms. Their strong scent made her dizzy. Rone paused at the side of a ragged boulder, stuck his foot into a chink in the rock, and hauled himself up. One more step and he reached the top, then lay down and reached for her. "Come up. I'll help you."

Hiking up her dress rather indecently, she managed to find the first foothold. From there, Rone took her hand and heaved her up beside him as easily as if she were a child.

Ilyenna glanced down at the other side of the boulder. The forest of roses was kept back by a flat expanse of rock. Dozens of fairies with rose-petal wings circled the flowers, coaxing the buds open and filling the air with their heavy scent. The aroma overcame the smells of the village—smoke and fish—yet there was still the taste of salt in the air.

Without pausing, Rone dropped down and looked up at her. "Jump down. I'll catch you."

For the first time, Ilyenna wondered as to his reasons for bringing her here. She looked back to the village with its cluster of tents spilling from the wall's entrance. She could still go back.

"Ilyenna?"

She sighed. She couldn't deny him, any more than she could deny herself water. She dropped into his arms. He held her aloft before gently sliding her down his chest to the ground.

Her heart raced, her senses suddenly full of only him. "How did you find this place?" she asked breathlessly.

He grinned his boyish, mischievous grin. "Last night, during the feasting, I happened to be walking back from the ocean when I saw a couple climb this rock and disappear. I checked it out this morning."

At the thought, old hurts rose within her. "A couple? So why bring me here?"

Rone released her and stepped back, but the roses walled them in like a fortress. He only had room to take two steps before they brushed against his back. "I wanted to speak with you."

Ilyenna raised an eyebrow. "And you couldn't have done that at camp?"

He looked away. "Not without the risk of someone overhearing us." He seemed to be battling with himself. "I need to make things right between us. In case . . . well, in case things turn out badly."

She turned from him, her fingers tracing the footholds she now saw someone had chiseled into the sides of the boulder. She wondered how many Cardens had used this spot for their trysts. "You mean in case we're not released as tiams?" Rone didn't answer. She turned around, her arms crossed over her chest. "I'm not sure we can make it right."

He threw his hands in the air. "By the Balance, Ilyenna, every time I try to talk to you about this, you flare up like a wildfire." He seized her by the arms and hauled her up so she was standing on her tiptoes. "Well, that's why I brought you here, so you couldn't run away, and no one can hear you shouting at me!"

Dumbfounded, she stared at him. "All right, I won't run away." She was careful to keep any promises of not shouting behind her teeth.

He released her and began pacing. Two steps in one direction, two back. "I mean, I know it was wrong, but I look at you and I start remembering. I want you so badly I can barely stand it. Then I'm so ashamed of myself I can't even bear to be in the same room with you."

She stared at him as he pressed his palms into the boulder, his face twisted as if he was in pain. "I know it was wrong, and I'm sorry." Rone finally looked at her, anger in his eyes. "But I wasn't the only one there that night. I wasn't the only one who wanted it. So will you stop blaming me and being angry at me?"

"Angry?"

He looked up at the sky. "Yes, angry! Every time I come near you, you're so angry, I can feel it rolling off you like heat from a fire."

She shook her head. "You—you said that you regretted it."

He looked at her like she'd suddenly lost her senses. "Of course I regret it."

"Then why do you keep feeding me false hope?" Ilyenna shook with rage. "If you regret it, then let me go!"

He appeared dumbfounded. "I was trying to apologize. To tell you how sorry I was, for shaming you that way."

What? She swayed. Rone reached out and held her securely. "Ilyenna?"

"I . . . I . . ." Closing her eyes, she tried to think. Was he really saying what she thought he was? "You regret that night . . . because of the shame it brought upon me?"

His brows gathered. "Why else would I have said . . ." His eyes suddenly widened with understanding. "Oh, Ilyenna, sometimes I think you're dense on purpose."

She punched his arm. It was an automatic reaction left over from their childhood. "I didn't know!"

To her exasperation, he didn't even flinch. "I told you I loved you," he said. "Could you really forget that quickly?"

She covered her mouth with her hand. "I thought you meant you loved me as a brother might. And in the moment . . ." She stomped her foot as he frowned at her. "We both thought we were going to die that night! I just thought that you were trying to—to—"

"To allow you to give away your first time, instead of letting it be taken from you?" Rone finished for her.

Blushing furiously, she looked away.

He took her hand. "Hey, it's all right. It was my first time too." He sighed. "And maybe you're right. Being together for our first times was part of my motivation."

"Then . . . why regret it?"

He clenched his eyes shut and backed away. "I regret the danger I placed you in. The selfish way I acted. The weakness I demonstrated. The shame I caused you." He studied her. "What do you think Darrien would do if he found out what you did—with me?"

Her hand moved protectively to her belly. Darrien would know soon enough. They all would. "The Council won't tolerate Undon's reparation. They can't."

"Even if they don't, if anyone finds out, you'll lose your chances for marriage, your title." Rone's voice dropped down so low she could barely hear him. "And I put all those risks on you, the woman I love."

Ilyenna was speechless. She could only stare at him. "We didn't think we'd live to see the morning."

He hooked his thumbs over his clan belt. "But we did."

She let herself absorb this news, let it chase away weeks' worth of misunderstandings. Still, she couldn't quite believe it.

Rone sighed. "You shouldn't love me back."

Her smile wilted. "Why?"

He took a deep breath. "You shouldn't love a man who can't protect you. All those years ago, if I'd have let you come hunting with us, or at the very least taken you home, you wouldn't have nearly drowned."

Ilyenna shook her head. "No. If it was anyone's fault, it was mine. I followed you. I chose to cross the river where I did, knowing full well that it wasn't where we'd crossed before."

He stared at her in disbelief. "All this time, you've blamed yourself too?"

She listened to the sound of the waves scraping unseen across the shore. "Rone, you saved my life."

He pressed his back to the boulder and slid down to sit on the ground. "I shouldn't have had to. I knew that trail was the only safe place to cross. I should've made sure you took it. And then your mother died trying to nurse you back to health."

Ilyenna sat down next to him, taking his hand in hers. "We were children."

"But I knew better. After all that, I failed to keep you safe from Darrien." His face darkened. "But I won't fail you again. Darrien will never lay another hand on you. I swear by—"

She pressed her hand over Rone's mouth. "You've never failed me. Never. You fed me from your own portions, saved me, tended me, took unnecessary risks . . . Rone, you've done nothing but show me love."

She thought she saw the first flicker of forgiveness in his eyes—forgiveness for himself. Being here with him like this, she'd never felt more complete. Since her childhood, she'd been told men and women were opposite ends of the Balance. When they came together, they created a perfect circle—the Link. She now understood what they meant. With Rone, she was complete. Whole. She leaned forward, her lips inches from his. "So, you really love me? More than as a sister?"

He chuckled dryly. "Brothers and sisters don't do the things we did."

Her insides squirmed deliciously.

"How could you doubt it?" He stroked her cheek.

The way her cheeks felt, it must have been a long time since she'd smiled this broadly. She covered her mouth.

Rone pulled her hands away. "By the Balance, I've missed your smile." He pressed his lips to hers. His kisses seemed to awaken a juxtaposition inside her, a delicious pain, like sweet, sour strawberries. His nearness, his love, left her stomach feeling squirmy and exhilarated—like when Rone and Bratton had dared her to jump from the topmost branch to a haystack below. All wrapped up in one overwhelming, wonderful pain—a hungering need for him.

As before, his kisses were gentle yet hungry. He pulled off the knot holding her hair back and gently unwound her braid. He ran his fingers through her hair. She shivered. Her mouth against his, she smiled and pulled him down with her. She felt her hair flaring around her. Felt his weight on her chest.

She reached up and started to undo his clan belt. Breathless, Rone grabbed her arms and held them down. He hovered above her for a moment, his face a myriad of emotions. "No. Not again." His voice was so low she could barely hear him. "I won't do this to you again."

"What if I want you to do this to me again?" Ilyenna murmured.

His brows drew down. "Then I'll love you more than you love yourself."

She grunted. Their shame, as he called it, would be perfectly obvious to everyone in a few months. But she couldn't seem to tell Rone about the baby. She'd just found his love again, and she wasn't ready to test it just yet.

Still, she wanted to argue with him, to demand. But it wouldn't do any good. When Rone had that stubborn look about him, she'd be better off to threaten the grasshoppers not to eat her garden.

"You can braid your hair on the way back." He started up the boulder. "Come on. The Council will be meeting soon. We've been gone long enough."

She stepped into the chiseled chink in the rock and took his hand. He loved her. He loved her, and everything would be all right.

20. The Council

"Where've you two been?" Varris huffed, her skirts gripped in her hands, sweat plastering her forehead. She bent down to the boy beside her and sent him off to fetch Ressa. Blowing a stray strand of hair out of her eyes, she grabbed Ilyenna's hand. "The last clan chief arrived just after you left. The Council might've already convened!"

Rone's dangerous look returned. Ilyenna had a sudden suspicion there was something he wasn't telling her—something bad. "Go," she prodded him. "We'll catch up." With a grateful nod, he took off at a sprint.

Her hand in Varris's vice-like grip, Ilyenna hustled toward the weathered houses beyond the city wall. She entered the village for the first time since they'd arrived. Grudgingly, she admitted it wasn't as bad as she'd thought. Rose bushes bloomed everywhere, masking the smell coming from the drying racks down by the docks.

Neatly ordered gardens resided on the west side of each house. Hanging from fishing lines, gorgeous, polished shells tinkled whenever the wind blew. Larger, conical shells lined the sides of the houses. The women wore a variety of pearls and shells around their necks or in their hair. They smiled kindly at Ilyenna as she passed.

At least until they saw Ressa storming toward them. Then they seemed to melt into side streets or houses. The clan mistress had the same look on her face as a dog herding a particularly difficult sheep. "Where've you been? I told you not to leave camp!"

Ilyenna bit the inside of her cheek. "I was safe. Rone was with me."

Taking Ilyenna's other arm as if afraid she might disappear again, Ressa started hauling her toward the clanhouse. "You . . . what? Why?" she asked, narrowing her eyes.

"How is that any of your business?" Ilyenna muttered.

"I suppose it isn't," Ressa said coldly.

Wishing she'd held her tongue, Ilyenna grimaced at the feel of Ressa's nails biting into her skin. "I'm sorry. I shouldn't have said that. You've been nothing but kind to me."

They arrived at the clanhouse, but Ressa didn't release her arm. "We've no time for this. The meeting started moments ago. Unless I've missed something else, all that's happened is Rone and Otec being restored as rightful clan chiefs. As if there was any doubt." She pulled Ilyenna past the two men posted at the door, released her, and moved into the shadowy room.

Her father and Rone. Hope lightened Ilyenna's heart.

Still, she hesitated in the doorway. She suddenly didn't want to hear the Council's verdict. Right now, she was safe, well-fed, clothed, and cared for. Her injuries were healing, and no one was threatening to add new ones. That could all change on the Council's whim. But refusing to listen wouldn't stop the decision from being made. Much as she wanted to run, Ilyenna knew that held no answers either. If she had to face this, she would face it as Rone had—courageously.

So, though her heart thumped madly, she moved through the room full of people. The voices slowly fell silent as she passed. It took a moment for her eyes to adjust. A few candles burned at the table, augmenting the light straining through the warped, pockmarked windows and open doors. The room smelled of tallow candles and lye soap. As always, the Council was seated before the empty fireplace, with clan chiefs on the left, clan mistresses on the right, and white-haired High Chief Burdin in the center.

As she came before the table, Rone smiled at her reassuringly. Some of the tightness eased from her chest at the familiar sight of him and her father in their seats. Perhaps she would be allowed to take her own place.

But then she saw Darrien standing behind his father. Their gazes locked. Horror and hatred burned inside of her. The Council could order her back as his tiam. With a shudder that shook her to her bones, she focused on High Chief Burdin. Though she could feel Darrien's eyes on her, she refused to look his way again.

"Ah, Ilyenna," High Chief Burdin said in his gravelly voice. "We've heard from your father and just now from Rone Argon. But we've yet to hear from you. Can you tell us of your treatment as a tiam?"

Ilyenna's blood seemed to freeze in her veins. She cleared her throat, her eyes tracing the grains of the floor. "In the short time I was a tiam, I was starved, beaten, humiliated, and—and . . ." She paused and shifted her weight uncomfortably.". . . and nearly violated, even though they agreed not to harm me by violence or neglect. I was only supposed to submit my sweat." She finished in a whisper.

More than one Council member shot Darrien and his father looks of disgust. For the term of their service, tiams were property, no better or worse than sheep or cattle. But Ilyenna wasn't a common criminal. She was one of them—a clan mistress. One who had taken her father's place in order to save his life, and the Council knew it.

"And were the other tiams treated this poorly?" Burdin asked gently.

Ilyenna managed a tight nod. "Even before some of the clanwomen were made tiams."

Her father gripped his axe as if he was considering using it. Rone glared at Darrien like he'd already made the decision to use his. Later. With a growing sense of dread, Ilyenna realized that's exactly what Rone had planned.

He spoke in a voice as calm as the stillness before a thunderstorm. "I would ask Ilyenna to relate to the Council what she saw at the Tyran clan house."

She locked gazes with Rone. She pretended he was the only one in the room, that she spoke only to him. "Darrien kept me in the attic above his room. One night, I saw three riders approach the clan house."

Out of the corner of her eye, Ilyenna saw Undon and Darrien exchange a quick glance.

She swallowed. "One held the horses, while the other two approached the house. When the door opened, I saw the men in the light—men with foreign cloaks and strange tunics. I believe they were Raiders."

A cry rose up from nearly every mouth in the room. Undon and Darrien remained oddly silent. She'd expected them to deny it, to accuse her of lying. Their silence frightened her more than their shouts would have.

"You saw the tattoos on their skulls?" asked Zenna of the West clan.

Ilyenna slowly shook her head. "They had their cowls up."

Conversations erupted throughout the room, so Ilyenna spoke a little louder. "I sneaked down to the kitchen to try to hear what they were saying, but I couldn't make out their words."

Rone leaned forward. "I can add my witness to Ilyenna's. Near Kebholm, two Raiders attacked her. I managed to kill one before the other escaped." He threw something that looked like poorly treated rawhide on the table. But this rawhide had writing on it.

Then Ilyenna stepped closer. The strange marks weren't writing, but tattoos. It was one of the Raider's scalps. She shuddered as she remembered the wet thing Rone had tucked out of her sight after he'd killed the Raider. She looked away, determined not to look at it again.

Clan Chief Shamaron of the Kebs cleared his throat. "A body was found, but it was rotted beyond recognition."

Samass stood to get a better view of the scalp. His face paled and he sat down heavily. "So there are Raiders about."

"That doesn't prove I was in league with them."

Every eye in the room turned to Undon, the tension so thick it felt like weight on Ilyenna's shoulders.

Undon wiped his mouth and leaned forward. "I would ask that the room be cleared of all but the Council and the doors be shut."

Burdin hesitated, his eyes narrowing suspiciously. "Very well." He motioned toward the door. People all around Ilyenna exchanged surprised glances, but no one argued. After they'd shuffled outside, the guards shut the doors. Without the breeze coming off the ocean, the room immediately felt stuffy. A trickle of sweat started down Ilyenna's spine.

Undon bowed his head, as if speaking were difficult for him. If Ilyenna didn't know better, she'd have believed his performance. "I struck the Argons because I believed they'd attacked my clan, killing many families."

What game is he playing? Ilyenna wondered. She glanced at Rone. Every muscle in his body seemed clenched tight enough to pull away from his bones.

Undon sighed deeply. "I now believe I was wrong."

In disbelief, Ilyenna swayed and had to catch herself to keep from falling over.

Her father grunted as though he'd been punched. "You're saying that killing and enslaving my clanmen—was a mistake?"

Many other Council members exchanged shocked glances.

Undon gestured toward the evidence lying on the table— evidence Ilyenna had already seen. A charred clan belt, a few arrows, and now the scalp. "If Ilyenna truly saw any men coming to my clan house in the night, they were scouts. A week after attacking the Argons, we found signs suggesting the Raiders staged the attacks on my farms to goad me into attacking the Argons, which would substantially weaken our borders and our defenses. I've had my scouts out searching for signs of Raiders ever since."

"Then how do you explain their cloaks?" questioned Tenna of the Kebs.

Undon made a gesture of dismissal. "Some of my men have taken to wearing them."

"But why the subterfuge?" asked Jenly the Cor. "The Shyle is too far inland to worry about attacks."

Ilyenna watched as realization dawned on her father's face. "Because of Shyle Pass," he muttered.

"Could an army of Raiders come down it?" asked Wynn of the West.

Otec nodded slowly. "There's a few months a year that the pass is traversable."

High Chief Burdin jumped in. "If there are Raiders coming down Shyle Pass, we need to know now, yes?"

All the clan chiefs and clan mistresses immediately agreed. Burdin stood, spreading his arms in midair over the table. "We'll send scouts immediately. They're to have access to whatever help they might need from the clans, especially fresh horses and food."

Every head in the room nodded assent. "Each clan, pick your best. In the meantime, I want every clan to send at least two hundred warriors. Two hundred more are to be at the ready in case the Raiders attack by sea. Clans Cor, Carden, and Delya are to have ships patrolling the waters. The orders go out now."

Ilyenna was completely forgotten as orders were sent out and men called for and dismissed. When the chaos finally died away, Burdin leaned back in his chair. "Now, what to do about you, Undon."

The Tyran clan chief bowed. "My apologies to the Argons, the Shyle, and even the Riesen."

Ilyenna's father jumped from his chair. "I'll accept no apology from you!" He turned to Burdin. "With enough time, our homes and herds can be rebuilt, our goods replaced. But the damage done by Undon goes much deeper. I have fistfuls of widows and fatherless children. Women violated. I go to bed at night to the sound of their weeping. Undon's hands are stained with the blood and tears of my clanmen and clanwomen. I have a price to extract for it." Otec turned to Undon. "I want you dead."

Undon seemed unmoved. "What would more bloodshed accomplish? Haven't enough died?"

"Because of you!" Otec shouted.

Undon slapped the table. "No, because of the Raiders!"

Rone spoke up, "You were in league with the Raiders. You only switched sides after your secret was discovered."

Ilyenna nodded furiously in agreement. "I'm telling you, the men were foreigners."

"That's preposterous," Undon huffed. "I'm a clan chief. Why would I do anything that risked my clan?"

"Money, power, jealousy. Why does any man betray those who would call him friend?" Rone shrugged. "Ilyenna has no reason to lie about the men being foreigners."

"Yes, she does." Darrien's voice was soft, but it struck a ringing silence through the room.

The whole Council swiveled to face him.

He stared at his feet. "For one thing, that attic doesn't have any windows. For another, it's far too high to climb down from, or to climb back up. If she'd have been able to manage it, she'd have slit my throat long ago."

Couldn't the Council see through this deception? "I considered it." Ilyenna locked gazes with Burdin. "I saw it through a chink in the mortar. Darrien had many skulls and antlers on his walls. I used them to climb down from the attic and back up."

Darrien spoke louder this time, his voice holding a hint of warning. "No, you didn't, because you never slept in the attic."

"I saw her there," Rone interrupted. "I brought her food and a blanket."

Darrien glared at Rone. "If that is true, you were there during the day, not at night."

Rone's hand twitched toward his axe.

Ilyenna's mind felt like a hammer that kept missing the nail. Darrien was setting a trap, but she didn't know how to avoid it. "I spent every night there."

He shook his head adamantly. "I won't let you lie, Ilyenna. I won't let you destroy my clan."

"I'm not lying!" She clenched her fists so tight she felt her nails cutting into her palms.

"You're trying to force me to confess? Fine!" Darrien turned away from her and said to Burdin, "She never slept in the attic. She slept in my bed."

All the air went out of Ilyenna. "That's not true."

He looked at her with false pity. "I tied her to the posts every night after I was through with her. There's no way she saw Raiders."

"I will have you and Undon's head for this!" Ilyenna's father shouted.

The Council members didn't even look at her. More than one face was flushed with rage or embarrassment . . . or both. Ilyenna finally understood Darrien's trap, but it was too late. None of them would believe her now. Not when her own father wouldn't. After all, what man would admit to forcing a woman? Especially after Ilyenna had just established violating women as a hobby of his.

She glanced at Rone, who was gaping at her in bewilderment. She felt everything falling away, like the last leaves wrenched from their branches before the first winter wind. She tried to keep her gaze open, to make him believe her. "If that were true, I'd have said it. Not some story about Raiders."

"Not if you wanted any chance at a marriage with Rone," Darrien said softly, his eyes glittering with hatred. "I've seen the way you two look at each other. But what man would take you after what I've done? You could be carrying my child right now."

His last words felt like a blow to her gut. She was with child, but not Darrien's. Would Rone ever believe that now? "Darrien is trying to destroy my honor," she said through her teeth. "To discredit me. Don't believe him."

The whole Council was looking at her now. She couldn't miss the pity in their gazes, especially her own father's, his guilt so strong she winced. Hadn't Darrien warned her? Hadn't he warned her that he would win? She glared at him, wishing she was a good enough aim to fling her knife into his gut.

"You are a poison! Everything you touch withers and dies." She hated the tears that started down her cheeks, hated that she couldn't stop them. They made her seem weak, vulnerable. She turned from Darrien to the Council. "Darrien threatened to dishonor me—he even tried once. That was the night I bashed him over the head with a rock and escaped." She blinked hard at the memory, hot tears plunging down her face. She felt them trembling on her chin. "But he never succeeded. He enjoyed torturing me. He's still enjoying it."

They all looked away. Darrien's story was winning. By the Balance, she'd fallen right into his trap.

Finally, Burdin took a long, deep breath. "This is a mess that won't be sorted out without some kind of proof." He blew the breath out. "What we know is there are Raiders, possibly coming down Shyle Pass."

"Trickery of the Raiders or no, Undon should have come to the Council with his grievances against the Argons," Wynn said, "not attacked them directly."

Ressa ground her teeth. "For that alone, Undon must be stripped of his role as a clan chief."

The other Council members nodded.

Undon shot to his feet and spread his palms on the long table. "Be warned, my clan is loyal to me, not to the Council. By unseating me, you risk the very discord the Raiders were trying to create."

Everyone went silent. Ilyenna locked gazes with Ressa. They both understood that with the imminent threat from the Raiders, the Council couldn't risk a civil war with its largest clan.

Burdin gestured for Undon to sit, and Ilyenna knew he was about to make his pronouncement. "The guilt for the many wrongs rests on more than one set of shoulders. For his grievous lack of judgment in attacking the Argon and Shyle clans, I remove Undon from his place as clan chief.

"For the damage to the Shyle and Argon lands, I hold the Tyran clan responsible and order reparation. For five years, a rotation of ten strong tiam clanmen will restore all damaged buildings and work at reestablishing the Shyle and Argon wealth. Undon and his son Darrien will be among those tiams.

"Clan Chief Burdin—" Undon began in a pleading tone.

"Silence!" Burdin roared. "The Tyrans will return everything taken—that includes Ilyenna and the other tiams. In addition, Clan Chief Otec and Rone will tally all the damage done and exact a price, to be paid in Tyran wheat and beer.

"Until we can determine Darrien's involvement with the Raiders, I will appoint a steward to manage Tyran affairs. For his unforgiveable treatment of Ilyenna, I order one hundred lashes, to be delivered in groups of twenty-five at each clan feast. He will also pay Otec her bride price. But she will remain free to marry any man of her choosing. "

Ilyenna swallowed her sob. Darrien's punishment wasn't nearly enough. She felt as if part of her soul had been ripped away. No man would have her now, not when they thought Darrien had taken her to his bed.

Burdin rubbed his whiskered face. "As for the allegation of treachery, we cannot make a ruling before we collect evidence. If it is found to be true, both Undon and Darrien's lives will be forfeit." Burdin leaned back in his chair. "What say you, Rone, Otec?"

Ilyenna's father shook his head. "You might not be able to take their lives without risking retaliation from the Tyrans. But I can. I've stated my claim. I want their heads. I demand a duel."

Ressa slapped the table. "You're an idiot!"

Ignoring her, Burdin pursed his lips, his beard bunching around his chin. "Don't do this, Otec. Don't risk yourself. Give the truth time."

Her father shook his head. "There is no other way to restore the honor Undon has taken from me and my family. I will not agree to the terms unless it is done."

Burdin sat in silence for a long time. He exchanged looks and words with the other Council members. Finally, they seemed to come to a consensus. "Tiams are taken so they might right the wrongs they have committed," Burdin announced, "not to be abused and violated. I do not approve, but neither will I deny you."

Rone jumped to his feet. "I was forced to serve as a tiam. During that time, I watched my fellow Argons and the Shyle beaten for no offense. The women were abused. By Darrien Tyran." He turned to Darrien. "I claim the same right of a duel. Only I want Darrien's head."

Burdin hesitated. "And if you lose? What then?"

Rone trembled with rage. "I won't."

Burdin shook his head, a sad, tired expression on his face. "Very well. You'll both have your chance." He pushed himself back from the table and started toward the door. The other Council members followed slowly. Ilyenna stood rooted to the spot.

Ressa marched right up to her. "Is what Darrien said true?"

Ilyenna didn't look at her. She was too busy watching Rone leave the room without so much as glancing at her. "No. Darrien tried, but he never actually violated me."

Ressa grunted. "Conniving son of a whore."

Ilyenna could no longer see Rone. "Where're they going, Ressa?"

The woman looked past Ilyenna through the doorway as the Council moved up the streets to a barren knoll east of the village. "They go to fight to the death."

Ilyenna swayed. Deep inside, she'd always known it would come to this. The room began to dim and tilt on its side. Ressa caught her arm. "Breathe, Ilyenna. Breathe!"

Ilyenna filled her lungs and the world steadied a bit. "I could lose them both—my father and Rone."

Ressa frowned. "Yes, child," she said softly. "You could lose them both."

Ilyenna wanted to faint, wanted the blackness to take her and never release her. But she stayed abominably awake. She was marked. There was no other explanation for this madness, for the death and pain that followed her like a shadow.

21. TO THE DEATH

Just beyond the village was an elevated cliff face.

"So that all might have a good view," Ressa mocked.

Ilyenna's mouth went dry. It all seemed so barbaric. Her father tossed his overshirt to the ground, his undershirt going with it. As a healer, Ilyenna understood. Men who wore clothing during battle stood a higher chance of fevers from their wounds.

The thought came unbidden. Ilyenna didn't want to watch the fight, but she had to. These could be the last moments of her father's life. She couldn't take her eyes off him. Didn't even dare blink.

Already shirtless, Undon checked the sharpness of his axe by brushing his thumb along the shining blade. A blade that could easily cut Ilyenna's father in two. Feeling sick, she covered her mouth with her hand.

It seemed every man or woman at the spring feast had heard about the fight. They came in solemn droves. Once they arrived, they began a slow, steady stomp with their right foot. Thrum, thrum,thrum. Ilyenna could taste the dust in the air.

No one said a word. Her father and Undon glared at each other with death written in their features. Ilyenna shivered as she looked at her father. Was this really the same man who'd hugged her for the first time yesterday? He didn't look the part of a killer. The wind ruffled his thinning gray hair. Already, a sheen of sweat glistened on a body that was still hard from work, but on which work and time had taken a toll. His skin sagged as if it had been made for a bigger man.

"Curse them all," she heard Ressa murmur under her breath.

Yes. Men and their abominable pride, Ilyenna thought. The crowd shifted as someone came up behind her. She turned to see Rone beside her. "Darrien is lying," she said through clenched teeth.

"I know," Rone said.

She felt the heat from his skin. What if that warmth changed to cold—a cold she could never banish? "You had this planned all along."

She sensed Rone's gaze on her, like a caress. "I've always known, from the day my father died," he said. "It's only been reaffirmed every day since. It's why I wouldn't commit to marrying you."

Agony filled Ilyenna's soul, so much worse than any physical pain. "And if you die? What happens to me then?"

"You'll be taken care of," he said with certainty.

She sighed. By now, Rone should know better than to underestimate Darrien. He'd win this game, a game that wouldn't be over for him until she'd lost everything. But she swallowed her protests. Rone would need every ounce of his focus. "You're right," she said softly. "I'll be taken care of."

"You understand?" he asked in relief.

No. How could anyone understand this madness? Ilyenna thought, but once again she bit back the words. "Of course."

He took her hand, squeezing it reassuringly. "Don't worry—I won't lose. Neither will your father."

Ilyenna wished she could believe it. But Darrien had snatched away her hope too many times. Her gaze shifted to Burdin as he came between Otec and Undon and raised both his hands over his head. The crowd hushed. "To first blood?" he said without hope.

"To the death," her father corrected.

Burdin pursed his lips as if he wanted to argue, but then he yelled, "Then may victory follow justice!" He dropped his arms and rejoined the crowd.

Ilyenna's father hefted his axe, testing the balance, and lifted his metal-studded wooden shield. Undon circled left. Her father mirrored the move, fury still smoldering in his gaze. They lunged at each other a few times, as if testing each other out. Then her father brought his axe in a high arch and lunged forward. Blocking the blow with his shield, Undon shoved her father's axe away and swung level. Otec raised his shield to block, but Undon shifted so his axe skimmed across the shield and sliced clean into the flesh of her father's upper arm.

First blood.

Ilyenna gasped in horror as her father staggered back, his axe hand going to his wound. He grimaced. Blood flowed freely between his fingers and ran down his arm. Undon took advantage, lunging this time with a much stronger strike.

Backing away, Ilyenna's father lifted his shield with his wounded arm, though Ilyenna could tell his grip was weak. He barely managed to deflect Undon's blow. Ilyenna bit her lip as Undon rained blow after blow on her father's shield. Blood dripped steadily from Otec's arm onto the ground. If he lost much more, he would have no strength to fight. Her father was losing.

She couldn't let him die. Gripping her knife, she started forward. A hand seized her arm. "You have to let this happen."

She turned to see Rone holding her, a solemn look on his face. She tried to break free, but he held her tight. Other men shot her warning looks. If she tried to interfere, she knew someone would stop her.

There was nothing she could do. Her father would die. Any of these men could stop it, but they wouldn't. Her mind echoed what Ressa had said. Curse them all.

Undon swung for her father's head. Otec blocked it with his shield, but the studs that held the shield together snapped, breaking it nearly in half. Her father managed to shove the axe away with enough force to make Undon stumble. Otec kicked Undon's wrist and swung his axe for the man's side.

Though he was off balance, Undon managed to draw back for a short, level chop. If her father wanted to avoid the blow, he needed to abandon his swing and twist away. Ilyenna thought she saw recognition flash through her father's eyes. But he didn't try to avoid the strike. Undon's axe bit into her father's hip with a sickening crunch.

Otec's face screwed up in anguish, but he followed his swing through. His axe disappeared, buried in Undon's fleshy side. Otec had sacrificed his hip for a killing strike.

Falling to the ground, Undon let out a scream that made Ilyenna cover her ears and cringe. But she couldn't look away as her father clumsily wrestled his axe free of Undon's spine. Undon clawed at the ground, fighting for escape. Otec drew his axe back again and brought it down on Undon's neck, severing the head from the body.

The screaming stopped. Ilyenna thought she saw Undon's eyes focus on her before they gradually went blank. She knew the sight would haunt her for the rest of her life.

She forced her eyes to shift from Undon's lifeless face back to her father. He was alive, but blood flowed freely from his arm and hip. His face was gray and bleak. He threw his axe down as though sickened by it. With a grimace, he went to his knees.

Ilyenna could lose him yet. She shoved her way past the men and knelt next to her father, propping him up. "Father?"

He rested his weight on his good arm, breathing heavily. "I did what I could to avenge you, my girl."

Tears ran down Ilyenna's face. "I know you did, Father."

Other clan mistresses arrived, pressing a cloth into Otec's wounds and helping Ilyenna ease him to the ground.

Ressa gestured to Burdin. "We need to get him to the clan house. Now."

With a word from the high chief, strong hands lifted her father and took him away. Stumbling to her feet, Ilyenna started after them. Ressa grabbed her arm and pushed her back. "I'll take care of Otec. Another set of fool men still have to hack each other to pieces."

Rone! How could she have forgotten him like that? She whirled toward the knoll. Already, weeping Tyran women had wrapped Undon's body in a blanket of Tyran blue; blood blotted the top of it red. Ilyenna saw an unnatural lump on Undon's chest. With a shudder, she realized it was his head.

"So passes a warrior," one woman intoned.

"So passes a Tyran," another answered.

Clanmen gripped Ilyenna, pulling her away from the bloody ground and back to the cluster of men and women. From the silence, the thrumming started again. Rone pulled his undershirt and tunic off. He looked so different from her father, his gleaming skin stretched over taut muscles. His body seemed to emanate youth and strength. It could all be gone in a moment.

She didn't think she could go through this again. Her soul would shatter like glass—shatter and never be whole again. Ilyenna searched for something to hold onto. Something to keep her from falling apart. Then Varris was there, squeezing her hand reassuringly. She searched Ilyenna's face and spoke over the sound of stomping feet. "You don't have to watch."

"Not watching would be worse," Ilyenna said tightly.

To her ears, the stomping sounded like a death march. For one more man, it would be. She stared at the bloodstained ground under Darrien's feet. Her gaze traveled up his hard body to his face. Rage twisted his features—rage aimed at Rone.

A new fury rose within Ilyenna. "Curse them all!"

As if in answer, Burdin stepped forward, his arms raised. The stomping ceased. "To first blood?" he said again.

"Please. Please, Rone. I beg you. Please," she whispered.

He shook his head. "To the death!"

She felt a splinter in her soul, like the ice cracking under her feet all over again.

Burdin eyed Rone and Darrien. "You're both young yet. No one else has to die today."

Rone's gaze shifted from Darrien to Burdin. "Step aside, High Chief."

Burdin dropped his head and slowly backed away.

As soon as he was clear, Rone and Darrien lunged at each other. They exchanged a series of quick, hard strikes. Rone attacked first. Darrien recovered and pressed him back. With a sick feeling in her stomach, Ilyenna realized they were well matched. Winning could depend on luck or endurance.

She squeezed Varris's hand harder. "Please," she heard herself whisper, "if there's any justice for the living, let the dead take Darrien."

As she watched, Rone slipped through Darrien's guard, his axe swinging diagonally from his left shoulder. Darrien jumped back, his shield barely managing to deflect Rone's blow, but Rone's axe grazed his cheek.

Rone had taken first blood. Darrien didn't seem to have noticed. Their axes tangled, and he threw his shoulder into Rone, making him stumble back. With their axes locked, Rone forced Darrien to either move with him or release his hold. Darrien fell forward, knocking Rone down with him. They rolled together, Rone on top first and then Darrien. Both men pushed against their axe handles, trying to gain the advantage.

Darrien spat in Rone's eyes. For a half second, Rone wavered. Darrien twisted Rone's axe out of his hands. It landed with a heavy thud, just out of reach. Rone grabbed Darrien's axe handle, pushing it steadily away.

Darrien jerked it up and to the side, slamming the base into Rone's temple. Rone's arms went slack. He groaned.

"No," Ilyenna gasped. She lurched forward. One of the men grabbed her collar. It dug into her throat.

Darrien reversed the momentum, and the axe bit into Rone's ribs. Darrien pulled it free. With a wicked grin, he slowly stood. His back to Ilyenna, he drew his axe over his head.

With a tearing sound, she managed to jerk free. "Please, no!" She threw herself over Rone, shielding him.

Darrien stood over her, Rone's blood dripping down his axe onto his face. Darrien hesitated, then slowly lowered his axe. "What will you give me?" he whispered, triumph in his eyes.

Ilyenna felt the second crack in her soul. "Whatever you want." The words came easier than she'd expected. It was so easy to betray her clan and herself to save the man she loved.

Darrien looked behind her. She followed his gaze to see Burdin cautiously approaching. Darrien smiled softly. "Swear it."

"I swear it." Her voice broke.

He nodded. "It's done then." He freed his hands from his shield and reached toward her.

She hesitated, staring at his hand, smeared with Rone's blood. Slowly, her gaze shifted to Rone. Though unconscious, he was breathing. He was alive. If she refused, Darrien would see those precious breaths ended.

Without taking her eyes from Rone, she slipped her hand into Darrien's. He pulled her to her feet. Burdin came up beside them and made sure Rone was indeed alive, then shot a questioning look at Darrien.

Darrien's act was firmly back in place. Loudly enough for the entire crowd to hear, he said, "Taking Rone's life will do nothing to erase the enmity between the Tyrans and Argons. My hope in sparing him is that he'll forgive the wrongs committed by my father and myself, allowing the business of healing to begin."

Burdin nodded cautiously. "I'm glad to hear it."

Darrien lifted Ilyenna's hand, stroking the thin veins with his thumb. "I cannot take back what I have done to Ilyenna, but I can do my best to make it right. I will marry her." He looked at her with something close to compassion in his eyes. Knowing how false it was, she shuddered. "That way, she'll have the chance for marriage—something my actions took away from her."

Burdin searched her gaze. "Ilyenna?"

"It's the only way."

Apparently surprised by her change of heart, the high chief continued to scrutinize her. "Children between the two of you would go a long way to healing the enmity between the Tyrans and Shyle," he finally said.

And guarantee Darrien regains his title as a clan chief, Ilyenna thought bitterly, because what good was saying it? Burdin would willingly throw a lamb to the wolves if it meant saving the flock.

Burdin's next words seemed more for himself than for her. "You're sure, Ilyenna?

Yes, the villain walks away the hero. And none of you know the difference. Still, she remained silent.

Darrien brushed the blood from his wounded cheek with his free hand. "Come, Ilyenna. Let us return to the Tyran camp."

She let herself be led away, but she couldn't stop herself from looking back. Varris was lifting Rone's head. His eyes blinked open. He glanced around in confusion before his gaze locked with Ilyenna's. Then the crowd blocked her view.

She still heard Rone's hoarse shout. "Ilyenna! Curse you!"

Her soul shattered into a thousand pieces.

22. A PROMISE

Ilyenna passed through the Tyran encampment with her head down. She felt the Tyrans' eyes on her. Soon, Darrien lifted the flap to the center tent and gestured for her to enter. He stepped in behind her and secured the flap. She felt his gaze on her back, but she didn't look up. She couldn't. She was the walking dead.

Finally, Darrien moved. She heard the scrape of wood on wood and the slosh of liquid in a mug. The unmistakable smell of Riesen whiskey burned Ilyenna's nostrils. She heard him throw it back, swallow, and let out a satisfied "ahh." The mug hit the table and he sat heavily. "Well, I have to admit this all worked out better than I dared hope."

"You had doubts?"

He chuckled. "A game as complicated as this rarely turns out so well." He was silent for a time. "Really, Ilyenna, you've done me many favors—favors I both love and hate you for. You killed my brother. Your father killed mine, allowing me to become the Tyran clan chief long before even I'd planned."

"You're not the clan chief. Not anymore."

Ambition glittered in Darrien's eyes. "I will be. Believe that."

She did. She turned and scrutinized him. "He was your father. Have you no sorrow?"

Darrien looked away. "It is unfortunate. But he would've died sooner or later." He sniffed loudly and shrugged. "For me, sooner was better."

She was going to marry a monster. A monster who would share her bed and raise her child—Rone's child. She pressed her lips together. If Darrien even suspected a piece of Rone grew within her, he'd kill it. That meant she had to share his bed. And soon. She shuddered. "What about me? Is sooner better for me, too?"

He studied her dispassionately. "We need children, Ilyenna. You know that." He poured himself another drink and threw it back, then stood and walked toward her.

Unable to stop herself, she backed away. "Why?"

Darrien smiled, the same cruel, wicked smile she'd seen him wear before he did something brutal. She backed up until she could go no farther. He took the last few steps slowly, drawing out her fear. His hot whiskey breath blew against her skin. She looked away. He tugged off the cord holding her braid in place, pulled it loose, and ran his hands through her hair.

Had Rone really done the same only a few hours before?

He brushed her neck with the backs of his fingers, then rested his hand around her neck. Just a little squeeze and he'd be choking her. "I've always been fascinated by you. You're so . . . different from the other clanwomen."

Ilyenna grimaced. She'd always been different. Dark eyed. Thin. She'd always hated being unusual, standing out when she'd wanted nothing more than to fit in. She hated it even more now.

He caressed the skin above the collar of her undershirt. "Not many things pull my attention away from my pursuit of power. And none of them fight the way you did." He bent down, nuzzling the skin he'd just caressed. "Won't you fight, Ilyenna? Just a little?"

She squeezed her eyes shut. "You cannot hurt one who is already dead."

He started undoing the laces of her underdress. "Oh, come now. I know the fire still burns in you. Let it flare up again. This won't be nearly as much fun without it."

She bit the inside of her cheek so hard she felt salty blood pooling in her mouth.

"Darrien Tyran!" came the shout from outside.

Ressa. Ilyenna nearly cried out in relief.

Darrien groaned and closed his eyes. "That woman will suffer a most abominable death." There was a promise in his words that took Ilyenna's breath away. He backed a step away from her and then another. She sucked in a deep breath and eagerly scooted away from him.

"Yes, Clan Mistress?" he shouted.

"It's against tradition for an engaged clan mistress to stay with her betrothed's clan. Since Ilyenna's clan isn't present, I offer the Riesens' hospitality."

"Traditions," Darrien growled under his breath.

Without invitation, Ressa entered the tent, letting in a fresh gust of air. Behind her came four of the Riesens' strongest men. Ilyenna practically ran to the woman's side.

Ressa took one look at Ilyenna's loosed hair and the laces undone below her throat and grabbed her like she'd never let go. "I could go speak to Burdin about this."

Ilyenna recognized Ressa's words for the threat they were. Apparently, so did Darrien. "Come, there's no need for that. Ilyenna and I've already shared a bed. What's the difference now?"

Ressa smiled, but it looked more like she was baring her teeth. "Whether or not that is true," she spat, "Ilyenna deserves to be treated with respect. After what you've admitted doing to her, I cannot imagine you would disagree."

Darrien narrowed his eyes into a glare. "Careful, Clan Mistress."

Ressa returned his glare as she backed away, still firmly gripping Ilyenna. "Oh, I'm always careful."

The moment Ilyenna left the stuffy tent, she sucked in air like she'd never get enough. Outside, twilight was coming on. Oblivious to her plight, the people had already begun their revelry.

Ressa didn't say a word until they were safely back in her tent. Her men followed. She guided Ilyenna inside, then walked back out. Through the tent flap, Ilyenna watched her round on the guards. "Darrien Tyran is the most despicable, lying tyrant to ever walk the clan lands," Ressa explained. "If I hear that any of you have repeated his lies, I'll have you all strapped so hard you'll wish Darrien was your clan mistress. Am I clear?"

All four men nodded like little boys eager to escape their wooden-spoon-toting mother.

Ressa grunted. "Good. Now all of you are posted outside this tent. No one gets in or out unless they sleep here or I've approved it." She shooed them away. "One on each side. Go."

Ilyenna could see the flickering shadows as the men took their positions around the tent. She took no comfort in their presence. They were all just delaying the inevitable.

Ressa rounded on Ilyenna, her fists planted firmly on her hips, but her words were as soft as a lamb's ear, "You must really love Rone."

Ilyenna closed her eyes. "How is he?"

The older clan mistress was silent for a long time. "His left lung collapsed." Ilyenna took a sharp breath and nearly choked on it. "We had to force some whiskey down his throat before he calmed down enough for us to heal him. We used a sea urchin spine to suck most of the air out of his lung cavity so his lung could fill with air again. Then we sewed it shut. When I left him, he was muttering threats to anyone who came near."

Ilyenna silently pleaded his wound wouldn't become infected. "Can I see him?"

"Ilyenna—" Ressa hesitated. "He thinks you've betrayed him."

Ilyenna bit the inside of her cheek, but it was so sore she quickly released it. "He would see it that way." She couldn't deal with it now. She didn't have enough strength in her. "Father?"

"Madder than a caged bear. But he's not moving very good, so he's complying."

Ilyenna slumped in relief. The men she loved were still alive, despite their own foolishness.

"Dying is a lot easier than living through hell," Ressa finally said.

"I know," Ilyenna replied, and even to herself, her voice sounded dead.

"I suppose you do." Halfway out the tent, Ressa turned. "I'll try, but I don't think there's anything else I can do for you."

Ilyenna lay down on her blankets. "I know."

***

"Wake up, Ilyenna. Come on, wake up!" Varris shook her shoulder.

Ilyenna wasn't sure how she'd managed to fall asleep. Perhaps giving up was easier than fighting after all. Still groggy, she sat up. The sounds outside revealed that the night's festivities were in full swing.

"I managed to get rid of your guards." Taking her hand, Varris led her out of the tent. "The Tyrans have announced they're leaving tomorrow."

Ilyenna had expected that. "Where are we going?" she asked.

Varris paused, glancing cautiously between tents before hurrying forward. "Rone's worse."

Ilyenna stumbled. "How much worse?"

Grim faced, Varris tugged her forward. "His wound is fevered. But it's not just that. It's like he's given up—like he wants to die."

Numb, Ilyenna allowed herself to be dragged through crowds of revelers, the different colors of the clans weaving around her like a living tapestry. Music, laughter, and mouthwatering smells danced on the salty air. Bright shells winked from the eves, and firelight flickered into sight between houses or tents before disappearing again.

Past the clan house's open doors, Varris led Ilyenna up the ladders to a bedroom. She nodded toward the closed door. "We've only got a few moments."

Ilyenna hesitated before pulling the latch and slipping inside. Rone lay on the bed, his face as white and shiny as a tallow candle. Breaths wheezed past his lips. He stared at her through bloodshot eyes fogged over with fever.

Ilyenna moved to stand before the bed. Neither she nor Rone spoke for an unbearably long time. Finally, she couldn't stand the silence anymore and said, "The Tyrans are leaving in the morning. They'll be taking me with them."

"It seems you sacrificed yourself for nothing," Rone rasped.

Ilyenna's legs lost their strength and she collapsed onto the bed. "Don't say that."

Rone's answering grunt transformed into a violent cough. He held his ribs as pain creased his face.

Ilyenna watched him helplessly, wishing she could take away his pain.

Spent, Rone lay back against the pillows, his eyes closed. There was blood on his teeth, his chin. "I would've given my life for you."

Ilyenna reached for his hand, but he pulled away. "I did give my life for you," she said softly.

He stared at her until understanding dawned on his face. He lay back against the pillows. "I'm dying, Ilyenna."

She leaned forward, suddenly terrified. "No! You can't. You have to try. You have to fight."

He studied her, anguish lining his face. Then he looked away. "I don't have anything to live for. Darrien took it all."

Ilyenna stared at the door, hating that she only had moments to say goodbye. Debate raged within her. Finally, she leaned down and said in her softest whisper, "You have a child to live for."

Rone's brows drew together. "A . . . child?"

She took his hand and pressed it to her belly. "Yes. Yours."

His gaze flicked from her eyes to her belly and back again. He pulled away, pressed his palms into his eyes, and groaned. "Oh, Ilyenna, what've I done to you?"

She rested her hands lightly on his, then pulled them away. "You gave me memories I'll cherish for the rest of my life." She smiled, wanting so badly to give him some sense of peace. "I'll raise this baby the way it should be raised. Someday, it'll change the Tyran clan."

Rone flashed the dangerous gaze she'd seen so many times. "Darrien cannot raise my child, cannot bed the woman I love. I'll come for you, Ilyenna. I'll start a war if I have to."

"The Raiders are still out there," she said furiously. "None of us are safe. Your clan and mine—" She stuttered to a stop when she realized the Shyle was no longer her clan. The Tyran was. She shook her head. "You are a clan chief. Your first responsibility is to your clan." Ilyenna opened her eyes and glared at Rone. "Don't forget that."

Varris tapped on the door. "Ilyenna? Please hurry."

Ilyenna couldn't bear to look Rone in the eye. "Try–try to forget me," she said as she stood up.

"Ilyenna, don't. Don't do this."

She bent down and pressed her lips to his forehead. "It's already been done," she whispered against his skin. She allowed herself one last look at him before she slipped out the door.

23. The Balance

Ilyenna waited at the edge of the Riesen encampment. Ressa and Gen stood silently at her side. She'd tried to say goodbye to her father, but he'd refused to see her. The few items she had—all gifts from Varris—were rolled into the blanket she held in her arms. She knew what she was going back to, but she couldn't bring herself to regret her decision to save Rone. Darrien might've won, but she'd make the best of it somehow.

She watched as the Tyran wagons slowly began winding away from Cardenholm. One horse broke away from the group and started toward Ilyenna and her friends. Long before she could make out Darrien, she recognized his bay horse. He pulled the animal to a stop in front of her. "It's time to go, Ilyenna."

Slowly, she turned to face Ressa and Gen. They'd done so much for her, risked so much. "Thank you. For everything."

Ressa gripped her in a fierce hug. "I'm so sorry we failed you."

Ilyenna stepped back. Gen's gaze held a mixture of anger and sorrow. She smiled at both of them. "You didn't fail me."

She turned to Darrien. He reached down to pull her up, and his face stiffened with pain. Ilyenna remembered that he would have been strapped sometime yesterday and a surge of triumph coursed through her.

Before she could take his hand, Ressa cleared her throat and said, "Of course, we must still honor traditions. My daughter, Varris, will accompany Ilyenna as a chaperone."

At that moment, a harried-looking Varris bustled out of their tent, a large bundle in her arms.

Darrien's fists tightened around his reins. "Though the gesture is appreciated, I refuse."

Ressa smiled haughtily. "I've already discussed this with High Chief Burdin, and he agreed that measures must be taken to ensure Ilyenna is treated properly. If Varris reports otherwise, you will permanently lose your position as clan chief."

Ilyenna felt such a surge of gratitude that she nearly wept.

Darrien surveyed Ressa. "Fine." He reached toward Ilyenna again.

She wet her lips. "I'd rather walk, if that's all right?"

Her question seemed to catch him off guard. He studied her beneath drawn brows. "Do as you wish. But keep up."

He turned his horse and kicked him into a lope. Varris squeezed Ilyenna's hand. "Don't worry. Mother and I have a plan."

"What of the steward?" Ilyenna asked.

Ressa blew out. "He's in Deliaholm, so it will take him a few days to arrive."

Her hand in Varris's, Ilyenna left Cardenholm. With every step, she was aware of the growing distance between herself and those she loved. But she couldn't bring herself to cry. Tears were for the living, not for one marked by the dead.

The group paused at midday to rest and water the oxen. A woman brought Ilyenna and Varris some dried fish and biscuits. They ate beside the river before moving on with the others. Just before dusk, the group stopped for the night. After the woman gave Ilyenna and Varris some food, she showed them to a wagon they could sleep under.

To Ilyenna's surprise, Darrien seemed to be keeping his promise. She didn't see him that night and only caught a few glimpses of him the next day. Just before going to bed on the third night, she saw him laughing with a Tyran girl. He glanced at Ilyenna before quickly turning back to the girl. Ilyenna thought she'd caught a glimpse of what her marriage would be like, women constantly shifting in and out of Darrien's arms. That was fine with Ilyenna.

As long as he was with them, he wouldn't be with her.

It took nearly a week to reach Tyranholm. Ilyenna was footsore and tired, but in better shape than she'd dared hope for. Breaking into a run as they entered the village, she searched for Narium. But the older clan mistress saw her first.

With a shout, she abandoned her work in the fields and ran toward Ilyenna. "Rone? Where's my son?"

"He's recovering," Ilyenna shouted back.

Narium gripped her in a fierce hug. "Recovering from what?"

Ilyenna looked away. "The Council sided against the Tyrans." Other Argon and Shyle women were arriving. Ilyenna noted how much better they looked since Darrien hadn't been around to beat them. If she wasn't mistaken, most had even put on some weight. Ilyenna didn't doubt Metha had something to do with that.

But something was wrong. She counted again. Three women were missing. "Where are Jossa, Wenly, and Kanni?"

None of the women would meet her gaze. Ilyenna turned to Narium.

The woman shook her head. "Kanni died from a fever from her whipping. Wenly replaced you in the clan house. Her skirts caught fire, and she died the next day."

"And Jossa?" Ilyenna's voice felt far away.

Narium folded her hands across her middle. "She made a run for it. She never came back."

Jossa had been the one to bring Ilyenna the washing at the river the day she ran away. She felt a tremor of pain inside her, but it couldn't gain purchase within her shattered soul. "She might have made it."

Larina shook her head. "I overhead the Tryans talking about it. They caught her."

Ilyenna didn't need to ask why they didn't bring her back. She waited for the pain to assault her, but felt only a hollow emptiness. Three women had died. Ilyenna had saved three others. That couldn't be a coincidence. Three were slated for death, so when Ilyenna saved them, the Balance had simply taken three others.

She closed her eyes. She should have known something like this would happen. After all, it had happened before, when she'd gone to the dead asking for her father and brother to be spared.

"You're all free." She meant to shout it, but it came out as a whisper.

The women sagged in relief. Some of them hugged each other. A few Argon women lifted their skirts and ran to tell the men.

Narium didn't seem relieved in the least. "What's Rone recovering from?"

Forcing herself to meet Narium's gaze, Ilyenna took a deep breath. "Father and Rone demanded a fight to the death. Father killed Undon. Darrien bested Rone but spared his life. He was recovering when last I saw him."

"Why would Darrien spare my son? He's been plotting his death for months."

Ilyenna winced. "I . . . traded."

"Traded what?"

"My life for his."

Narium's eyes went wide. "You came back to this, for Rone?"

Ilyenna didn't answer.

Narium stared at her for the longest time. "Such devotion can't go unrewarded. The Argons will be ever in your debt. I will ever be in your debt. It is a debt we will repay with your freedom."

Ilyenna could see where Rone got his fierce determination. "No," she said softly. "I'm afraid Undon and Darrien's treachery went deeper than simply against the Shyle and Argon clans. He's in league with the Raiders. Raiders who will be coming over the Shyle Pass."

Narium pursed her lips. "The Council—"

"Didn't believe me." Ilyenna's cheeks burned in shame. "Because Darrien claimed I was seeking revenge after he violated me. That the Raiders staged the attack on the Tyrans, that it was their doing all along."

"After all he's done, they believed him over you?"

Ilyenna shrugged. "He was very convincing."

"Narium!"

Ilyenna started at the sound of Darrien's voice. He galloped his horse toward them. He jerked the animal to a halt, then jumped down and faced Narium. "Clan Mistress Narium, Burdin has ordered you home as fast as possible to raise what's left of your clanmen. You're to send them to Shyle Pass." Darrien bent low and said mockingly, "You have my apologies at the death of your husband. It was all such a tragic misunderstanding."

Narium balled her hands into fists. "This isn't over."

Excitement flashed in Darrien's eyes. "Give my regards to your son. If he's still alive, that is."

Narium took a threatening step forward. "You would have done well to remember the difference between an enemy and an ally. Now it's too late."

He rested his hand on his axe hilt. "There is no difference."

Narium's gaze shifted to Ilyenna. She could see promises in the Argon clan mistresses's eyes—promises Ilyenna knew she was in no position to keep.

Without another word, Narium turned and walked away. Varris stepped closer and squeezed Ilyenna's hand reassuringly.

"Where are we to stay?" Ilyenna asked.

"In the women's house," Darrien said. He grabbed Ilyenna around the waist and kissed her hard.

Trying to imagine herself somewhere far away, Ilyenna let him.

He pulled away with a look of triumph. "Tradition," he scoffed with a glare at Varris, "dictates we have a wedding. I'll come for you tonight."

Ilyenna watched him go. Wagons full of goods were being unpacked and repacked as preparations were made for war. Several recently freed tiams from the Shyle and Argon clans were gathering their things to leave.

Ilyenna stood motionless in the center of it all—certain that she was drowning all over again.

Tonight, she would marry her enemy.

24. SUMMER'S GIFT

I lyenna lay on the only bed in the women's house, staring at the tiny beams of light coming through the holes in the roof. She held one beam in her hand. It left a tiny pocket of warmth on her palm.

"We just can't leave her! You know what he'll do," Larina argued with the other women.

Ilyenna grunted softly. "As if you can stop him."

"She's your clan mistress," Varris said hesitantly. "If she wants you to go, you should obey."

"She won't be my clan mistress much longer!" Larina blurted before clapping her hand over her mouth. "Oh, Ilyenna, I'm sorry."

Ilyenna held back a smile. While she'd been away, Larina had taken it upon herself to become the Shyle clanwomen's leader. It was an unexpected but pleasant surprise. But if Larina wanted to be a leader, it was time she learned some of the harder lessons. "Larina, you know the saying 'Sometimes you have to lose a sheep in order to save the flock.'"

Throwing her hands in the air, Larina started pacing again. "You're not a sheep!"

The other Shyle women watched her nervously. Ilyenna knew how desperately they wanted to run, how much they feared Darrien would change his mind and stop them. But they stayed. Partly, she guessed, out of loyalty, and partly out of guilt over leaving her behind.

With a sigh, Ilyenna released the little ray of light. She stood and gripped Larina's shoulders, halting her pacing. "Don't you understand? Raiders are coming over Shyle Pass. You have to warn our clan. You have to make sure your families are safe. Larina, if you're going to be a leader, you must learn to put the clan ahead of the clanwoman."

Wasn't that what High Chief Burdin did? a little voice inside her nagged. What they'd all done? By the Balance, it was hard to be the one thrown to the wolves.

Ilyenna looked at each of the women in turn before her gaze settled back on Larina. "You have to help Bratton. He'll be alone." Larina had loved Ilyenna's brother for years. Ilyenna had never approved, but if it got Larina out, all the better.

With a wistful look on her face, Larina gazed out the door, toward home. "But how can we leave you here with him?"

Remembering something her brother had said, Ilyenna released her. "Let the dead take care of themselves. You must concentrate on the living."

Larina gaped at her. "You're not dead!"

"I may as well be."

Larina stared at her for a long time before she finally nodded. The other women kissed Ilyenna goodbye and slowly shuffled outside.

The last one out, Larina paused at the threshold. "The Shyle are strong as stone," she whispered.

Ilyenna closed her eyes and took a deep breath. "Supple as a sapling," she finished. She lay back on the bed and waited for death or sleep—anything to take her away from her fate, if just for a moment.

Unfortunately, Metha came instead, barreling into the room with a bundle under one arm and a fat baby in the other. She set both down on the table and looked Ilyenna over with a critical eye. "No Tyran bride is going to look like she just walked a few hundred miles. Especially not one marrying the clan chief."

To Metha's credit, her voice didn't waver. Ilyenna studied her, looking for hidden remnants of jealousy or anger. But Metha simply looked bossy.

Well, that's nothing new, Ilyenna thought.

Ilyenna introduced Varris and Metha, then said, "And I did just walk a few hundred miles."

"That's no excuse for looking like it." Metha shook out a wedding dress. This one was old, simple, and beautiful. Sky blue, the Tyrans' color. Intricate embroidery lined the hems. Judging by the size, it had obviously been meant for Metha's wedding.

"I can't take your dress," Ilyenna said.

"Humph," Metha grunted. She hauled Ilyenna out of the bed. "Try it on so this girl of yours and I can get to taking it in." She started pulling Ilyenna's clothes off.

Helping only as much as was absolutely necessary, Ilyenna studied Metha. The woman was obviously flustered, but not about seeing Ilyenna's bare skin. "I thought you hated me," she said as they tugged the dress over her head.

Metha pulled pins out of her mouth and stabbed them into the dress. Ilyenna looked away. If she was going to be jabbed, she'd rather not know about it until it happened. Metha had almost finished them all before she finally spoke. "You were right. Darrien nearly killed me and Harrow. If he loved me, he wouldn't have done that, especially to his child."

Varris gasped and stared at Metha and Harrow. Metha stopped her fussing to frown at her. Varris quickly looked away. "Why didn't he marry you?" she blurted.

Pain crossed Metha's face but was quickly replaced by anger. "Because he'd already taken what he wanted from me. I didn't have anything else to offer."

Varris studied Ilyenna. "Then what does he want with you?"

Ilyenna folded the sleeve for Metha to pin. "To break me. And he wants claim to the Shyle." Her voice dropped to a whisper. "And revenge for me killing his brother and for my father killing Undon."

Metha froze, staring at Ilyenna. "Hammoth was a good man!"

Ilyenna looked away. "No. He was better than Darrien, perhaps, but good men don't murder women and children and band with Raiders."

"I don't believe he did any of that." Metha wiped her eyes as she struggled to pull herself together. "Even as a child, Darrien made sure anyone who crossed him paid dearly." She shrugged. "I thought it would make him a good leader. It might have, if he cared about anything other than power."

With quick, sure fingers, she undid the shoulder laces. The dress dropped to the floor, exactly as a wedding dress was meant to. Ilyenna shivered as her skin adjusted to being bare—and out of sick dread.

From the bundle Metha had brought with her, she pulled out a long sheet and a bar of soap. Normally, a procession of women would have accompanied Ilyenna from her home to the river. They would've helped her bathe, rubbed scented oils in her skin, and put flowers in her hair. Ilyenna was glad that part was not to be. She didn't want the ministrations of unknown women.

Metha handed the sheet to Ilyenna. "You'll be all right alone?"

She nodded. The only Tyran she had to fear was Darrien, and she couldn't see him moving up their rendezvous. No, he'd make her dread every second of the wait. She wrapped the sheet around herself and hurried to the river. She did a thorough job, not for Darrien, but for herself.

Numerous fairies spun around the flowers. The blooms grew bigger, their scent stronger. It was almost as if the summer fairies were giving Ilyenna a wedding gift. Still, she left the flowers where they grew. She was halfway back to the women's house when Hanie appeared. The girl's face was red from crying. Ilyenna knew she'd just learned Undon was dead—by Ilyenna's father's hands.

Hanie shyly handed her a fistful of brightly colored flowers, saying in a voice thick with tears, "I picked these for you. No one else would."

Ilyenna's heart sank at the child's honest words. It appeared the other Tyrans wouldn't be eager to accept Ilyenna. "Thank you, Hanie, for your kindness. It means a great deal." Her voice tripped over the last few words, and she realized how much she really meant them.

Hanie and Metha. The only friends she had in this place.

With a small smile, Hanie turned and ran away. Ilyenna walked slowly back to the women's house. Now that her wedding was so close, she wanted to delay as much as possible. She kicked rocks and stopped to gaze into the woods. When she arrived at the house, she sighed and went inside.

Metha looked up. "We only had time to do a running stitch. It'll have to do."

Ilyenna smiled for Metha's and Varris's benefit. "No one will notice." She didn't care what she looked like on her wedding day, but she wanted them to know she appreciated their efforts.

Metha yanked the sheet off and tugged the dress over Ilyenna's head. She ran a broken-toothed comb through Ilyenna's damp hair. She weaved a stalk of wheat in a thin braid from ear to ear across Ilyenna's head. The only time a clanwoman wore her hair down was on her wedding day.

"Where did you find all those flowers?" Varris asked as she took them one by one and handed them to Metha, who wove them through Ilyenna's hair.

"Hanie brought them," Ilyenna replied.

Metha's fingers slowed and she said, "I knew she'd come around."

When they'd finished, Metha held up a mirror that was so old the outer edges had black, spiderweb-like cracks around the edges.

"You did a good job," Ilyenna said. Her black hair hung to her waist, dotted with flowers. The dress's blue was the color of the winter sky. Though the seams were a bit rough, it fit her well. It was snug across her bust and waist. There was no overdress—nothing to hide or distract. A clanwoman's wedding dress was meant to show off the bride. Unfortunately, it made Ilyenna feel more vulnerable. She wished Rone could see her like this, with flowers in her loose hair.

She wished it was him coming to her door. Instead, Metha left to tell Darrien that Ilyenna was ready.

While Metha was gone, Varris's gaze darted from the door to Ilyenna. "Listen to me, Ilyenna. Mother sent Riesen clanman to the border. They're waiting for us."

Ilyenna bit her lip. "We'd never make it."

Varris gripped Ilyenna shoulders and shook her. "Rouse yourself, Ilyenna! I know you're fighting the sadness. I know it's overwhelmed you, but you have to keep trying! You can't give up and go quietly."

Tears stung Ilyenna's eyes. "How will I get away?"

Varris gripped her knife and held it out, hilt first.

"You want me to kill him?" Ilyenna gaped at the weapon. "They'll hang me!"

Varris shook her head. "Mother and I spoke with Clan Chief Burdin. You're a clan mistress. Any crimes you commit will be tried before the Council. They would never convict you. In fact, they will claim you killed Darrien for treason."

Ilyenna tried to piece the fragments of her soul back together. "I'd have to escape first! There are Tyrans everywhere. How will I make it to the Council?"

Varris nodded toward the stable. "I'll have horses waiting. After Tyranholm sleeps, we'll run for it."

Ilyenna took the knife and stared at it. It felt heavy in her hand. "I'm a healer, not a murderess."

Varris closed her hand over Ilyenna's. "How many innocent people are dead because of Darrien? How many more will die if he lives? This is the only way the Council can do away with him without stirring up a civil war."

Ilyenna shot to her feet. "You've had this planned for days! Why did you wait until now to tell me this?"

Varris winced.

Ilyenna's fingers tightened around the knife. "The Council planned this from the beginning."

Varris pursed her lips. "I'm sorry, Ilyenna. They're just trying to save the lands."

Ilyenna threw her hands up. "They're using me! If keeping me alive sparks the civil war they so fear, they'll hang me anyway, despite their promises."

Varris went stiff. "That won't happen. Mother and I would smuggle you out before it got to that point."

Ilyenna tipped back her head and laughed. "You really are as naive as I was. If you smuggle out a murderess, they'll hang you in my place. Are you willing to risk that for me, Varris?"

Tears filled the girl's eyes. "I risked my life to come with you. And I'll risk it again when we escape. Isn't that enough?"

Ilyenna's shoulders sagged. "I'm sorry. It's not your fault."

A knock sounded. Ilyenna started and stared at the door.

Varris took the knife and shoved it up Ilyenna's sleeve. "The Council came up with a way to ensure your freedom. Take it."

Ilyenna waited for her emotions to drown her, for tears to well in her eyes. But nothing came except an immense sadness. When a man and a woman came together, they joined the opposite sides of the Balance, making a circle. The Link. Marriage to Darrien was anything but balanced. It was a mockery of what she'd had with Rone.

The door flew open. Darrien gave a slight nod of approval and stepped inside. Ilyenna's mouth suddenly went dry. She stood rooted to the spot, unable to move.

He smiled wickedly at her. "You can come on your own or be dragged."

His obvious delight at the prospect finally did it. He would never touch her. Just before she left the house, she turned to look at Varris. The woman stood rooted to the spot, her face ashen. "Take it," she mouthed.

Ilyenna gave a slight nod. Walking past Darrien, she started toward the clan house. Already, twilight was coming on.

He hurried to catch up. "Eager are we?"

She wanted to vomit. "Let's just get this over with."

He grabbed her arm, steering her away from the clan house. Just below his fingertips rested Varris's knife. Ilyenna felt sweat bead her brow. If he felt it . . .

But he hadn't noticed it yet. "It's not often a clan chief marries," he said. "We have people to greet."

He was actually going through with the traditional parade? Would his foolishness never end? "Your clanmen are leaving for war, and you want them to celebrate? Give you gifts? Besides, as soon as the steward comes, you'll be disposed."

"That," Darrien said, his voice slung dangerously low, "will never happen." He led her down a street.

Little girls ran ahead of them, throwing flowers and shouting, "The bride comes!"

People came to the doors. Women shouted well wishes, while the men called out innuendoes. Gifts were handed out, gifts which young boys carried ahead, shouting. More girls came from the houses to throw flowers at Ilyenna's feet.

It was all for show. Ilyenna could see fear in the clanwomen's faces, and annoyance in the clanmen's. The knife felt heavy above her wrist. "You're just doing this to draw out my fear," she said to Darrien.

Turning down yet another street, he waved. "Of course, now smile."

She didn't bother. He could pretend all he wanted, but she refused. "Don't you understand? You've already taken everything," she said. "You've nothing to threaten me with. Nothing to hold hostage."

They passed the last of the houses. The boys' arms were loaded with gifts, everything from barrels of beer to burlap sacks of grain. Darrien bent down to her, his lips brushing her ear. Clanmen shouted and hooted at the sight. She felt his lips pull into a smile. "Everything? Oh, no. I have one more thing to take from you."

She smiled to herself and thought, Oh no you don't. I already gave it to Rone. And you'll die before you ever touch me. She longed to say the words out loud, to wipe the smile from his face.

Just before they entered the clan house, Darrien turned to the crowd. Ilyenna saw Varris standing at the back, her hands crossed over her stomach. Darrien smiled at her as two men took up positions beside her. "Because you are an honored guest on this momentous day, Varris of the Riesen, I've ordered an honor guard to see to your safety and every need."

Varris's hands dropped to her sides and her gaze met Ilyenna's. Ilyenna's head spun until she was sick. Darrien gripped her arm again, pulling her inside and shutting the door to the shouts outside.

Ilyenna wondered how he'd known she and Varris were

planning to escape—and if he already knew about the knife a finger's breadth from his hand. As he pushed her up the ladder, Ilyenna noted Metha's blankets rolled up beside the wall. Harrow's basket lay next to it. This was Metha's home. Her gifts. Harrow's heritage. Ilyenna was a thief here.

But she hadn't taken away Metha's place on purpose. At least the woman seemed to understand that now, though Ilyenna doubted Metha would ever forgive killing Darrien.

Darrien opened the door to his room. Ilyenna was numb. Unfeeling. Dead. She felt the outline of the knife against her skin. She studied Darrien's face, looking for any sign of humanity. "You don't have to do this."

He grunted. "I've been looking forward to this for a long time. Now, you can come in by yourself or screaming."

She stared into the room full of dead things and took a hesitant step forward. The rest weren't so hard. She found herself beside the bed, staring out the window into the night sky. Could she really go through with killing him? What other choice did she have?

"So, what can I do to rile you up?" Darrien asked. "I like you better when you're feisty."

Yes, she could kill him.

He pulled her hair over her shoulder and began kissing her neck. She eased the knife down between her fingers.

"What if I said you were right, that my father and I were in line with the Raiders? That they promised us all of the Shyle and Argon lands if we crippled your clans and kept the pass clear. Would that make you fight?"

That explained why he'd taken a clan chief and two clan mistresses. A leaderless clan was a weak clan. Anger coursed through Ilyenna with such heat that she wondered how it didn't consume her. She calmed herself before asking, "Then why bother with me?"

Darrien slowly tugged at the laces at her shoulders. "If the Raiders fail, the Shyle will still be nearly destroyed. Of course I'd step in, take care of my wife's clan. I'd have claim to."

"And if the Raiders defeat the clans, you'll kill me?" she said.

He chuckled. "No. I don't think I will. You're much too amusing to kill."

She thought of all the people dead because of Darrien, and how many more would die in the future. She wanted to fight him, to scratch his eyes out and feed them to him. Her insides quivered with rage. Spinning, she plunged the knife toward him.

Darrien caught her arm and twisted it behind her back. She cried out in pain.

He laughed. "Took you long enough to use that knife."

He tried to pull the knife from her, but she tightened her grip. He twisted her arm so hard he lifted her from the ground. She felt something tear in her shoulder. He jerked the knife from her hand and threw her on the bed.

Her breath coming hard and fast, she stared at the knife in his hand. She'd failed.

"I figured you'd try something like this," Darrien said matter-of-factly. "I would have."

"I'll tell the Council what you've done."

He shook his head. "By then, it will be too late. The Raiders will be here." As he took a step toward her, a knock sounded at the door.

"Not now!" Darrien shouted.

"I'm sorry Clan Chief, but one of Burdin's men has come from Shyle Pass. The Raiders are almost through, and their numbers are overwhelming. They're calling for every able-bodied clanmen to move out as soon as word reaches them. You have to give the order now."

Darrien let out a low, guttural growl. "There's no way my clanmen can be ready to move out tonight. Tomorrow. Maybe the next day."

"Clan Chief, the man has orders from Burdin himself."

Darrien ran his hands through his hair. "I'll be right back. Don't move."

When the door slammed behind him, Ilyenna felt the first tremor. Then her whole body started to shake so hard she had to clench her teeth to keep them from chattering. Using the dress, she scrubbed Darrien's saliva from her neck and shoulder. Tears started down her face as she yanked the laces of her dress tight.

She remembered Varris's words, "Don't stop fighting."

Ilyenna glanced around, looking for some kind of weapon. Then she remembered. Her clan belt still hung from a nail above the bed. She scrambled onto the bed, grabbed her belt, and jerked the knife out of its sheath.

She heard Darrien coming. She whirled away and cradled the dagger to her breast, her heart throbbing in her chest.

She flinched when the door banged open. He grabbed her from behind. "Let's get this over with."

Ilyenna whirled and pressed the dagger into his middle. She tried to force herself to kill him, sink it into his flesh, but she just couldn't.

Darrien raised his hands. "We've been over this. You're a healer, not a killer. Now give me the knife." He reached for it.

Ilyenna pushed harder. He backed away. She moved with him. "You keep forgetting I killed your brother."

Darrien's expression hardened. "You kill me and they'll hang you."

Ilyenna smiled. "I know."

He pivoted away from the knife and tried to bat her hand away. She braced herself and charged him. The knife slipped easily into his belly.

He stared at the blood dripping down his shirt. "I—you—"

She pulled out the knife. Blood gushed onto the floor. Ilyenna's healer instincts kicked in. She could staunch it. If she'd missed his intestines, he might even survive.

But she made no move to help him.

Darrien collapsed onto the floor, blinking up at her. Ilyenna gaped at the bloody knife in her hands. She wanted to throw it away, but it was all that stood between her and Darrien.

She imagined facing Metha in the morning. The Tyrans would kill Ilyenna. She glanced down at Darrien and realized he had either passed out or died. She threw the knife onto the bed and wiped her bloody hands on her wedding dress. She felt like she was suffocating. She threw open the window, gasping for breath. She looked down. Too far to jump, but not far enough to kill her.

She closed her eyes and felt the warm breeze on her face. The smell of flowers was so strong. She'd only smelled them that strong twice before. Could it be? She peered into the gloom. Leto stood at the edge of the woods. She was plump now and her flesh seemed to glow with golden light.

She was staring at Ilyenna with something close to fury in her gaze.

"Please," Ilyenna choked out. "Please help me."

A flash of pain crossed the summer queen's ebony face. She began slowly backing away.

"No!" Ilyenna gasped. "No! Come back!"

Leto was gone. Somehow, Ilyenna knew the queen hadn't just slipped into the forest—she had truly disappeared. Ilyenna could feel it. She leaned against the windowsill. For the first time, she almost wished she'd let Rone die.

Hating herself for the thought, she let out a sob. She took a breath of the cold air. She felt the cold seeping into her skin, into her muscles. It felt so comforting, so good. Collapsed against the windowsill, she tried to come up with a plan. But she could see no way of escaping her fate. Truly the dead had marked her as their own.

Her cries were so hard she didn't hear it at first. It was a loud whisper before she finally swallowed a sob and listened. "Ilyenna."

She straightened and glanced around in shock. In a matter of moments, clouds had rolled in, covering the stars with threatening gray swirls. A frigid gust blew her hair behind her before enveloping the room. When had it turned so cold?

"Ilyenna."

Leaning out the window, she looked up at the sky. A single snowflake sped toward her. Ilyenna's heart stuttered. Could it really be one of the winter fairies, in the middle of summer?

The snowflake twisted and twirled toward Ilyenna. She stretched out her hand. She didn't know why, but she had to catch it. Suddenly, the snowflake shot forward and landed on Ilyenna's hand.

Some part of her was aware of Darrien bleeding on the floor, but the rest of her was focused on the snowflake. It didn't melt, and hope soared in Ilyenna's chest. Then the snowflake vanished. In its place was a tiny, ice-blue fairy with rabbit-fur wings. Chriel.

Her voice sounded like singing crystals. "I know you, Ilyenna. Know you as I know the language of the storms, the frost flowers that bloom in the ice, the sleeping sighs of the bears in their caves. You think of yourself as a healer. But as a winter queen, you will become a destroyer."

Ilyenna could only stare at the terrible beauty of the fairy.

Chriel fluttered her wings. "The powers of winter will allow you to save yourself and the ones you love. But there is a price. Before, you hadn't become winter yet. To do so is to be reborn. And after that, you'll never break free."

"I'll no longer be human?" Ilyenna asked.

Chriel cocked her thimble-sized head to the side. "You will give up your humanity. All of it—your memories, your emotions. You will be shattered, melted down, and reformed into something new." The fairy paused, looking sad. "To save yourself and the ones you love, you will have to lose them."

Ilyenna thought of her clan. Even now, the Raiders were coming down the pass. High Chief Burdin had called for every clanman in the lands. That meant it was bad. And the reinforcements might not make it in time.

Ilyenna shook her head. "I've already lost them."

Chriel fluttered off Ilyenna's palm and pressed her lips to Ilyenna's.

25. WINTER'S KISS

With the power of an avalanche, winter raged in Ilyenna's ears. Her already shattered soul was ground to powder and melted, then remade and reformed. She was Ilyenna no more. In an instant, winter had transformed her from a thinking, feeling woman into a force of nature. As cold and wind and snow embraced her, her fears and memories were frozen beneath a thick layer of ice.

She stood, reveling in her power and her oneness with winter. Her connection with millions of winter fairies snapped into place. She felt their joy at reuniting with her, their thrill at the chance for an early summer storm. They were an extension of herself. Their emotions were her own. The beating of her heart fell into rhythm with theirs.

Hefting her skirts, she stepped onto the sill.

Rough hands pulled her back. "I knew you had magic! I knew it. You will share it with me."

A man pointed a bloodied knife at her. She blinked at him, an unnamed distaste on her tongue. Who was he? What madness made him think he had the right to threaten her, the winter queen? But she was not one for violence. Especially against one so weak. "You don't want my anger, human."

He shook her. "Heal me!"

She cocked an eyebrow. "Don't try my patience."

He shoved the knife under her chin. "I'm dying. Heal me or I'll take you with me."

As one, Ilyenna felt the fairies' emotions turn with hers, from playful to rage. That rage roared in her ears like a thousand blizzards. "A fairy's kiss has the power to heal," she said.

The man hesitated as if some part of him sensed his peril, but then he grasped Ilyenna's head and pulled her mouth to his. When their lips met, she breathed out a full blizzard.

One snowflake was nothing dangerous, but Ilyenna spit out thousands. The man coughed and sputtered as they invaded his lungs. He tried to push away from her, but she held him fast, filling him with wind cold enough to freeze the sap in the trees. When she finally released him, a ring of hoarfrost coated his mouth. His lips were blue, and jagged bits of ice hung from his chin. His eyes wide, he clutched his throat, his mouth working like a fish. He no longer had the ability to draw breath, for she had frozen his lungs.

"A fairy's kiss also has the power to kill," she said.

His veins stood out on his neck. He stumbled, panic on his face.

She reached toward him. She felt no more enmity. He'd paid with his life. "Tell the dead the winter queen wishes them well. After all, we serve the same side of the Balance." She pressed her fingers to the man's neck and allowed her cold to surge into him.

He froze, a rictus of pain on his face. Ilyenna cocked her head to the side. Such a horrific sight. With a gentle push, she tipped him over. He shattered into a million pieces.

"Now he knows how it feels." She wasn't sure why she'd said the words, but they felt right.

The fire snapped in the hearth. It was making the room unbearably warm. Ilyenna held out her hand. Ice flowed from her palm, freezing the flames in place. "Ah," she sighed. "Much better."

But her relief over the man's death was short lived. The fairies were still furious—unlike Ilyenna, their anger hadn't been assuaged by his death. They wanted their own vengeance. Entwined as their minds were, their emotions overwhelmed her. Their need became hers.

She heard voices and turned. Qari, Tanyis, and Ursella flew into the room. Ilyenna let out a squeal of delight. Each of them came and pressed their lips to hers. Winter embraced her more tightly.

Qari, her wings like frost flowers, beamed. "Summer has withdrawn."

"We are free to dance!" Tanyis fluttered her wings in excitement.

Beating her wings like shards of ice so fast they blurred, Ursella zoomed across the room and hovered above what remained of the dead man. Her tiny nose turned up in disgust. "Your kind will pay for that."

Ilyenna heard the other fairies outside the window. They'd come quickly, filling the air with the sound of their wings. They'd brought the blizzard on their backs. If she didn't let them release their anger, they'd be sullen all summer. "Very well," she told them. "Let's dance."

She closed her eyes and let winter take her over, transforming her into a thousand flakes. She roared from the room. If any of the humans happened to look up, they'd only see the snowy outline of a woman raging through the heavens. Instead of wings, they'd only hear the rush of the wind, the clash of the flakes.

Calling the storm, she sped across the land. Her fairies joined her. But there was malice as they drove the storm. They sent the snow pelting against the buildings, howling down the chimneys to snuff out the fires. They pelted any wayfarers.

As they raged, Ilyenna happened over high mountains. She saw many, many men. At first, her fairies attacked them as they had the others. But for some reason, the sight of them made her memories churn beneath the frozen barrier that held them back.

A word bubbled up from the frozen ice that held the memories of her past life. Raiders.

Her fury built, piling up inside her like the snow on the ground. Her fairies reacted to her rage. Ilyenna forced her mouth open wide and swallowed the men, driving them into whatever shelter they could find. She rooted them out of hollowed logs, from beneath blankets. She showed no mercy, sending them to the dead in droves.

The more she raged, the more she became it. The cold and the storm enveloped her so completely she knew nothing but the storm, at one with her fairies' shared fury.

When the men were buried beneath a thick layer of snow, she moved on, looking for others. She didn't find many. Few caught out in the open had survived her initial fury. But she still wasn't satiated. "Find more," she ordered. The fairies fanned out, searching. Alone, she trolled the land. Then she saw a solitary traveler. She attacked, driving him back.

His horse ducked its head, its sides quivering. The man booted it, trying to drive it into the storm when it knew it needed to turn its tail to the wind and find others of its kind to huddle with for warmth.

Another cruel man. Ilyenna pummeled him again and again, until he finally abandoned the trembling horse and stumbled forward alone. Frustrated, she pulled back and blew with all her might. The wrappings around the man's face caught in the wind. He reached out, trying to catch them, but her wind jerked them away. He turned his face to the storm.

She stopped short. Somehow, she knew this man. Something within her broke the barrier. Her fury faded as her memories floated free. She could see them all. But it was like looking at someone else's life. Her past life. She remembered, but she felt nothing. She pulled away from winter, retaking her human form.

Using her wings that shimmered with the iridescence of an aurora, she fluttered curiously toward him. The man groaned, hunching unnaturally even for the cold. She came a little closer and a word came unbidden to her mind. "Rone."

More memories swelled inside her, bursting into her mind so fast she nearly fell from the sky. As it was, she barely caught herself from crashing. Still, she landed with enough force to shatter human legs.

Ilyenna hurried forward. Rone lay face first in the snow, his eyes closed. Her emotions were still frozen. She felt no fear, no sadness. But she remembered him—remembered loving him. The memory alone was strong enough to drive her to save him. She bent down, drawing the cold from his body into her own.

His eyes fluttered open. "Ilyenna?" he asked.

"The Ilyenna you knew is dead," she answered.

His head rolled back. She felt him again and sensed an unnatural heat in his body. "Fevered." Her other life supplied the word. She added a bit of cold, just enough to make him feel right.

Other fairies arrived. Though they didn't know the source of her new emotions, they felt them. Her compassion had swallowed their fury.

Holding the man called Rone in her arms, Ilyenna took to the skies. She found a house—the same one she remembered borrowing a draft horse from in her previous life—and landed on the doorstep. She knocked on the door. The humans inside opened it. They took one look at her and gaped, too afraid to even close the door.

Ilyenna shoved past them. She lay Rone down before the fire. Even the heat from those meager flames made her feel sick and wilted. She turned to find the humans gaping at her wings. Though she couldn't resurrect any emotions, she remembered enough to understand how ethereal she must look to them. With a thought, she made her wings disappear.

They blinked in disbelief and begin to rationalize what they'd seen in low, harried voices.

Ilyenna dug around in her jumbled memories. It was like sifting through the contents of someone else's life. Then she found the right memory. "He's sick. I need qatcha. Do you know what it is?"

The woman shook her head.

"Garlic, oregano, and onions, simmered with a silver spoon, salt, and chicken organs." Ilyenna recited. "I also need juice from crushed garlic. And clean rags."

As she started pulling off Rone's layers of clothing, she could smell the rot. Finally, she saw the source of the smell. The wound was swollen and red, obviously infected. "Give him whiskey. As much as he can hold."

The woman knelt next to Ilyenna and began pouring whiskey down Rone's throat by the spoonful. Ilyenna bathed the wound with whiskey while she waited for the alcohol to inebriate him. When his mumbling went from tight with pain to loose and random, she figured it was close enough.

She enlisted the help of the man and one of the older boys to hold Rone down. Pressing on the skin, she forced out the puss. Ilyenna rubbed and pushed and wiped and poured warm whiskey over the wound until only clear liquid and blood came out. Then she carefully separated the wound, sticking a silver spoon in sideways to keep it open. She scoured it with whiskey and a rag, cut off any dead tissue, and dripped pungent-smelling garlic juice inside.

Leaving in the spoon, Ilyenna left the wound open to the air. "Keep him warm, and keep as much of the qatcha down him as possible." She started toward the door.

"Wait," the woman cried.

Ilyenna turned expectantly.

"Where are you going?" The man asked. "That storm is no place for a woman like you."

Ilyenna smiled. "The storm is exactly the place for a woman like me."

She stepped outside. With a thought, her wings appeared. She shot into the thinning clouds. She heard the door being thrown open behind her, heard the confused shout. But she was already in the clouds.

Chriel appeared. She'd obviously been waiting for her. "The man?"

Ilyenna shrugged. "I hope he lives." At least, she thought she did. She felt regret for not loving him, but she didn't think she was capable of love anymore. "My memories knew what to do to heal him. He'll have to do the rest."

Ilyenna felt it then, the press of summer against her. It was strong and unbearably hot. She couldn't help but shrink before it.

Chriel looked to the south. "She's much stronger than us. It's her season."

Ilyenna followed Chriel's gaze and saw her, Leto, the summer queen. She had left when Ilyenna had begged for help, so that winter might come and restore Ilyenna.

Leto came to her with wings like maple leaves. They were trembling with the cold. In contrast, the heat made Ilyenna shudder. But in this half space between winter and summer, both could stand before each other for a brief time.

"Thank you," Ilyenna said simply.

Leto smiled. "In years past, I've fought with winter. Perhaps with you, fighting will not be necessary."

Ilyenna dipped her head in acquiescence. "I do not wish to fight you."

Hesitantly, Leto bent forward and touched Ilyenna's stomach. "Every year, I have a child. But winter never has. Strange."

Ilyenna felt the life within her, still growing, still strong.

Leto withdrew her hand. "It is summer."

Ilyenna understood. This was not her realm, not her time. Part of her wanted to fight, to stay and revel in winter a bit longer. She'd eventually lose, but she could draw out her time. Yet she respected the summer queen and was grateful for what the woman had done for her.

"Until summer ends, winter will not come again," Ilyenna promised.

She called her fairies to her with a thought and sped away. Behind her, she felt summer's heat spreading through her cold like a drop of milk in water.

26. AURORA

Ilyenna cut through the night sky in the form of an aurora. She pushed back winter's borders, directing her warrior fairies to act as sentinels. There was no moon tonight, only sharp stars that pierced the sky behind her. She shimmered at the center of the aurora. She tried to press further south, but her strength was dissipating before summer's power. It was as far as they would manage before the warmth of morning drove them back.

Ilyenna pulled herself back to her human form. The aurora condensed into her wings, which shimmered with color. An army of fairies took shape around her. The starlight gleamed dully off hundreds of their lithe bodies.

Ilyenna searched the forest below until she found a clearing to land in. She flared her wings, catching pockets of the wind to slow her descent. She landed gently on the ground, dry leaves crunching beneath her feet. Within moments, they were rimmed with frost. She crouched, letting her senses settle around her. In this land, the harvest was weak. Many of the trees had died from a late touch of winter. The animals would struggle to survive until next season. Even mankind, with their cursed fires, would find this winter a difficult one.

Ilyenna felt no joy or sorrow in their hardship. It was the way of the Balance. Good years and lean.

Her fairies awaited her orders. They had until morning and the day's heat to do their work. "Prepare the land for winter," she commanded.

Her frost fairies danced across the green leaves, sending tendrils of cold into the trees to warn them of winter's coming.

Chriel and the rest of the creature fairies sought out the animals. Ilyenna heard their whispers. "Hurry, hurry. Eat and grow fat, for sleep and rest and cold are coming."

Ilyenna watched as a rabbit lifted its nose to the air, listening to the fairies' warnings. When it saw her, it darted away. Closing her eyes, Ilyenna sent ribbons of her power outward, pressing against summer. "It is my time," she reminded Leto softly.

Ilyenna felt summer shiver. It instinctively dug deeper, trying to resist, but the season was shifting. Winter's power spread farther by the day. Ilyenna slipped through the forest and came across some of her frost fairies working on an apple tree.

The winter queen cocked her head to the side. In the darkness, the tree seemed to be made of layers of shadow, but she made out the heavy globes weighing down the boughs so they trailed along the ground.

Reaching out, she pulled an apple free and held it to her lips. She breathed out, letting winter's kiss sweeten the apple. She remembered promising Jablana that the winter fairies would spare her trees. It was a foolish promise to make. It went against the Balance.

But the promise had been made; there was no use in regret. Ilyenna bit into the apple, reveling in the cold sweetness on her tongue. She loved apples.

"My queen."

Ilyenna turned to see one of her warrior fairies flying downward. He was naked except for a loincloth of fur. He held the tip of his spear against a summer fairy's back. Ilyenna noted how careful he was not to touch her. Male fairies had no magic, and the heat from a summer fairy's touch could kill him.

The fairy had her arms wrapped tightly around her body. She was shivering. Her translucent wings seemed wilted.

"What would you have us do with trespassers, my queen?"

As part of their treaty, the summer fairies were to retreat when winter came. This fairy had broken that treaty, and Ilyenna was within her rights to execute her. But she knew how possessive fairies were of the trees and animals they tended throughout the season. "Take her to her side of the border and let her go. Do the same with any others you find. Only fight them if you must."

The warrior fairy bowed. "My queen."

She watched him fly away. The land was frozen from a late winter storm, yet the apple trees remained. With a sudden flash of clarity, Ilyenna realized where she was. She tossed the apple to the base of the tree and flared her wings.

"My queen, we only have a few hours before the heat of the day drives us away," Qari reminded her.

"I have something to attend to. Keep preparing for winter."

Qari's wings arched in question, but she bowed anyway.

Ilyenna pumped her wings, pushing herself into the air. She noted her fairies dancing joyously among the trees. A road flashed beneath her. She followed its winding path deeper into mankind's holds.

Eventually she came to a village. She landed among the cairns of the dead. They walked on her side of the Balance and welcomed her presence. Ilyenna nodded a brief greeting and searched the windows of the clan house.

As if he sensed her, a man appeared. She could see his face bathed in the golden glow of a candle. Blinded by the light, he could not see her. His flesh was flushed and warm, full of life. Rone. He had survived. She remembered everything. But she was a force of nature now. A woman no longer.

Still, she watched him, fascinated. His pale hair was tied back. She wanted to loosen it and see for herself if it was as soft as she remembered. She recalled his kindness—sharing his food with her, gently caring for her wounds, foolishly risking his life again and again to save her. But most of all, she remembered his lips on hers, his hands on her body.

The word mankind used to describe what had been between them. Love.

Behind her, Ilyenna felt heat, as if she stood too close to a fire.

Another of her warrior fairies darted to her, his wings stiff with alarm. "My queen, Summer comes."

Ilyenna nodded. "Let her come."

The fairy took up a defensive position beside her. Other warriors came down, their ice spears gleaming in the night.

Heat blasted the winter fairies. They wilted before it.

Ilyenna flared her cold outward to protect them. Winter and summer mixed, creating a sudden gust of wind.

A nimbus of power arrived in front of Ilyenna. It condensed into a white-hot form that brought with it the smell of desert-baked sand and spices. That form darkened to Leto. She was heavy with child. Male summer fairies surrounded her, their spears made of dark wood instead of ice.

The summer queen smiled. "We meet again, Ilyenna."

Ilyenna nodded. "Leto."

The woman glanced at the house behind Ilyenna and smiled knowingly. "By nature, winter is cold and unyielding. But the woman you were before was not. She was the kindest woman I had ever seen, which is why I helped you become queen."

Ilyenna wished Qari were here. She would know what the summer queen was hinting at. "Why do you tell me this?"

Leto smiled. "I have a consort, winter queen. You could as well."

"A winter queen has never had a consort before," Ilyenna said. Qari had made it clear that winter queens were too cold to feel something as fiery as love.

Leto rested a hand on her stomach. "Or a child."

Ilyenna refused to look at the clan house again, refused to acknowledge the bitter regret that cankered inside her. How could she be surrounded by hundreds of fairies and still feel completely alone? "He would never survive." Not in her castle made of ice.

"There is power in a fairy's kiss."

"A winter kiss?" Ilyenna eyed Leto carefully. "But what human would ever give up the power to dwell freely in both winter and summer?"

Leto nodded toward the clan house. "That man would."

"Why would you tell me this?" Ilyenna asked, narrowing her gaze.

Leto smiled. "You spared my fairy. A kindness returned for a kindness given." With that, the summer queen began to shine. She fragmented into swirls of light that withdrew with a sound like the wind through leaves.

As Ilyenna spread her wings to fly away, she cast a final glance at the clan house. Her gaze met Rone's. In the fading light from Leto's departure, he could see her through the window. Ilyenna wondered if Leto had done that on purpose.

The extinguished candle in his hand clattered to the floor. "Ilyenna."

At the sound of his voice, more memories stirred within her, and she realized that she, queen of all winter, was jealous of the girl she'd been before. Of the love she'd felt.

She nodded to her warrior fairies. "Summer is truly gone. Back to the border."

The warriors exchanged glances before bowing. "My queen."

Ilyenna looked back at the window, but it was empty now. She felt strangely hollow. But then the door cracked open.

Favoring his side, Rone ran toward her. His face was wan, his skin nearly as pale as hers in the moonlight. He stumbled to a halt before her, his breath hitching oddly. He shook his head, looking both amazed and afraid. "It's you, but then again it isn't."

She knew what he meant. She'd seen her reflection. Her skin was paler, white with a silver undertone. Ice blue tinged her lips. Her hair was loose and a little wild, with colorful wildflowers frozen in the strands. Her dress was made of a snow and ice. On her head, she wore a headdress of ice and diamonds.

And that wasn't all. An otherworldly aura of power shimmered around her.

He reached toward her but then stopped. "Is—is it really you?"

Ilyenna crossed the gap between them, pausing just before her skin touched his. "I will try to hold the cold back. You will tell me if it hurts you?"

Rone nodded. She brushed her fingers across his warm cheek. His breath caught.

Touching him tugged at something deep within her. "It didn't hurt?"

He shook his head and dropped to his knees. "It is you!" His breath misted the air. "Please forgive me for failing to save you."

He was shivering. With a touch, Ilyenna drew the cold away and helped him to his feet. "I saved myself."

He nodded slowly. "I know, but it cost you so much."

She glanced into the trees, watching her fairies dance. "I gained more than I lost."

She brought her other hand out and ran her fingers carefully across the planes of his face. "It is strange. I remember you. I know you. At one time, the soul that is mine loved you." She dropped her hand. "Now all I feel is regret. Regret because, though I live my life, the memories of the woman I was will not let me forget."

Rone caught both her hands under his own. "Ilyenna?"

She closed her eyes. "Yes?" she breathed.

She was surprised when his lips met hers, and even more surprised when she responded. Gasping, she stepped back and pressed her fingertips to her mouth. Though her lips felt pleasantly warm, she felt a surge of disappointment. "It's not there anymore. The love I had for you."

It wasn't entirely true. She felt something. A possibility, a chance for something to grow from the ashes of what had been their love. Perhaps even something stronger and more beautiful than before. But could she ask any man to give up everything for a mere possibility?

No. It wasn't fair, especially not for one who'd already give up so much. "The Balance protect you, Rone Argon." Ilyenna spread her magnificent wings.

He grabbed her hand. "I don't care what you've become. You are mine, and I am yours. That will never change."

"Rone—"

"Stay with me."

She studied him. "I want what she had. I want to love again. But I'm not even sure I'm capable of love." He took a step toward her. She backed away. "Do you think it is possible for you to love me as you once did her?"

He reached out tentatively. When Ilyenna didn't pull back, he cradled her cheek in his palm. "You still have the same soul."

Rone took her in his arms. She felt his warm body against hers. He kissed her with a longing and regret that made her hurt for him.

When she finally pulled away, the hard edges inside her seemed softer. "That I remember very well."

He smiled and moved to kiss her again, but she shook her head. She tipped her head up to the sky. "Tell Chriel to bring Elice here."

Rone's happy expression changed to one of disbelief as their daughter came, born on the backs of a hundred creature fairies, Chriel in the lead. Elice was wrapped in white fur. Slate brown eyes were set in a round face with pink lips, soft brown hair, and creamy skin.

"This is your daughter," Ilyenna said.

Rone simply stared. "She has your eyes and lips."

"And your chin and cheeks."

He cleared his throat and said thickly, "But how? The time couldn't have come yet."

Ilyenna cocked her head to the side. "Qari says we are never with child longer than a season."

He shook his head. "Can I hold her?"

Ilyenna took her daughter in her arms. The fur blanket fell back, revealing soft, delicate skin. Ilyenna handed her over.

Rone held her carefully, as if afraid she might break. "Elice?"

The girl reached up and patted his face. He flinched in pain.

Ilyenna tisked and touched his cheek, instantly drawing away the cold of Elice's touch. "We must teach her to keep her cold inside. Until then, you must be very careful."

His eyes wide, Rone rubbed his cheek. "What did she do?"

Ilyenna grinned and took Elice from his arms. Bending down, she let her child's chubby fingers skim the top of the nearby lake. Intricate, swirling patterns of ice fanned out. Quickly, Ilyenna withdrew Elice and wrapped her in the furs.

"Summer wouldn't approve," she said with a hint of pride.

Rone hesitated before tentatively taking Ilyenna's hand. "You can't stay here?"

She shook her head. "I am a queen. I live with my fairies."

"Then I will go with you."

Ilyenna watched Elice. "And what of your people?"

He looked sadly back at the clan house. "I never really came back to them." He touched her face again. "You're not the only one who has changed. I don't belong here anymore. I belong with you."

Ilyenna searched Rone's gaze for signs of doubt. All she saw was relief, as if a great pain inside him had eased.

"The transformation will make you impervious to the cold, but you shall never again feel the warmth of the summer sun on your face. Never smell a freshly mowed field. Never taste the sweetness of a juneberry. And you will never see your family again."

Rone didn't hesitate. "Since you left, I have felt none of those things. I have been empty."

"Chriel," Ilyenna called. The fairy with rabbit fur wings moved to take Elice. "I have chosen Rone Argon as my consort. Make him a friend of winter."

"Wonderful, my queen!" Chriel changed direction, fluttering forward and pressing her lips to Rone's.

He stopped shivering as golden sun spilled over the valley. "I—I'm not cold anymore."

Ilyenna smiled. For the first time since she'd been reborn as the winter queen, she felt whole.

Rone took her hand in his. He was smiling and splitting his gaze between Ilyenna and their daughter. "I love you," he said.

In response, she called an aurora to dance before the stars. Spreading her great wings, she drew him to her and took to the skies.

ACKNOWLEDGEMENTS

I first began Winter Queen in 2008. It would be nearly impossible to name every person who had a hand in the direction of the book during that seemingly interminable time span, but I would like to mention a notable few.

Thank you:

God—for letting me borrow Tolkien (literally) every once in a while.

JoLynne Lyon, Cami Checketts, Steve Diamond, Michelle Argyle, Chris Loke, and Julie Slezak—for always pushing me to create something more powerful than I thought possible.

Andrea Winkler, Cathy Nielson, Tiffany Farnsworth, Stephanie Jensen, and Rachel Newswander—for making my prose as transparent as Ursella's wings.

Kathy Beutler, Laura Sava, Robert Defendi, and Linda Prince—without your artistic talents, my readers would be forced to endure drawings of stick figures and read novels with pregnant sentences (inside joke—you'll have to ask me sometime).

My family and friends—for seeing "author" as only a small part of me (because in reality, it is).

ABOUT THE AUTHOR

Amber Argyle grew up with three brothers on a cattle ranch in the Rocky Mountains. She spent hours riding horses, roaming the mountains, and playing in her family's creepy barn. This environment fueled her imagination for writing high fantasy.

She has worked as a short order cook, janitor, and staff member in a mental institution. All of which have given her great insight into the human condition and have made for some unique characters.

She received her bachelor's degree in English and Physical Education from Utah State University.

She currently resides in Utah with her husband and three small children.

CPSIA information can be obtained at www.ICGtesting.com
Printed in the USA
LVOW05s2142061014

407482LV00038B/2189/P